I0831696

A TEXAS TAIL

A TEXAS TAIL

Jeff Guinn

Fort Worth, Texas

Library of Congress Cataloging-in-Publication Data

Names: Guinn, Jeff author
Title: A Texas tail / Jeff Guinn.
Description: Fort Worth, Texas : TCU Press, [2025] | Includes bibliographical references.
Identifiers: LCCN 2025031311 (print) | LCCN 2025031312 (ebook) | ISBN 9780875659350 hardback | ISBN 9780875659442 ebook
Subjects: LCSH: Middle-aged men--Fiction | Halloween costumes--Fiction | Tail--Fiction | Texas--Fiction | LCGFT: Fiction | Tall tales
Classification: LCC PS3557.U375 T49 2025 (print) | LCC PS3557.U375 (ebook)
LC record available at https://lccn.loc.gov/2025031311
LC ebook record available at https://lccn.loc.gov/2025031312

Fort Worth, Texas

TCU Box 298300
Fort Worth, Texas 76129
www.tcupress.com

Design by Bill Brammer
Cover illustration by Becca Waugh

For Mary Ann McKenzie and all the other librarians
who help children learn to love reading.

A TEXAS TAIL

If you're from Texas, then you probably know someone like this.

1.

Plunk Landy found the tail that became his peculiar destiny while poking around a costume shop a few days before Halloween, his favorite holiday. He liked to dress up right after dark and go prowl the residential streets of Crowley, Texas, the Fort Worth suburb where he lived, doing what he could to encourage other grown-ups to be generous with the candy they handed out to trick-or-treaters. Normally forty-two-year-old Plunk wouldn't have shopped for his annual Halloween getup in a store. He preferred putting together costumes for himself, like the year he went out all got up like Dak Prescott, quarterback for his beloved Dallas Cowboys, and swore to grown-ups that he'd win them a Super Bowl if they filled each kid's Halloween sack full of good stuff. That was one of Plunk's favorite Halloweens, even though getting the black body gel off his skin took forever. That crap cost a lot of money, and the tube it came in promised it would wash off right away, which it didn't; though the extra hard scrubbing was still worth it.

But last year things didn't turn out happy, which was always Plunk's goal, to have fun and help other people have fun, too. He got himself up as President Trump, an easy costume that required just a bushy blond wig, orange-y mascara smeared on his face, a droopy red tie, and an especially thick pillow under his shirt. He also wore a genuine used red MAGA hat he'd bought for fifteen cents at a garage sale. Plunk-Trump followed kids up to houses and when doors opened he told the people handing out goodies, "None of this liberal sugar-less gum stuff. Give 'em real candy or I'll go MAGA on your ass," obviously a harmless joke that almost all of them laughed at. But a couple wimpy mothers trailing after their kids griped about language and bad taste, and somebody else giving out candy must have called the police. Plunk knew both of the cops who came, he'd gone to school with their older brothers. They suggested that Plunk go home, and he did, because his favorite holiday had been spoiled. He was pissed. What was wrong with having *fun* on Halloween?

So this year Plunk figured he'd play it safe and go out wearing something nobody could possibly object to, and he walked over to the costume shop—which was only a couple blocks from his apartment—on the Saturday before Halloween to pick it out. Only there didn't seem to be much interesting. Lots of clown gear, which Plunk didn't like because if you wore it right, nobody knew it was really you underneath the red nose and green wig. Harry Potter crap. *Star Wars* outfits, mostly Darth Vader, but the masks were cheap flimsy plastic, and what self-respecting lover of Halloween would want to be seen in something no class like that? Plunk briefly considered gender-bending—a nurse's outfit maybe—but decided not to because he'd heard experts on *Fox & Friends* say that seeing a man in women's clothes might make kids go crazy or turn gay. Or something like that.

And then he saw it, up on a shelf in a back corner: a full-sized lizard outfit in three parts, all yellow with big black irregular spots. There was a head made out of heavy plastic, a shiny body suit, and the best thing of all, up on that high shelf, a thick, long, heavy tail that seemed like it was made of vinyl and just looked freakin' great. Plunk didn't find out until later that it was supposed to be a leopard gecko costume. All lizards were the same to him. In fact, at first he thought it might even be some kind of dragon from that TV show Plunk had only watched a couple times because there was too much talking between the sword fight scenes and hot stuff involving the blonde girl. He felt immediate, all-consuming longing, like he'd felt as a kid when a fantastic new toy got advertised on the Saturday morning cartoons. He usually didn't get the toy, because Pop worked for peanuts at the Crowley sanitation department, but now Plunk was a grown-up who was going to have that lizard costume, or at least the tail, which fascinated him though he couldn't have said why. He reached up and gently touched the tail, excited and nervous at the same time, sliding his fingertips along the smooth surface and admiring the texture and the color, not pale lemonade-yellow but a deeper near-gold, the black spots offering perfect contrast. It seemed like the tail was solid inside, maybe rubber in there, making the tail a hefty, substantial thing, nothing cheap or ordinary about it. Special.

A salesgirl almost young enough to be Plunk's daughter if he'd been having sex right out of high school, which he hadn't, was ringing up a couple Harry Potter costumes at the front register. Plunk waited until she'd handed the packages to the kids and their mom before calling her over.

"I want this," he said, gesturing at the lizard getup.

"You do?" she asked, sounding surprised.

"Yeah, I'll rent it for Halloween," Plunk said, already imagining himself slithering up to doors alongside trick-or-treaters, though how exactly he'd slither would be something he'd have to work out later.

The girl shook her head.

"That's for sale only, not for rent," she said. "Guy last year saw some TV commercial for car insurance that had lizards in it. He came in and asked us to special make it for him, not green like you'd expect, but like a yellow one with spots. We did, had to order it from this place in Hong Kong, and then he didn't want it, said it was all a mistake. The manager said we'd sue him, but we really wouldn't because that would like just cost more money. So if you want it, you got to buy it."

Plunk considered. That amazing tail just fascinated him.

"How much?" he asked. The girl wasn't sure because nobody had ever asked before. She went to the front counter and looked through some papers. A minute later she came back and said nine hundred dollars.

Plunk made a minimal living selling bolts and screws and other small fastener items to construction crews. Nine hundred was more than he could afford. But he had to have that tail.

"How much for part of it?" he asked.

The girl's eyebrows shot up.

"What part?"

"The tail," Plunk said.

"Why not the head?" she asked. "Something you would actually wear."

The head didn't do all that much for Plunk. He was surprised and somewhat offended that the salesgirl couldn't see the wonders of the tail.

"You can wear the tail," he told her. "It's got a belt I guess you buckle around your waist."

The girl looked doubtful and said she'd have to call Mr. Davenport, the store manager, who was at home. She got on her cell phone for a minute and then told Plunk that Mr. Davenport said it was the whole costume or nothing; the tail was part of the complete outfit. Plunk took the cell phone from the girl and told Mr. Davenport it was better to sell part of it and get some money rather than none of it and nothing. They argued back and forth for a few minutes, not mad at each other or anything, just guys haggling, and finally Mr. Davenport said okay, five hundred for the tail, and Plunk talked him down to four seventy-five.

"No return on this," the salesgirl cautioned as she took Plunk's credit card and ran it through the little machine on the counter. He never understood exactly how that credit card stuff worked, but a few seconds later the machine buzzed and chattered and she gave him a slip to sign.

"I'd never return it," Plunk said and knew it was true. The girl had some trouble getting the tail down from the shelf where it was displayed, so Plunk helped her pull it down and wrap it up in brown paper. The tail was at least four, maybe five feet long and heavier than you'd expect, which Plunk liked because that probably meant it would last forever. Because of its shape and weight the package was awkward for Plunk to carry the half-mile home, but he didn't care. He had his tail. It belonged to him. He slung the package over one shoulder and started walking, enjoying the curious glances from passersby who obviously wondered what was in that odd-looking parcel. They'd know soon enough if they lived in his part of Crowley and went out with their kids on Halloween.

2.

Plunk lived in a small one-bedroom apartment. The rent was eleven hundred a month, and utilities came to another hundred or so when it was summer and he had to run the window air conditioners a lot. North Texas summers always lasted a long time. He didn't need a big place. It was just him. The apartment complex was called The Jacksonian, probably after Andrew Jackson, who Plunk remembered from mandatory Texas history class in junior high was a friend of Davy Crockett's and fought alongside Sam Houston at some important battle or other. To Plunk, Jackson was mostly the guy on the twenty-dollar bill, where Davy Crockett's face would have been better, dead animal hat on his head and his rifle, too. The rest of the people living in The Jacksonian were mostly like Plunk, singles who were a little too old for any fancier apartment pickup scene or folks who didn't have a whole lot of money and never would, so they settled for living somewhere that the owners kept pretty clean on the edge of a neighborhood where crime wasn't yet much of a problem. Plunk had a parking space right outside his door for his battered million-year-old Ford Ranger pickup truck, which he'd bought a couple years back to replace an even older Ranger that finally broke down for good. His so-called new truck was so ancient that Plunk had to lower and raise windows by cranking handles on the inside of the doors. So what? As long it was a truck, which all real guys in Texas drove, it was fine with Plunk. Most of the time he'd rather walk anyway, unless he was on the job, which required him to drive to lots of construction sites. Walking was better because you were out among the people.

But Plunk sure didn't mind being by himself when he brought his lizard tail home, because he felt excited about having it to wear on Halloween night and nobody else knowing yet. Plunk Landy's secret that only Plunk Landy would reveal to the amazement of all at a time and place of his choosing—he knew he'd heard that saying somewhere before. When he strapped that baby on and hit the Halloween streets, everybody would look because they'd never seen anything like it.

Plunk himself was a familiar sight to most people in Crowley. He'd been living in the midsize Fort Worth suburb since he was eight and his folks moved over from Burleson because Pop got the sanitation department job. Before that Pop had worked for Burleson Sanitation, a fancy name for garbage man, and the Crowley job paid a little more. Crowley wasn't fancy, mostly a place families lived while hoping life got a little better and they could afford moving up to Arlington or even Fort Worth itself. Never Dallas or the Dallas suburbs, which were for rich people. A lowish rung on the moving up ladder is what Crowley was, and Plunk's folks never did get up any higher, though it was fine with him. Even when he was grown up, he never thought about leaving his hometown or state. You might as well live where you already lived, and besides, everybody in Texas was lucky because much of the rest of the country was weird and against anything regular people believed in. Crowley was also fine because Plunk liked watching sports on TV and this neck of the woods had baseball's Rangers and basketball's Mavericks and college football's TCU Horned Frogs and especially pro football's Cowboys, even though Plunk actually going to any of those teams' games never happened because tickets cost so much, parking alone for one game would have been almost as much as his weekly beer budget. For ballgame-watching Plunk had a massive eighty-one-inch high-def widescreen TV, his one indulgence and favorite possession prior to acquiring the lizard tail.

Which he now placed on the card table where he always ate his microwaved dinners. The table sagged a little under the weight of the long package. The table's legs never had been real sturdy. Plunk didn't care because he only took about a minute to sit there and eat every night, bolting his food and then popping a beer to sip as he moved to the couch to watch ESPN.

The ends of the package drooped over the sides of the table. Plunk had to pull it over some because one end, the wide tail side, was so much heavier than the side where the tail came to a point that the table was in danger of tipping. He tugged at the brown paper wrapping, popping the tape apart carefully, opening the package with reverence and nearly cheering out loud when he saw his yellow tail with black spots revealed in all its magnificence. A real costume connoisseur, Plunk especially liked that the inside of the tail was solid. You poked it with a finger and it dented in a little but then puffed right back out. Vinyl outside, sure, but that was just the outer covering, the skin. There was good industrial-strength rubber inside, not Styrofoam or anything. Built to last. Three separate sets of straps protruded on the thick end, and one of them was a belt to buckle around your waist, just like Plunk told the salesgirl. But there were two other thinner belts, and Plunk figured out you passed those by either side of your junk and buckled, and those straps around each upper thigh held the tail solidly in place. Okay!

Well, of course he had to try the tail on. Couldn't wait. At first he thought the waist belt wouldn't be quite long enough, Plunk had put on some pounds over the years, not a lot but some, all the beer and good greasy food added up and the belt wasn't adjustable. But he sucked in his stomach and got the belt notched on the very last possible hole, and the thigh straps fit okay. Most of the tail was still splayed on top of the card table, it was that long, and Plunk felt the solid connection of it to the place on his back where the end of his spine met his ass, and then down some over the tops of both cheeks. He twisted to glimpse himself in the mirror by the door and the part of the tail that was still on the card table swung over and the weight of it tilted the shaky table, which toppled over with a crash. Plunk turned to pick it up and the weight of the tail, which now went from his ass to the floor, made it hard to turn. The thing was *heavy*, which in no way upset Plunk. He loved its heftiness.

And, when he finally got his look in the mirror, he marveled at the sight of the spotted tale hanging down and dragging behind him. There was a balance issue, but it wasn't major. Plunk had to lean forward just a little to compensate for the new weight, kind of the way school kids did when they hefted backpacks crammed with books. The adjustment to the weight was a sort of validation—something substantial was involved.

Plunk took a couple tentative steps and the tail made a sloofy sound dragging along the cheaply carpeted apartment floor. He could only go a couple steps in any direction because then he'd walk right into the wall. So he turned to walk the short distance to the opposite wall and it was damn near impossible because the end of the tail was still pointing the other way. Plunk twisted his hips impatiently, thinking the tail would whip right around, but it lay flat and he could feel the belts around his waist and thighs straining. The belts were not of as high quality as the tail itself and Plunk was scared they might break. So he bent over and picked up the tip of the tail in his hands, turned it in the right direction and walked to the other side of the room, the tail sloofing again. He decided he liked the noise.

Another look in the mirror made Plunk decide the beautiful yellow-black tail didn't look real good jammed up behind his faded blue jeans, which were the pants that Plunk always wore when not at work. A pair of black jeans would look better; there was no question the rest of Plunk's Halloween costume would be intended to complement the tail and not vice versa. That meant a trip to Target, which Plunk didn't want to take right then because he only had about forty bucks in cash and didn't want to put anything more on his credit card this soon after the four seventy-five spent at the costume shop. Plunk got behind on his card payment a few times and now VISA kept a sharp eye out. It was hassle he didn't need. This late in the month his bank account wasn't flush, but he could probably go fifty for black jeans and maybe some inexpensive black tennis shoes, just to stick with the color scheme. He'd run by the bank Monday and make a withdrawal. There was time. Halloween wasn't 'til Thursday.

A faded yellow sweatshirt already hung in Plunk's closet. If it wasn't too cold Halloween night, he could wear that. It would sort of match the tail. And he thought he'd stick to only the best-lighted residential streets that night. Why have a freakin' tail if it was too dark for people to properly see it, feel awed by it and maybe a little jealous of its owner?

So Plunk stood in front of the mirror awhile, turning his body a degree or two from side to side, admiring the color and line and solidness of the tail, until he finally thought, *Geez, I can't wait 'til Halloween to show this baby off.* Gratification delay had never been one of Plunk's attributes. He reached down to adjust the angle of the tail and went out the apartment door into the street.

3.

Just about everybody in Crowley really did know Plunk Landy. He'd spent long enough trying to make sure they did. From the day he arrived in town and entered third grade at Renfro Elementary School, he'd been the kid who made everybody look and laugh. Nothing mean, ever, or even intended to offend. Fart noises with hand in armpit. Crossed eyes and tongue stuck out. Inappropriate behavior sometimes, but nothing indecent, because Plunk was not a dirty-minded guy. In fifth grade Jeremy Hollins got suspended for unzipping his pants and getting Sylvie Sanders to stick her hand in, but Plunk would never have done something really wrong like that. He knew the difference. He just wanted to make people notice him and everybody have fun because of it, himself included.

Which is how he got the nickname. Plunk's real first name was Delbert, which he hated. His mother named him that because it was her father's name, not realizing Delbert was of course the kind of name other kids mocked. But Plunk was stuck with it, even though at ages eight and nine he tried going by Del and then Bert, but those two names were kind of skuzzy, too. Then in Little League when he was eleven, Plunk was in this baseball game and doing kind of bad as always. In school his grades were average, but on ball fields of any kind he was below average, though he loved to play. So in this game he came up to bat for the third time after striking out the first two, and the pitcher hit him right in the ribs with a fastball. Some kids would have fallen over and cried, or maybe acted brave like it didn't hurt at all. The same things everybody did. But he put on a show for the parents in the stands, hopping around, contorting his face, and hollering, "He plunked me! He plunked me!" The next day somebody called him Plunk as a joke but it stuck, and so the joke turned out to be a good one. Plunk loved his new name, the coolness of the popping P it started with and the crispness of the K at the end. Best of all, none of the other guys had that particular name, which was great if you were Plunk and lousy if you were Delbert. Being named Plunk meant sticking out in the right way.

The nickname was Plunk's best showcase for a couple years, and then in high school came a big break. The South Crowley High sports teams were nicknamed the Warriors, and of course Plunk wasn't good enough to play on any of them. It wasn't like Little League where the coaches had to play any kid who wanted. But the school not only had cheerleaders, it had a mascot who dressed up in headdress and warpaint and jumped and danced on the sidelines, trying to get everybody in the stands fired up and yelling. Before Plunk, the mascot had always been some boy from the senior class, but after blowing all the other contenders away in tryouts Plunk held down the honor from tenth through twelfth grade, loving every minute. Everybody agreed he was the best mascot ever. He would have worn the headdress and warpaint to class if they'd let him. Plunk ended up buying his own flashier headdress when the one from the school just wasn't eye-catching enough. He saved up his allowance almost a year to afford it.

His high school social life was okay. Plunk was pals with practically everyone and best friends with no one, a kid who sat comfortably on the fringes of the popular crowd without ever being invited to completely join. At parties he'd be the first one to try to chug a beer and have the stuff spurt out his nose. He knew not to ask out any of the cheerleaders, but sometimes he'd have a date with somebody from the lower ranks of the pep squad. Plunk and a couple of those girls went steady but never for more than a week or so. They always promised him they'd stay friends and usually they did. Girlfriends paled anyway compared to the awesomeness of being the official Warrior Mascot. All three years, there were plenty of Plunk's pictures in the school yearbook.

High school graduation was a sad time for Plunk. Not that he'd miss the classes. He'd pretty much known all along what the school guidance counselor suggested the beginning of his junior year, that not everybody had to go to college, and perhaps Plunk's people skills, as she called them, could bring him a very successful career in some kind of sales job. Also there was the fact he hadn't made a grade above B and earned mostly Cs in all his years in high school. Studying was not Plunk's thing. Being Warrior Mascot was.

After graduating he got his first job in a Kroger grocery store, stocking shelves, which was not a sales position or even very important, but Plunk had hopes of getting promoted to cashier where he could talk to people a lot more. He went home feeling low every day—he still lived with his folks, you can't afford your own place on a few bucks an hour—not because of the tedious work but because Matt Foley was Warrior Mascot now, and a sorry one at that. Matt let his mother help with the face paint, and she put on these wimpy delicate thin lines and not good thick ones, the kind people in the stands could actually *see*. Matt's yells were more like girly screeches. He hopped instead of jumped. Plunk went to all the football games his first post-high school fall and he was decent about it, he didn't criticize Matt a whole lot, but he could also tell any sense of real school spirit was gone from the stands. Everybody sitting around him told him over and over that he'd always be the best Warrior Mascot, Matt or anybody else would never come close. And Plunk knew this was true. But he yearned to be more than a memory.

Plunk thought about it for weeks, by far the longest in his life he'd ever brooded about anything besides his original given name, and then he had it. When the South Crowley High Warriors took the field for their first home game of the following season, Warrior Mascot Ricky Hardesty who'd replaced the now-graduated Matt Foley was amazed to look in the stands and see a *real* Warrior Mascot there, in headdress and war paint jumping up and down and getting some of that long-lost spirit back in everybody. Poor Ricky. Some people said he cried. Plunk didn't want to hurt the guy's feelings. When he heard, he called the principal and suggested he and Ricky team up on the sidelines: he was volunteering to teach the kid how to do it right. But the principal said only students, coaches, and officials could be down there, no non-school personnel on the playing field. Sorry, it was a district-wide rule and not his decision. Halfway through the season Ricky quit as Warrior Mascot, supposedly to concentrate on his trumpet-playing since he hoped for some kind of musical scholarship, and the school didn't replace him. By default Plunk was once again Warrior Mascot, even though he was up in the stands instead of on the sidelines. It was still all right.

Three years out of high school Plunk finally got promoted to cashier and then came the news the high school was officially going to "discontinue" having a student elected official Warrior Mascot, obviously in the sure knowledge that proud South Crowley graduate Plunk Landy would do the job right forever up in the stands. He turned twenty-one and was happy again, even though cashiers didn't make enough for their own place, either. His folks didn't seem to mind. As for Plunk, well, where he lived was a minor concern now, if any. He was a cashier during the week, talking to everybody, joking, having a little fun, helping the store's customers enjoy shopping at Kroger, and then on weekends he was the unofficial but still unquestioned Warrior Mascot at fall football games. Plus Plunk had started thinking he could do the spirit stuff at basketball games too, after football season was over. And after basketball, then maybe even baseball games. Warrior Mascot all school year long! Perfect life!

And then, a month before the next football season, two disasters. First, at work, Plunk got canned. It wasn't really his fault. The store manager knew Plunk liked to josh with the customers whose purchases he rang up at his register. No harm was intended, and everybody seemed to enjoy it, until old Mr. Carpenter complained Plunk was making fun of him for always buying laxatives. "Stopped by 'cause you're stopped up?" wouldn't have offended anybody else, surely. But the manager issued Plunk a warning and put him on probation, company rules when a customer complained. Two days later Mrs. Vandiver griped he had said something mean about her hair color, which changed every freakin' week and everybody in town made fun of it behind her back, Plunk was just letting her in on the joke. But that got him what he thought of as "double secret" probation like in his all-time favorite classic movie *Animal House*. Even if he wasn't from Texas, Belushi was a god.

Week after that, Plunk told a customer he bet he was ready to chomp into that watermelon, about as innocent a remark as anybody could make. But the guy was Black. There weren't many Black people in Crowley, but Plunk had never been prejudiced against any of them and nobody had ever accused him of it before this. Plunk just thought the watermelon the guy was buying looked particularly fine—he would have jumped at an offer to eat some of it himself. But the guy told the store manager if something wasn't done he was going to take his complaint to the district supervisor and also to court if he had to, so Plunk got fired. It was just some woke shit years before anybody heard that term.

"Nothing personal, Plunk," the manager said, and Plunk understood it wasn't the manager's fault that some people had no sense of humor. Still, he hated starting over professionally in a WalMart warehouse, where he stacked boxes and pried open crates for minimum wage and never got to have contact with customers at all.

Which Plunk could have handled, but on the heels of that came news the Crowley school board had given in to some assholes who thought the team nickname "Warriors" was offensive to Native Americans, which is what you were now supposed to call real-life actual Indians. What was the deal? "Warrior" was a compliment! Anybody should love to be called a warrior, including Indians and dumbass Indian-lovers. But the board voted to change the team name from "Warriors" to "Tornadoes," in honor, they said, of a monster twister that once flattened downtown Fort Worth while mostly sparing nearby Crowley. This was an example of a few whiny liberal socialists getting their way even though regular people liked things fine the way they were. It was troubling to realize that something like this could happen even in Texas. Plunk always did his best not to hate anybody, but this time it was hard not to. Try as he might, Plunk couldn't think of a way to dress up like a tornado short of wrapping himself in bands of tin foil or something, which would look stupid rather than entertaining. He went to the first couple football games that fall dressed as Warrior Mascot like usual, but it seemed to make a few lame-ass people uncomfortable and so he quit doing it, and in fact quit going to the South Crowley High football games altogether. He moped until Halloween, when on a sudden whim he broke out the Warrior Mascot costume and ran around the streets urging trick-or-treaters to show some holiday spirit and for grown-ups to give them lots of candy. Good old-fashioned regular people yelled out it was great to see the Warrior again and Plunk did the same thing for three more Halloweens, until the compliments subsided in favor of polite nods and eventually suggestions to maybe try something different. The feathers on the headdress were getting raggedy anyway. So each subsequent year he took to the Halloween streets in homemade costumes, and it became a tradition. Plunk tried to keep up with the sports and cultural times, like the Dak Prescott costume, though sometimes it fell flat like when he was Mulder from the *X-Files* TV show, but nobody seemed to catch on, because to them he just looked like a guy in a suit. The big X he'd taped on his back apparently wasn't enough of a clue. Plunk had already known the *X-Files* costume wasn't close to his best, but it was what he'd thought of that year and you couldn't be inspired every time. Besides, he loved that old TV show. Plunk felt pretty sure there were aliens around somewhere, and that the government, the Deep State, was lying about it like it lied about everything. Mulder was an American hero; Plunk was almost as proud to be him as he was to be Dak Prescott.

There was one good thing. Even though Plunk was right there with all the little kids on every Halloween, their parents didn't worry he'd try any sex stuff. Nobody from Crowley thought Plunk was a perv. He played to the grown-ups as much or more than to the small fry—it was the adults' attention he was really after, because on Halloween the kids themselves just cared about candy, and who could blame them? But it was also the one night of the year Plunk could do his costume thing and people would think that was just great.

So the citizens of Crowley were accustomed to seeing Plunk in some kind of attention-getting outfit every Halloween, but that still didn't prepare anyone for his appearance this particular Saturday before the holiday with a gigantic lizard tail apparently growing out of his ass and dragging along behind him.

4.

Plunk and his new tail were an instant sensation in the Jacksonian apartments parking lot. When he stepped out his front door, taking a little longer than usual to close it behind him—because *he didn't want to catch his tail!*, was that great or what?—all the people hanging around in the lot, the guys working on their cars, the women chatting to each other and pushing hair out of their eyes, whipped their heads around to stare. It was one of Plunk's greatest moments, you better believe it.

"What the hell's that, Plunk?" Eddie, his best friend living in the apartments, hollered and Plunk, ever the showman, knew exactly how to react. He knitted his brows in a puzzled look like he couldn't understand what Eddie was talking about, and Eddie pointed to the tail and Plunk turned around and looked behind him, but straight back and not down at the pavement where the tail rested in all its gleaming glory, and Eddie yelled, "No, the *tail!*" and Plunk raised his arms in the universal gesture for confusion and everybody was laughing by the time Eddie—the best-ever straight man, Plunk just loved the guy—screamed, "What's with the goddamn *tail?*" and then Plunk with perfect comic timing looked down and pretended to see the tail for the first time and made a little startled hop.

Well, after that everybody just had to walk over and take a closer look. Plunk joined in the laughter when Eddie asked if he'd bought that tail or just *grew* it, and after a while he explained about finding it in the costume store where he'd gone because of those liberal crapheads complaining about President Trump last year. It was a good story and maybe Plunk made it even a little better, adding bits about the salesgirl refusing to touch the tail since it looked so lifelike, so Plunk had to pull it down off the rack by himself and nearly dislocated both shoulders, the thing was so heavy, and maybe he also claimed it cost him six hundred instead of four seventy-five, but what was the harm. Everybody agreed the tail would be a sensation on Halloween and a couple of the men, divorced dads who didn't live with their kids, asked if Plunk would pose for pictures that night when they had their ex-wives' permission to trick-or-treat with their sons and daughters and of course Plunk said he would.

Then somebody asked what kind of lizard tail it was and Plunk admitted he didn't know. Darlene from one of the apartments across the way, a woman who in Plunk's very limited experience around her always acted like she knew everything, said she thought it was a leopard gecko tail.

"They call it leopard because it's yellow, see, with the black spots like leopards have," Darlene said. "I know because I saw a program about them on PBS."

"What's the difference between a regular lizard and a gecko?" Plunk asked, figuring it would be good to know if on Halloween night somebody asked him that question. But Darlene had no idea, though she didn't exactly admit it, mumbling it involved claw length and then remembering something she had to go do so nobody would try to pin her down on it. Plunk knew she was faking both the answer and the excuse to leave, but it didn't make him mad. Everybody liked to feel important, not just Darlene with her glasses and old-fashioned ponytail. And probably nobody else in the whole world besides him was at that very moment wearing a leopard gecko tail except for the leopard geckos themselves.

It had been fun goofing with the neighbors, but Plunk wanted a fresh audience. What passed for downtown Crowley was just a few blocks away, a short walk, and so, like Darlene, Plunk suddenly remembered something to do and started to head off. He thought he'd be making a jaunty exit but that didn't happen. When he turned to go down the sidewalk, the tail was pointed the wrong way like it had been in his apartment a few minutes earlier, and the belts strained and Plunk was sort of stopped short. Everybody laughed again but this time Plunk wasn't pleased they did so, because it was *at* instead of *with*. He made the best of it, muttering "Dumb tail," loud enough so they all heard it, maybe they'd think the stop-short stumble was intentional, part of the act. He bent down, got the tail properly aligned, and started to walk off again. Then, more trouble.

Back in the apartment on the carpet, the tail sloofed right along. But the sidewalk was different, a little rough and uneven, so now there was this scuffing sound. The weight of the tail behind him was all right, Plunk could handle that, but he couldn't stand the idea of his beloved tail getting all scratched or maybe even cut up by gravel.

So with everybody still looking, Plunk moved off the sidewalk onto the grass and for the first few steps it was better, the sloofy sound again. But then Plunk saw right ahead a pile of dog shit, people walked their dogs and let them go wherever and left the crap for other people to step in. Plunk was not about to let his outstanding—hell, *magnificent* tail get smeared with dog shit. No way.

But if he couldn't tail-walk on the sidewalk or on the grass, then what? Maybe he should grab the pointy end of the tail in his hand and sort of carry it. Keep the thick part off the ground. That might work. Plunk reached down and grabbed the pointy end, straightened up and walked. That worked okay in one way, the tail was off the ground, the weight of it was evenly distributed and all. But now the tail was also kind of wrapped around Plunk and he knew it didn't look nearly as good,—the effect was spoiled. And the effect was the whole point.

"I gotta fix this thing," Plunk admitted to the parking lot onlookers, and, feeling a little deflated, grabbed the pointy end and hurried back inside his apartment.

5.

It took Plunk all the rest of Saturday evening and trips to two different stores before he got it worked out. The tail dilemma forced him to miss watching college football on TV, but the emergency was such that he didn't even think too much about the games. The problem itself was simple: how to walk around with the tail without subjecting it to wear from gravelly sidewalks and smearing from dog shit. Also it would be good to not have to reach down and turn the tail by hand whenever he wanted to change direction. The solution, however, proved to be a puzzler.

First thing Plunk did back inside the apartment was take the tail off and look it over for damage. Damn it, there was some. Just from being dragged a few yards over pavement, there was dust covering the pointy part, also some scratches on the shiny vinyl. Plunk wet a paper towel and wiped the tail down. The dust came off, and the scratches were shallow enough not to show when he was through. But the risk was clear. Inside on carpeting, or outside on shit-free grass, the tail could be pulled right after him. But he couldn't walk over pavement dragging the tail behind him unless he wanted it to get all torn up. So he had to find a way to lift it up when going some places, then let it all the way down in others.

Plunk rummaged through some kitchen drawers and found leftover wire from when he set up speakers for his widescreen TV. The wire, which he'd picked up at one of the construction sites where he called as a salesman, was thin and dark and covered with a clear plastic coating. It seemed to Plunk like he could loop one end of the wire to the tail's pointy part, the other end of the wire to his wrist, and just raise his hand whenever he wanted the tail off the ground. But the coated wire wouldn't tie snugly around the tail tip or his wrist. The plastic made it slip, and the knots kept coming undone.

So Plunk took his old Swiss Army knife and methodically stripped the coating off both ends of the wire and tried again. This time the wire knots held, and that was fine on the tail tip, but around his wrist the thin wire cut into his skin and hurt like a mother, and if Plunk was wincing half the time he wore the tail it would spoil the effect. So wire wasn't going to do.

Next he tried string, which worked but looked like crap. Plunk intended his tail costume to be first-class all the way. Which made him think of duct tape, something Plunk truly loved. You could do almost anything with duct tape. It currently plugged a hole in his pickup's windshield, covered another hole on his couch, and held together the inner works of the toilet in Plunk's bathroom. Very useful stuff. But when Plunk tried using it to hook up the tail tip and his wrist, the shiny silver duct tape just did not go with the shiny gold-and-black of the tail.

So Plunk regretfully left the tail behind and walked a quarter mile to the hardware store. There he looked at some different lengths of chain, finally selecting one that was copper-colored with small pliable links. He paid nearly five bucks for six feet of it, went back to the apartment, got out his pliers, and fashioned a loop for the pointy tail end and another for his wrist. The copper-colored chain looked great on the tail and not bad on the wrist (Plunk's right one because he wore a drugstore wristwatch on his left). He figured he had the whole thing solved, only he didn't. When he got up to walk and try it, the minute he raised his wrist to lift the tail the links in the wrist loop pulled loose and the tail plopped back on the carpet. Plunk thought maybe it was just a couple faulty links, but the same thing kept happening and Plunk eventually figured out that chain links soft enough to twist weren't going to be able to take much strain at all, and the heavy tail was considerable strain.

At this point it was nearly 7 p.m., well after dark since it was fall, so Plunk zapped a macaroni and cheese TV dinner and brooded while he gulped it down. The whole effect of the tail had to be perfect on Halloween. There was no way he could drag it on the ground during his rounds with trick-or-treaters, because he couldn't stand the thought of the tail being permanently damaged in any way. Already he was thinking of it as something to treasure far beyond this one Halloween.

Yet he couldn't just pick up the tip of the tail and carry it because that looked so sorry, so amateur. Plunk had a certain position in the community. People had expectations of him on Halloween. He couldn't let everybody down.

So he turned on the TV, figuring to watch a few minutes of football, and flipped through the sports channels. One had on this dog show. Normally, Plunk hated it when they put on crap like that instead of real sports like football or at least monster trucks or pro wrestling that regular people wanted to watch. But then the dogs made Plunk think, and minutes later he was hustling to the pet store, which in Crowley was really just some aisles in the Tom Thumb grocery store, and there he found what he needed—those retractable dog leashes where you snap one end to the dog's collar, hold this handle on the other end and push a button when you wanted the leash to pull out or pull in. The leashes were kind of pricey, $12.95 each, but Plunk bought three different ones because he didn't know what size would work.

Back at the apartment again, Plunk experimented. There was no collar on the tip of the tail to attach a retractable leash to, but if Plunk carefully wrapped the original wire he'd tried in a snug loop around the tip, he could then hook the catch on the one end of the leash around the wire. That held okay on the first leash, but when he took the leash handle in his right hand and depressed the button, the leash wouldn't retract at all and the tail stayed flat on the floor. Now Plunk was discouraged, but then he figured out he was using the leash for small dogs, and the tail weighed a lot more than some weenie little dachshund. He switched to the Great Dane/Doberman retractable leash and damn if it didn't work perfectly! Plunk positioned himself in front of the mirror and practiced, pushing the button with different amounts of oomph and watching as the tail behind him lifted up an inch off the ground or six inches or all the way to shoulder height: It was Plunk's to control, and best of all the tail just looked great, twitching like it was stuck on the ass of a real gecko. Over and over Plunk pressed the button and waved the tail up and down, even as ESPN broadcast late Saturday night college football, which Plunk always watched but not this time. For once it was just flickering background light and noise as far as he was concerned, at least compared to the wonder of the tail.

Plunk was in front of the mirror for a long time, until all of a sudden he realized his bladder was stretched to the breaking point. So he unbuckled the tail and laid it carefully back on the couch. Then he checked his watch as he hustled to the john. Jesus, it was almost 1 a.m.!

Plunk slept well that night, just waking up once around five, coming out of a dream he couldn't remember the minute his eyes were open. Then he thought of the tail. Could that have been part of the dream and not something real? Panicked, he scurried to the couch in the living room and ran his hand over the smooth vinyl covering of the possession he now prized most. When he returned to bed, he was sure he was too excited about the tail and Halloween to go back to sleep, but he did anyway.

6.

Sunday mornings during pro football season, Plunk always went to visit his mother, Ida, who lived in an old folks' home. She'd moved there three years earlier when she was seventy-eight. Plunk was taken by surprise. One day Mom was living in the house he'd grown up in, had lived there alone since Pop died of the stroke in '21, and the next thing you know she'd had a garage sale, sold most of the furniture, and moved into Pleasant Valley Residential Community. Her friend Helen had moved there a few months earlier and talked Mom into joining her. They shared a room. Pop's pension covered most of it, and Mom had some Social Security. She liked that they served meals there and she didn't have to cook anymore. As far as Plunk could tell, she spent her days playing bridge and nights watching TV. At first he'd offer to take her out for dinner or a movie, but she was always pretty busy with Pleasant Valley activities. As long as she was happy, so was her only child Plunk.

He got in the habit of weekly visits, Sunday afternoons in the spring and fall and Sunday mornings during football season so he could spend an hour or so with her and still get back to his place in time to watch the Cowboys game. Plunk didn't resent time spent on Mom visits. It was what you did, go see your mother in the old folks' home. Though in the last year or so it seemed like Mom's mind was getting a little mixed up.

"Where's Annie?" she'd ask, and Plunk hadn't seen or heard from Annie for nearly fifteen years since she moved to Wichita Falls after their divorce. Mom used to know that. She hadn't mentioned Annie for years, and now she wouldn't stop doing it at least once every visit. At first Plunk would say, "We got divorced, remember?" and Mom would, but then she started to look confused when he told her that, so now he'd just say she was out shopping or something and Mom would nod and talk about something else. One of the Pleasant Valley administrators took Plunk aside and said Ida was showing some signs of dementia and maybe soon it would be good to move her to another wing of the building where there was twenty-four-hour care and supervision. Of course, there was some additional expense involved, and the administrator told Plunk they should talk about insurance issues and so forth, some things weren't covered by Medicare. Plunk agreed they'd talk, then resolutely put off the discussion. He believed you didn't go looking for trouble until there was no doubt it had already found you. Right now answering questions about Annie was simpler than having Mom move rooms, which would upset her since she liked sharing with Helen. Let her be happy as long as she could.

Otherwise, the Sunday visits during football season fell into a comfortable routine. They lasted an hour. Plunk got to Pleasant Valley at 10:30 a.m. At 11:30 a bell jangled to signal lunchtime for the residents. Mom would say she needed to meet Helen in the dining room. Plunk would hug her goodbye, and on days when there was a Cowboys game, if he walked fast he could be back in his apartment right at noon kickoff. Sometimes they played the late game midafternoon, or even the big Sunday night game, and once in a while it was on Monday or Thursday night. But no matter when the Cowboys played, on Sunday mornings Plunk did his sonly duty and Mom got her visit, good for both of them.

On this particular Sunday, Plunk looked forward to seeing Mom so he could tell her about the tail. When he was a little boy, she'd helped him rig up Halloween costumes. She understood how he loved the holiday. Pop thought it was a nuisance, kids hammering on the door wanting candy. Being at heart a good guy, he still went out and gave them candy, but really he would have been happier if Halloween disappeared forever. The wonder of the tail would have completely eluded Pop. But not Mom. Plunk didn't bring the tail to show her, because now that he had the dragging problem solved he wanted to keep the tail out of sight until Halloween. Maybe next Sunday Mom could get her look at it.

When Plunk got to her room, unfortunately Mom greeted him as usual: "Where's Annie, son?"

Plunk shrugged.

"Shopping again. So how you been this week?"

Ida Landy kept her gray hair pulled back in a tight bun, which she patted while she talked.

"Helen and I played lots of bridge."

"You win?"

"Well, some of the time." Pat. Pat. "We had a real nice meal last night, pot roast with brown gravy. What did you have?"

It took Plunk a second to recall.

"Macaroni and cheese."

"You were watching some ballgame, weren't you? Macaroni and cheese isn't a real meal." Pat. Pat. "I wish Annie would fix you something better."

This was a bad sign, Mom bringing up Annie again. Plunk tried to change the subject.

"Halloween this Thursday, Mom. I can't wait."

"You always did love Halloween. Do you remember the costumes we used to make?"

Plunk grinned.

"You bet. That one time you cut up the mop so I'd have hair like the guy in *Pirates of the Caribbean*. And Pop spilled a beer and went looking for the mop and it was on my head. He got mad but not really. You sure made great costumes."

"All through school the teachers would wonder about you," Mom said suddenly. "Acting out for attention, they'd say." Pat. Pat. "They'd ask questions about how you were at home. I'd tell them you just liked people to look, you didn't mean any harm."

This was news to Plunk.

"No kidding? When did they do that?"

Mom rearranged some knickknacks on her small square dresser, trying to get the framed photos and tiny plaster figurines lined up right.

"It was all the teachers right up through high school. I remember you wore those feathers and painted your face. You wanted to go to class dressed like that."

"When I asked, the principal said no. I didn't know they called you about it."

"I was used to it by then. I told them there was no reason to worry." Mom got everything on the dresser the way she wanted. She sat back on the bed—Plunk was in the room's only chair—and resumed patting her bun.

"I got a great costume this Halloween," Plunk said, trying to steer the conversation back to a more cheerful subject. "Last year wasn't that good, you remember, some people didn't like the President Trump thing."

Mom nodded like she sure did remember, though Plunk was sure she didn't. The discussion with the administrator couldn't be put off much longer. But it could at least wait until after Halloween.

"So I went to this costume store and I found a great lizard tail," he continued. "It's real big and yellow with black spots. You put it around your waist with some belts, and I rigged this thing out of a dog leash so I can carry the tail instead of dragging it when I need to."

Mom patted her bun, apparently considering things.

"A lizard costume," she finally said. "Does it have a face with teeth?"

"No face. Just the tail. It's a great tail."

"How can you tell it's a lizard from just the tail?"

Plunk didn't want to explain about a head and bodysuit coming with the tail but costing too much, and how the tail all by itself was better anyway, so he repeated what Darlene said in the parking lot about it being a leopard gecko and not actually a lizard tail. Mom smiled and listened and patted her bun, and when Plunk was done telling the gecko thing she asked, "Does Annie like it?"

Three Annie mentions in one visit. Trouble had definitely found its way to Pleasant Valley.

"You know Annie," Plunk said evasively. "She's like Pop about Halloween."

"Your father liked beer," Mom observed. She was like that now, switching unexpectedly from one thing to another.

"Well, that was Pop," Plunk said, since he couldn't think of any better response. "How's Helen? What's the menu here been like this week?"

Mom patted her bun and talked about Helen playing bridge and also about a disappointing breakfast omelet. Plunk was relieved when the lunch bell rang. He loved Mom but was ready to get back to his tail.

7.

The guys usually congregated at Plunk's apartment on Sunday afternoons to watch the Cowboys. It was a good place for guys to be. Somebody'd bring beer, somebody else might have popcorn for the microwave, Plunk had his widescreen TV, and he didn't have a wife or girlfriend to tell everybody to keep their feet off the couch. You could burp when you wanted and fart when the urge struck.

Eddie was a Sunday afternoon regular ever since he'd moved to the Jacksonian apartment complex three years ago. Eddie was maybe a year younger than Plunk, "between women" as he called it, though Plunk was beginning to wonder if there had ever been a time when he wasn't. Plus now they had Larry B. (called that because he had a strange, long last name nobody could pronounce or spell or even remember) and Red from where Plunk worked, guys like him who sold nuts and bolts to construction companies. They were a good bit younger, late twenties maybe, and not that different from Paulie and Mack and Donnie, three twentyish guys who'd been Sunday afternoon regulars for a while and then stopped coming 'cause they got married or found girlfriends who put demands on their time. There had been other guys before them. Plunk understood. It didn't hurt his feelings. It seemed like for a long time now most of the guys he hung with were younger. They rotated out when they moved away from Crowley or hooked up permanently with women, and new guys took their place. Plunk would have been hard pressed to name even one old high school pal that he still saw except to nod at in the grocery store or the gas station. They'd left for other places or else had families, responsibilities. Most of the time Plunk was glad he didn't, so he could watch his football games and drink beer and not have to justify it to a woman. He told himself he was free.

Eddie was outside the apartment door when Plunk walked up. He was always the first to arrive on Sundays, probably because he had the shortest distance to come, just a couple doors down across the parking lot. Red and Larry B. lived elsewhere in Crowley, another apartment where they were roommates, something Plunk didn't want anymore. He liked not having to ask permission before switching channels.

"Christ, you about made us miss the kickoff," Eddie griped. He hefted a paper sack full of beer while Plunk unlocked the door. "Your mom okay this week?"

"Yeah, she was fine," Plunk said, even though the three mentions of Annie had him spooked. He wanted to forget about that and start thinking about the Cowboys. "You bring enough beer?"

"I got twelve in here," Eddie said. "Red's supposed to bring some, too, if the butthead remembers."

Plunk got the door unlocked, and Eddie handed him the bag of beer to put in the fridge, first taking out a can for himself and one for Plunk. Plunk went on into the kitchen, which wasn't far since the kitchen and living room were right there together. He was putting the beer in the fridge when Eddie whooped.

"Look at me! I'm Lizard Man!" and Plunk turned to see Eddie marching around the room holding the gecko tail up against his ass. Plunk had left it carefully arranged on the couch before he'd gone to see Mom. Now he felt a terrible white hot flash of rage, seeing Eddie with his hands on it.

"Put my goddamned tail down," Plunk roared, an unusually nasty note in his voice. Eddie, though not the sharpest blade in the knife drawer, picked up on it. He dropped the tail on the floor.

"Shit, what's the matter with you?" Eddie asked in a defensive kind of way. "I wasn't hurting it."

Plunk picked the tail up off the floor, checking for scratches. For a moment Eddie wasn't there at all, just him and the tail. It felt good to be holding it. Then Plunk remembered Eddie, who was staring at him like a puppy would look at somebody who'd just been mean to it.

"I didn't hurt it any," Eddie repeated. "I was just looking at it."

That made Plunk feel bad, though he still didn't want Eddie wearing his tail.

"Ah, hell, sit down and drink your beer," Plunk said. "I'll put this in the bedroom. I just don't want anybody screwing with it so it'll be in good shape for Halloween." He took the tail in and put it on the bed, stretching it out to pretty much full length. The tail still felt heavy and good.

There was a knock at the door and Plunk opened it to find Larry B. He also had a paper bag from the store. There were packages of microwave popcorn in it.

"Where's Red?" Plunk asked. "He didn't come with you?"

Larry B. grinned.

"He went on a date last night with that waitress at the burger place and never did get back home," he said. "He called me on my cell a couple minutes ago to say he wouldn't make it here for the game."

"Well, good for Red," Plunk said, but Eddie wasn't happy about it.

"Butthead was supposed to bring beer," he griped. "Now we've only got twelve."

"I'll go get some more if we need it," Larry B. said good-naturedly. Plunk switched on his widescreen and it was right at kickoff, the Cowboys against the sorry-ass team from Arizona. Dallas wasn't very good this season, they were 3–4 so far, but as usual the Arizona Cardinals were even worse and Plunk and his buddies expected a Cowboys win, which they got. Not having to worry about losing gave them plenty of time to comment on the play-calling of the Cowboys coach, the charms of the Dallas cheerleaders, and the resonance of their respective burps, which were facilitated by the beer. Turned out Eddie's twelve cans were plenty, nobody was really trying to get drunk as such. There was just the man-comfort thing of watching sports and ogling women and slamming down some suds. During halftime, secure in the certainty of a Cowboys win and prideful because of it, they briefly discussed an ongoing national issue, the wall partway across the US-Mexican border. Libs kept bitching that the section already built should be torn down because it was cruel or something, but the commentators on Fox News insisted that the whole border ought to be walled off immediately to protect America from mobs of illegal immigrant killers, drug dealers, and rapists. Plunk, Larry B., and Eddie were all on the Fox news side, how could anybody argue against such common sense, and now the other two agreed when Eddie said he just wished they'd build walls all around the borders of Texas, not let any bad illegals or crazy liberals in, which would solve all kinds of problems so far as real Texans were concerned. They toasted this brilliant solution, clinking their beer cans together and dripping foam on Plunk's musty-smelling carpet. When the game was over, all three were feeling relaxed and happy. Good times.

"You know about Plunk's goddamn gecko tail?" Eddie asked Larry B. They were both slouching on the couch draining the last few drops from beer cans. Plunk was lounging on the living room chair, one that came with the apartment. Plunk didn't like it all that much, it was covered in rust-colored fabric and had a spring that stuck in your back—well, the couch did, too—but it was there to sit on and the other guys had the couch.

"Plunk's got a tail?" Larry B. said, all curious. He made a big deal out of going over and taking a good look at Plunk's ass, the beer he'd consumed helping the degree of the pretend inspection. Plunk laughed and told Larry B. to get away from his butt, was Larry B. a goddamn dog or pervert or something, but then Larry B. really wanted to know. So Plunk told him the whole thing again, the visit to the costume shop, the three-piece leopard gecko costume, the store manager insisting Plunk buy all three pieces or none and how he talked the guy into selling him just the tail for seven hundred dollars.

"I thought it cost six hundred," Eddie interrupted, and Plunk wondered why the dickwad had to be spoiling his good story.

"Six hundred, seven hundred, whatever," Plunk said, and to move on he started telling about his struggle to keep the tail from dragging over gravel or in dog shit. After that, Larry B. of course had to see the tail all rigged up properly, so Plunk went into the bedroom and strapped it on, loving the heft of it up against his ass, the nice secure feeling of the retractable collar handle in his right hand.

He went out in the living room and showed the guys how it worked, and they loved it, exclaimed over and over how impressive it was. Plunk told Larry B. how he was going to wear it on Halloween night, and Larry B. said he might just have to come along and watch.

There was a second football game on TV, but Larry B. said he probably ought to get going, Red would surely have some great stories to tell about his night with the waitress. Did Plunk and Eddie want to head back with him?

Eddie did—he loved stories about people having sex, and neither he nor Plunk ever had much to talk about in that regard. Plunk said thanks, he'd pass. The other football game looked good, Denver and Las Vegas, and he wanted to watch.

So Eddie and Larry B. took off, and it was only after he shut the door behind them and went to sit down on the couch that Plunk realized he still had the tail strapped on, funny how he'd forgotten for a minute it was there.

8.

Plunk worked at Campbell Bolt & Screw, in the farthest southwest corner of Fort Worth. The office was a twenty-minute drive from his apartment in Crowley, thirty minutes if traffic piled up. He had to get in to work by 8 a.m. because construction crews got going at first light and what Plunk's company did was sell them bolts and screws and flanges and items like that. It wasn't high-ticket stuff and Plunk didn't get paid that much for selling it, $500 draw a week plus 5 percent of what he sold. On good weeks he took home maybe $800, but usually it was more like $650, sometimes even less. Probably he could have done better someplace else, but Plunk had worked at Campbell now for nine years and he didn't need that much money anyway, living as he did on microwave food and beer. It was easier to stay where he was.

Plunk and the other Campbell salesmen made their site calls in Fort Worth sometimes, but more often in its suburbs: Crowley, Benbrook, Keller, Weatherford, Burleson, sometimes as far south as Cleburne or even east as Arlington. There were only five of them selling for Campbell, which in truth was a kind of a raggedy-ass outfit. They didn't sell in Fort Worth much because that's where the big parts companies did their business, selling huge shitloads of bolts and screws to major contractors building skyscrapers. Campbell's customers were the little guys, the ones building some new rooms on houses in Benbrook or expanding a Mom-and-Pop cafe in Weatherford. Even then, Plunk didn't get to call on the ones who might order a couple thousand dollars' worth of stuff at a time. That honor with its bigger commission payouts was reserved for Kevin Eldridge and Broc Sears, who were buddies with company owner Austin Campbell. Kevin and Broc didn't even leave the office most days—they worked with phones and computers at their desks. Plunk and his Sunday football compadres Larry B. and Red got the small fry, the ones who might need a few hundred bucks' worth of bolts this week, fifty bucks' worth of screws the next. The little guy customers usually liked doing business face-to-face rather than on the phone or by computer.

Which meant Plunk spent most of his workdays hustling in his Ranger pickup from one town to another, checking in with foremen running projects to see if they needed anything that day. If they did, Plunk called the order in on his cell phone and office manager Jessika

Ortiz would notify the guys at the warehouse, which for some reason was a couple miles away from the company office. The Campbell truck would make the delivery within ninety minutes or the cost of the order was cut by 20 percent. Sometimes Plunk forgot to charge his cell phone and had to find a place to plug it in and partially recharge it, cutting delivery time perilously close to the full ninety minutes and Plunk didn't want that. The couple of times it happened, Austin took the loss out of Plunk's paycheck.

Plunk usually headed back to the office around noon so that Jessika, who handled both the phone and the daily accounts, could enter his sales in her special computer program for that and make them official, so he'd get the 5 percent commission in his biweekly check. Then, after Plunk ate something—a sandwich if he'd remembered to make and bring one, more often a handful of cookies from the stash he kept in a drawer of his desk—he'd head out again and try to sell some more.

Plunk would come in one last time every day to log afternoon sales; then if things felt right, he might go have a beer with Larry B. and Red before heading home. The thing he liked about his job was that you kept moving around a lot, no being stuck at a desk inside all day, and he got lots of chances to josh a little bit with all the different foremen he saw on a regular basis. They were mostly good guys who liked to take a break for a minute and swap jokes. Plunk had a good new one this week about a redhead, a brunette, and a blonde in the waiting room of an obstetrician's office and he was looking forward to telling it lots of times until he had no fresh audience left.

So he only expected to be in the office for a minute on Monday morning before heading off to Benbrook, where Joe Don—who was putting up a small parking garage by a doctor's office—had asked him last week to come by first thing Monday. But Jessika told him that Austin needed him, so Plunk went into his office. It was a nice office, very roomy, which you wouldn't have expected looking at the smallish Campbell Bolt & Screw building from the outside. Go through the front door, though, and you'd see Jessika had some space around her desk in front but Plunk and the other sales guys, even Kevin and Broc, were all jammed together in a corner, their beat-up metal desks bumping together at the corners. Ausin said he needed a private office with lots of room for meeting with clients, which was bullshit. Maybe twice a month a customer actually came to Campbell Bolt & Screw to place an order with the boss. Austin just wanted room to practice his putting, which he did constantly, knocking one golf ball after another across the floor into a metal glass, the ball making a little clinking noise when it went in, which it didn't often because Austin was a suckass putter, at least in the office. Kevin and Broc said he was great out on the course, and they would know because they played golf with him almost every Saturday morning. They said he always beat them fair and square, but Plunk had his doubts. Whatever, it wasn't really his business and he didn't mind never being invited to play because golf was boring. Also, Plunk had no golf clubs.

So Plunk went in, first knocking on the closed door because that was what all the employees except Kevin and Broc were supposed to do. He was told to come in, and of course there was the boss bending over a putt, not even looking up as he said good morning.

"What's up, Austin?" Plunk asked. They all called him "Austin" instead of "Mr. Campbell" because that was supposed to make them feel they were part of the same team.

"I need you to run out to the store sometime this morning and get a cake," Austin said, wriggling his putter back and forth before striking the golf ball. It rolled across the carpet and missed the mouth of the metal glass by at least two inches. "It's Jessika's twenty-sixth birthday and the cake's for her, so she can't do it."

Whenever somebody at the office had a birthday, Jessika went out and got a cake. Then at lunchtime everyone would gather around and sing "Happy Birthday." Plunk enjoyed it because he liked cake.

"Well, I gotta go over to Benbrook," Plunk said to the top of Austin's head, which was bent over another golf ball. "Joe Don says he'll be making a pretty good order. After that I thought I'd hit Wayne in Cleburne since I'll be out that way anyway, and also Celeste in Burleson."

"The dyke," Austin muttered as he missed another putt. Austin always assumed every female foreman was a dyke. Plunk didn't know if Celeste was dykey or not. Her business, not his. That's how Plunk felt about anything that wasn't normal, so long as he was left alone to live his own life the way he wanted. What he didn't like was when liberal buttheads took up against the things regular people believed and said and did. Why couldn't they just live and let live, like he tried to do?

"Anyway, I don't know where grocery stores are out that way," Plunk continued. "Maybe somebody else could get cake."

Austin looked up briefly. His face was puffy and several chins dangled underneath. Nobody liked cake more than he did.

"Sales aren't that great," he said. "So everybody's got to pitch in everywhere. You can find a cake someplace."

According to Austin, sales were never great, though that hadn't stopped him from building this reportedly bigass house in the best part of Keller where all the houses had three-car garages. Kevin and Broc had been there and told everybody else about it.

"Okay, I'll find one," Plunk said agreeably, though he thought if sales really were bad it would make more sense to let the salesmen just concentrate on selling, not buying birthday cake. But what the hell. Boss told you to do something, you did it. Life was that way.

And it turned out getting Jessika's birthday cake was just about the highlight of Plunk's workday. He got to Benbrook to find Joe Don was out sick and his number two thought they had all the stuff they needed, so Plunk should come back Tuesday to talk to Joe Don if Joe Don was back on the job. Wayne in Cleburne didn't need anything either, though he liked the joke about the blonde in the obstetrician's office (the punchline of "Oh, no, I'm gonna have *puppies*!" really cracked him up). Celeste in Burleson actually bought a bunch of stuff, $535 worth, $26.75 added to Plunk's next paycheck, but the whole rest of the day's seven more site calls only got another $75 or so from one piddly additional sale. Austin liked his salesmen to bring in at least $1,000 a day. For Kevin and Broc that was easy because they got the big accounts and could sell two or three times that, no sweat, but Plunk and Larry B. and Red really had to hustle and frequently didn't make it. Once a month Austin would get everybody together and read out individual sales totals. This was Plunk's least favorite time. On his worst sales months Austin would call him aside for a pep talk that included very little pep and lots of talk about the failing local economy and how hard it would be to find a new job at Plunk's age and minimal qualifications. But the great thing about Plunk, he could walk out of the office after that feeling real depressed and somehow still be cheerful by the time he joined Larry B. and Red for a cold one in a nearby bar before heading home.

Anyway, he found a bakery as opposed to a grocery store in Burleson and he bought Jessika one hell of a birthday cake, a couple layers with flowers and other shit made out of sugar and "Happy Birthday" across the top in pink. Girly, but so was Jessika. Everybody said it was a great cake, and Plunk got reimbursed from petty cash for the thirty-three dollars he paid for it. On the way home from work he stopped at the bank and withdrew seventy-five dollars from his checking account. Then he went to Target and bought the black jeans and tennis shoes to wear on Halloween night. Sometimes Plunk flat out forgot to do errand-y things like pay bills and shop for TV dinners, but there was no chance he would have forgotten getting the jeans and shoes. All day long he'd been smiling, even after the string of unsuccessful sales calls, because he knew that at the end of the day he was going home to his tail.

9.

Halloween was just freakin' spectacular. Plunk and his tail were a sensation. In his wildest dreams he couldn't have imagined it turning out as great as it did.

The wonderfulness commenced right when he walked out his apartment door, dressed in the yellow sweatshirt even though it was chilly enough for a coat, and also the black jeans and black tennies. Plus the tail, the fabulous miraculous tail, and Plunk already knew enough to pull the sweatshirt way down so that if you didn't know to look for the belts holding it on you'd swear the tail was growing right out of Plunk's ass. The retractable leash let him have the tail up off the concrete when he began to stroll across the complex parking lot, but he didn't get far because the handful of parents who lived at The Jacksonian had their kids waiting for Plunk and his tail to appear. All the grown-ups wanted to take pictures of the kids with Plunk. It was already full dark even though it wasn't 7 p.m. yet so the sudden sharp lights from their cell phones hurt Plunk's eyes, but he didn't care. And the kids, well, they were just peeing themselves with excitement, all of them in Harry Potter outfits or characters from the latest Marvel movie. Some of the little girls were plain vanilla fairies or princesses. They clustered around Plunk and it was very lucky he had the leash holding the tail mostly out of their reach, because they grabbed at it with hands already sticky from early Halloween candy.

"Just touch it real easy, don't yank on it," Plunk instructed, and the kids minded very well. It must have taken twenty minutes for all the parking lot pictures to get taken, and when the last cell phone photo flash had burned spots in his vision Plunk hollered, "Now who's ready for trick-or-treat?" and the kids screamed back that they were.

So Plunk ended up sort of a Pied Piper leading this bunch of kids, really a *throng*, on a double-time march to Crowley's nearby residential streets, where there were other gangs of kids already knocking on doors but one by one they quit that when word spread about Plunk and his tail. All the kids wanted to look at it, touch it, and every trailing parent with a cell phone begged Plunk to pose with Jason or Molly, and being an agreeable guy of course he did. Streetlights on some blocks helped reveal the tail in its glory, but still there wasn't a lot of light. So most everybody missed the belts around Plunk's waist and between his legs and he kept getting asked how he kept the tail on. After a while he'd respond, "Whatcha mean, how do I keep it on? Ain't ya seen a guy with a tail before?" and every time he said it, bad grammar but who cared, Plunk would then roar with laughter, because of course he knew nobody had ever seen anything like it.

All the grown-ups handing out candy on their porches loved the tail, too, no crap like last year with Plunk's President Trump. Several of them insisted Plunk take some candy too, even though his whole purpose in being there was to increase candy take for all the kids. It would have been impolite to refuse, and soon enough Plunk felt the pulse-pumping onset of sugar rush from all the miniature Milky Way bars and mini-packs of Skittles, not that he needed any extra energy boost. This night was just great, Halloween the way Plunk always wanted it to be, people laughing and having extra fun all because of him.

And there was this nice thing where everybody was impressed with the tail but they seemed respectful of it too. Mostly Plunk walked around with it lifted just off the grass or sidewalk to keep it unmarred and shiny, and every kid wanted to touch it, but they usually didn't pull at it and most of the parents cautioned them to be careful with it. Every other block or so Plunk would pause to demonstrate how he could raise and lower the tail using the retractable leash, though after the first couple times he realized it was more impressive just to do the raising and lowering without explaining how it was done.

Though everybody wanted to look at the tail, nobody bothered with questions about what kind of tail it was or anything. It was as though the tail itself was enough, pedigree had no bearing, which was good because if somebody had asked Plunk for more details about leopard geckos he wouldn't have known any. But nobody asked. They just loved the tail.

As if things weren't already great enough, ninety minutes into Plunk's Halloween night a reporter and photographer from Crowley's weekly newspaper showed up. Plunk knew the reporter, heavyset Linda whose day job was working a bank's drive-up window. She wrote for *The Crowley Observer* on the side, little stories about local events. The paper's only full-time employee sold ads. Linda and a couple others supplied the stories, receiving a few bucks for each one. Called "stringers" in newspaper lingo, they did it in hopes of jump-starting careers as full-time journalists. Plunk knew for a fact Linda periodically sent what she called her "clips" to the daily papers in Fort Worth and Dallas, hoping she'd get hired on as a reporter, which was her lifelong goal. She'd been chasing that dream a long time—she was at least ten years older than Plunk, which put her on the sorry side of fifty—but she never gave up. Plunk knew her from back in his days as Warrior Mascot. She'd written a couple stories about him then.

"Hey, Linda, what can I do for ya?" Plunk hollered, as if he didn't know.

"I'm supposed to write a Halloween story about Crowley trick-or-treaters, but all everybody is talking about is you," Linda said, fumbling with a pen and notebook. "This tail, Plunk. All the kids are just loving your tail."

"Yeah, well, I think maybe they're getting more candy because of it," Plunk said modestly. He noticed how Linda was trying to look him in the eye, but her gaze kept slipping toward his side and ass where the tail hung down. "It's a pretty nice tail, I guess. Hey, no yanking! Touch it gently!" He said this not to Linda but to a little girl in a princess getup who'd run up with hands outstretched.

"All of the children want to get a closer look," Linda said. "Can I interview you for a minute?"

Plunk pretended to think it over, but he didn't really. He was pleased about being in the paper. He hadn't been for a long time, and he couldn't understand it. He should at least have been every Halloween with all the great costumes. But nobody at *The Crowley Observer* had thought so. Now Linda was asking for an interview, pleading really, and Plunk liked the sensation of importance, of *mattering*.

"I don't know if I got the time," he said, just for the fun of making Linda squirm. "These kids are depending on me for help with their trick-or-treating."

Linda scribbled in her notebook, getting the interview going even though Plunk hadn't exactly agreed to it. That was the way of pushy journalists, he thought. Their kind of attitude was one reason Plunk seldom read a newspaper: He depended on Fox News for his political and cultural information, because Fox always made things easy to understand. But he'd sure look at the next edition of *The Crowley Observer* if he and his tail were in it.

"You dress up lots of Halloweens, don't you?" Linda asked. "When did you start doing it?"

Plunk acted indignant, and it wasn't all an act.

"I do this every Halloween, not just lots of them," he said. "I want to help everybody have fun. I been Dak Prescott, and also the guy from the *X-Files*, and last year President Trump and some people complained about that one because they got no sense of humor. There's nothing wrong with having fun. That's what Halloween's for, fun and candy for the kids."

"About the tail," Linda said. "How did you come up with that?"

Plunk had to caution a couple more kids not to pull on the tail, and that gave him a second to reflect. He wanted the tail to be entirely his own doing, not something he'd gotten from somebody else.

"I was just looking for something different," he said. "So I fixed it up with this leash and all so I could get it to go up and down." That wasn't a lie. Plunk tried never to lie, though he wasn't above stretching the truth to make something sound more interesting.

"So you made the tail yourself?" Linda persisted. Damn nosy reporters.

"Well, actually no, not really," Plunk conceded. "They made it at a costume store–"

"Quality Costumes from right here in Crowley?" Every October, Mr. Davenport the store manager bought some Halloween ads in the *Observer*, and Linda and the weekly's other stringers were on constant alert to mention advertisers in their stories whenever possible.

"Yeah, there," Plunk said, feeling testy. "But those buttheads at the store didn't really appreciate it. I guess you can't write 'buttheads' in your story, so pick another word." Linda nodded. "Anyway, somebody ordered the costume and then didn't want it."

"A lizard costume of some kind?"

"Right, but not a lizard. It's a leopard gecko because it's yellow with black spots. They had other parts of it, but the tail was best and I bought that."

"What's it made of? How do you keep it on?"

So Plunk told her about the vinyl outside and good solid rubber inside, and about the three sets of belts, and then about his experiments with how to keep the tail from dragging on gravel or dog-messed grass, and Linda kept nodding and scribbling in her notebook.

"You're such a hit with your tail this year, what are you going to go out as next Halloween?" she asked.

Plunk had no idea. He loved his tail and it somehow seemed like being unfaithful to it to speculate about a future costume.

"I'll worry about that later," he said. "Right now I got to help these kids get all the candy they can."

"I'm going to interview some kids and parents about the tail," Linda said. She gestured to the guy standing by with the camera. "Jesse's going to take a few pictures, okay? And my story will be in the *Observer* when it comes out next Monday."

Linda pulled some kids and parents aside, jotting down whatever it was they were telling her, and Plunk knew it had to be good because they kept pointing at the tail and laughing. Even better was how Jesse the photographer must have spent fifteen minutes posing him this way and that, sometimes with kids clustered around him, sometimes Plunk and the tail alone, and then Jesse asked Plunk to walk up to somebody's door leading a pack of trick-or-treaters. He took what seemed like a hundred shots of that, the lady giving out the candy was so pleased to have her picture taken that she gave the kids on her porch with Plunk all the candy she had left, and it was a lot. She said she was going to have to go inside and turn off all the lights afterward.

Plunk stayed out until every last trick-or-treater was done, it must have been 10 p.m. or later before he got home with his tail proudly following behind him. What a Halloween! What a night! Plunk stood in front of the mirror for a while admiring the tail before he finally took it off, his ass instantly feeling much lighter without the weight but not *better*. If Plunk had followed his usual Halloween tradition he would have stuck the tail in the closet where he kept remnants of previous costumes, but he just couldn't do it. Instead he laid the tail on his couch and near-reverently used dampened paper towels to wipe off dust and the occasional child's chocolate-y handprint. Then he sat in his chair, sipping a beer and smiling at the tail and wondering what picture of him might be printed in the *Observer*. Good times, nothing but good times, and Plunk had a sense they were going to get even better. The tail was lucky for him, he just knew it.

10.

As good as Plunk felt when he went to bed Halloween night, that was how lousy he felt when he got up for work the next morning. Reflection was not what Plunk was all about, and he rarely analyzed his equally rare bad moods, but he knew why he was in this one. Halloween had been great, had been spectacularly good, and it was over. His tail was going into the closet or something. The winter months looming ahead meant only work, an ongoing mediocre season from the Cowboys, and Mom asking about Annie with increasing frequency.

So Plunk fixed breakfast, instant coffee and a couple Pop-Tarts. He put on a knit shirt and some khakis—Austin didn't insist on coats and ties but he wouldn't go for his salesmen in jeans and T-shirts—

then sort of gave the tail, which he'd left on the couch, an affectionate pat on his way out. In the car on the way to the office he listened to the country station, but Willie Nelson and Carrie Underwood didn't get him singing along like they usually did.

But when he got to the office everybody else was pretty happy because it was Friday, and Plunk perked up a little because of that. Larry B. asked how his Halloween went, adding that he was sorry he hadn't gotten there with his camera to take pictures of the tail. And Jessika asked what tail was that, which got Plunk describing it and everybody else gathered 'round to hear, Austin even quit putting for a minute to come listen. Plunk ended up sort of acting out how he led kids up and down the Crowley streets on their trick-or-treating rounds, and the decision was made that Plunk would have to bring the tail in to work on Monday so everyone could see it.

That had Plunk feeling considerably better when he went out on his morning calls, and damned if every place he went didn't put in orders, pretty good ones, too. He was already a couple hundred over two thousand for the day when he went back to the office around noon, and then the afternoon calls brought in another thousand or so. Plunk wasn't real hot at math, but he knew he'd have some fine extra in his next paycheck.

Which made the Friday afternoon beers with Larry B. and Red taste just that much greater. At Larry B.'s suggestion, Red described his date with the hamburger place waitress to Plunk, including a couple pretty interesting things she liked to do in the dark. Plunk didn't really care about other people's sex lives, their business and not his, but if somebody wanted to tell about it, it would be impolite not to listen, and this gal apparently was something else.

"What's her name again?" Plunk asked.

"Susie. Suzanne. Shit, I'm not sure," Red confessed.

"So when you gonna do her again?" Plunk asked. "I mean, when you gonna *see* her again?" That wasn't anything dirty, just the way guys liked to joke around.

"I'm gonna see her a lot, I guess, since I like the burgers where she works," Red said. "I don't know about doing her anymore, though. She acted kind of funny when I went in for lunch a couple times last week, saying shit like where were we going to go the next time and everything. Besides doing it with her, the rest of it wasn't anything special. She talked about her feet hurting and how she wants to be a hairdresser as soon as she gets together the money to go back to school. Like I cared or anything."

Plunk and Larry B. sipped their beers and nodded in agreement. This was typical of women, talking about superficial stuff and expecting you to listen.

Saturday Plunk spent just screwing around; he didn't have any plans beyond watching some college football and doing whatever else he felt like. Which ended up involving his tail, or rather where to store it until next Halloween, when he was certain that he'd wear it again. The one closet in the apartment held bits of past costumes as well as Plunk's meager supply of clothes, but it would have been disrespectful, even sacrilegious, to stick the tail in with that lesser stuff. But it couldn't just be left out on the floor, where somebody might step on it, or Eddie might even puke on it after too many beers watching a game on TV. He'd had a couple accidents like that before.

So Plunk went to the hardware store and then to Target looking for some kind of plastic packaging the tail could be stored in, but there wasn't anything to fit a long pointed tail, no surprise. The trip wasn't wasted because Plunk splurged and got himself a whole bucket of extra-crispy KFC, his favorite food ever and something he usually couldn't afford. But he'd had that big sales day Friday, and besides there was the great Halloween to celebrate. So he got the chicken plus a couple family-sized sides, slaw and mashed potatoes and gravy and a half-dozen warm biscuits, how about that? Plunk went home, put the feast on the card table, popped a beer, and ate himself half sick while watching some football. The tail was stretched out on the couch and seemed to provide a kind of companionship, which Plunk appreciated. He was glad not to have a roommate; he hadn't lived with anybody since Annie took off fifteen years ago. He'd lived with his folks, then with a wife. When he was a kid, Plunk usually didn't like being alone, hell, like the high school counselor said, he was a people person, nothing wrong with that, but after Annie left it seemed like he wouldn't be comfortable sharing a place with somebody else. They'd been married just over three years when she decided to get out, which didn't surprise Plunk since he knew things weren't great, but still it hurt his feelings. There hadn't been a serious woman in his life since, and Plunk thought if two men roomed together it sort of seemed gay even when it wasn't. Plunk didn't mind gays, hell, what people did to each other and who they did it with wasn't anybody's business but their own. Thing was, he just didn't want anybody thinking *he* might be gay. This was Texas, after all. So he had his buddies over to watch ballgames, he told them his place was their place, but at night when he turned out the lights it was only him. Plunk liked being host because everything revolved around him. With a roommate you had to ask before having people over. Eddie had made some noises about layoffs rumored at the Miller beer plant in south Fort Worth where he worked, and maybe he and Plunk should think about sharing a place to save them both some money, but it wasn't going to happen.

Plunk thought, as he enjoyed a tasty burp combining beer and fried chicken flavors, that the tail might be the all-time best roommate. It looked good, it was nice to have around, and it didn't talk when Plunk was trying to concentrate on the ballgame.

"Shit, I oughta marry it," he cracked, and laughed at his own remark when the tail didn't respond.

The tail was still on the couch when Plunk got up Sunday, and he was feeling a little rocky because maybe he'd had one too many beers the night before. But it was still Sunday and time to go see Mom, so he got dressed and had coffee and a cold piece of leftover KFC and started out the door. But his eye fell on the tail, and he remembered he'd told Mom he might bring it by to show her. So he picked it up and carried it outside in the crook of his arm.

It being Sunday morning, nobody was out in the parking lot. Plunk's neighbors generally liked to sleep in on Sundays, few of them cared about church or anything. Plunk himself liked the idea of church but not actually going to it. Now he crossed the street and already his arm felt a little tired from lugging the tail, it was after all long and heavy with the weight of it unevenly distributed when carried because one end was real wide and the other pointy. But then Plunk thought hey, why not, and right there in the street he strapped the thing on and got the button end of the retractable leash in his hand to pull the tail up off the sidewalk. The heaviness on his ass was just so right, he now realized that when he wore the thing he immediately felt better, happier, and as he walked the few cars passing on the street slowed down so the people inside could get a better look, some of them even called out hearty hellos, and if one clown bitched, "Halloween's over, pal!" well, there was bound to be a butthead in every bunch.

Mom and everybody else at Pleasant Valley just went nuts over the tail, or as nuts as worn-out old people could get. The aides in the constant care wing heard the commotion, and one of them asked if Mr. Landy would mind bringing his costume over so some of her patients could enjoy it too, and naturally Plunk obliged. He felt really touched at how these out of it geezers—the men and women looked almost identical, patchy hair and lots of drool—widened their eyes in amazement and gently reached out to touch the tail, which Plunk had polished up to a nice gleam during some of his Saturday downtime. The aides wanted to know how the tail stayed on and Plunk showed them the belts and also how the retractable leash worked. There was such a drawn-out fuss that Plunk didn't get home until a half-hour after the Cowboys' kickoff, and boy was Eddie pissed about that. He and Red and Larry B. had downed about two beers each waiting on Plunk's apartment porch, but they hadn't left because he was the one with the widescreen TV. Plunk apologized and everybody went inside, and they had a good time even though the Cowboys lost to the Eagles.

After the guys left, Plunk polished the tail again—some of the old folks had left handprints on it, unintentionally of course—and decided that after taking it to work tomorrow he'd maybe just leave it on the couch for a little while longer until he decided how to store it properly. He really hated to put it away until next Halloween and was glad he'd gotten to wear it one more time before he did.

Then the Monday edition of *The Crowley Observer* came out, and Plunk didn't have to figure out how to store the tail after all.

11.

On Mondays the *Observer* didn't get put into sales racks until afternoon, and then only in Crowley and a couple other south Fort Worth suburbs. Plunk resigned himself to not seeing the story about himself until he came home after work. He'd pick up a copy outside the 7-11 then.

But it was sure something to look forward to. As he put the tail in the front seat of his pickup, actually using the seatbelt to keep it safely in place—sometimes Plunk skipped wearing his own seatbelt because nobody had the right to tell him that he had to wear one, but he was taking no chances with the tail—Plunk wondered what photo the *Observer* would run. He hoped it would be one of the ones Jesse snapped on the old lady's front porch, because those captured it all—Plunk wearing the tail and helping everybody have more fun, and the kids getting more candy because of it.

During the drive Plunk played a pop music oldies station, good stuff always and this particular morning better than usual, "We Are the Champions" and other great tunes. He sang along loud and off-key with them all. When he arrived at work everybody wanted to see him put the tail on right away, but Austin from his office hollered out that sales had been down, there were lots of sales calls to make, and everybody could do whatever at lunchtime if they wanted. Plunk had no place to leave the tail so Jessika offered to keep it by her desk.

"Don't let anybody mess with it," Plunk pleaded, and Jessika gave him a kind of odd look before promising she wouldn't let anyone even look at it until he got back. Still, Plunk felt uncomfortable leaving the tail under anyone's supervision but his own.

This meant he felt distracted while making his morning rounds, hitting some minor league contractors in Keller and Saginaw, places north of Fort Worth itself. Plunk made some sales but just small ones, maybe $350 total. Worse, because he'd gone so far north he didn't get back to the office until twenty past twelve, and he worried the whole way that everybody else couldn't wait to see the tail and maybe it had gotten messed up somehow.

But when he got there, he found Jessika had kept everybody away and they were all waiting respectfully until Plunk arrived. He appreciated it, and immediately went to strap on the tail when Jessika said, "Don't you want to read about yourself first?"

"Whaddaya mean?" Plunk asked, and Jessika waved a copy of the *Observer* at him.

"Larry B. knew you wouldn't want to wait, so when he was on a sales call he stopped by the *Observer* office and picked this up for you," she said. Jessika added something else but Plunk didn't hear her, because when he held the paper in his hand he saw his picture on the front page, and it was great. There he stood on the lady's porch and the whole tail was stretched out behind him, and the kids were looking at it wide-eyed and the headline read, "Local Man Spins Halloween 'Tail.'" Some might have wished the *Observer* could run photos in color instead of just black-and-white but that didn't occur to Plunk. He loved the picture exactly the way it was. After a minute he realized Jessika was urging him to read the whole story out loud, and he wanted to but worried that would look stuck up. He also wasn't great anyway when it came to pronouncing words while reading out loud; he'd sucked at that all during school and didn't want to embarrass himself doing it again now. So he told Jessika she should read it to everybody, and she did.

It was a good story though it had its share of mistakes, the kind Linda always made. Jessika read:

"*Local Man Spins Halloween 'Tail.'* That's the headline."

"I know that already," Plunk blurted, and everybody else laughed because he sounded so impatient. "Read the rest of it."

Jessika grinned; she was having fun with him.

"*By Linda Prescott.* Oh, I guess you already knew that, too."

"Read the damn story," Plunk pleaded.

Jessika took a deep breath and began.

"Halloween trick-or-treaters in Crowley got a special thrill Thursday night when longtime resident Plunk Landy appeared on the streets in costume. As is his annual custom, Mr. Landy dressed up to help urge grown-ups to be generous in giving away candy. In recent years Mr. Landy has dressed as Dallas Cowboys quarterback Dak Prescott, as Mulder from the TV series X-Files, *and last year as President Trump, which upset some of his neighbors."*

"They just didn't have a sense of humor," Plunk moaned. "Why did she have to even mention that?"

"Don't interrupt while I'm reading or I'll stop," Jessika warned. "Okay. Here we go again."

"*On Thursday Mr. Landy topped them all by wearing a colorful lizard tail that he identified as belonging to a Leopard Gecko because of its gold color and black polka dots. The long, wide tail delighted the trick-or-treating children, who Mr. Landy allowed to touch the tail as long as they didn't yank on it.*

"Mr. Landy found the tail at Quality Costumes in Crowley, which Mr. Landy says has some of the finest Halloween costumes anywhere." Plunk knew he'd never said that, but he wasn't about to interrupt Jessika again to point it out. "*The tail was part of a three-piece costume, but Mr. Landy insisted on purchasing only the tail because he felt it 'had class.' No one meeting Mr. Landy on Halloween night could recall seeing anyone wearing a tail before.*

"'I like the way it looks,' said Trixie Bressoud of Crowley, who gave all her remaining Halloween candy to the children accompanying Mr. Landy when they appeared on her doorstep. 'And I like a man who's happy to dress up and have fun with little children. America needs more people like him.'

"Mr. Landy says he might wear the Leopard Gecko tail again next Halloween.

"'You bet I'll be out here again,' he promised as all the children around him cheered. 'There's nothing wrong with helping other people have fun. That's why I do this.'"

Everybody waited a second until Jessika said, "Well, that's all of the story," and then they clapped Plunk on the shoulder and urged him to strap the tail on, which he did, showing the three belts and how he pulled the tip of the tail up and down with the retractable leash. All the while, he was thinking about how many copies of the *Observer* he should buy for a dollar each when he got back to Crowley. He could bring one to Mom and also give some to the other old people at the home. Maybe Eddie would want one, too. Somebody would.

Plunk paraded around the office in the tail while everybody else finished eating their sandwiches and drinking their sodas or coffee, everybody having fun until finally Austin came out of his office, putter in hand, to ask about the commotion. But he, too, was amazed by Plunk's tail, and also the story in the *Observer*, which Jessika gave him to read.

"Let's have a look, Plunk," he ordered, and Plunk sidled over. Austin inspected the tail and also the belts, asked if it fit snug, and then knitted his brows together in thought.

"Say, Plunk, what you doing Saturday afternoon?" he asked.

Plunk said he had nothing planned besides watching college football, which was the truth.

"Okay," Austin said, "my boy's having his sixth birthday party at two at our place in Keller. We've got a pony ride and things. My wife hired that Tex guy who does kids' parties."

"I've heard about him," Jessika said. "Two-Gun Tex is what he's called. A woman from my church had him come to her niece's birthday party maybe two years ago."

"Is he any good?" Austin asked. "Costing me money, and my boy and his buddies get bored easy."

"I think she said that besides bringing the pony, he also dressed like a cowboy clown and had toy guns that shot bubbles or something," Jessika said. "He had the kids have a water pistol fight."

"Sounds pretty good," Plunk said, thinking he would have loved having some cowboy with bubble-shooting guns come to one of his birthday parties.

"Actually, the lady from my church said it didn't go too good, but it wasn't really the Tex guy's fault," Jessika said. "The girl having the birthday was turning ten, and I guess she and her friends thought they were too grown up for clowns and bubbles and stuff. Your son's turning six? That ought to be just the right age."

Austin frowned. "It was my wife's friend's idea for us to hire this guy, but if the kids hate him, she'll blame me." He pointed to Plunk's picture on the front page of the *Observer*. "Kids definitely like the tail. Plunk, how about you come over and wear that thing at the party on Saturday? Make sure the kids have a good time."

"You already got the Tex guy." Plunk said. "He probably wouldn't want me in his way."

"It's my call, not his," Austin said. "Hell, it says in this newspaper story that on Halloween all the kids cheered for you."

Plunk didn't exactly remember the cheering, but it probably happened if Linda put it in the story, unlike what he was supposed to have said about the costume shop.

"I guess I could come," he told Austin, pleased that there was a new reason to keep the tail out a while longer.

"Well, Jessika'll get you directions," Austin said. "Two p.m., remember. If I tell my kid you're coming and you don't show up he'll raise hell."

"I'll be there," Plunk promised.

"I'll take this story home to show my boy and my wife," Austin added. Plunk really wanted to keep the copy of the *Observer* for himself, but what the heck. He'd get more copies after work.

Everybody had one more good laugh when Jessika had to remind Plunk to take off the tail before he went out to make his afternoon sales calls.

12.

Monday night Plunk sat on his couch rereading the *Observer* story while he waited for the NFL game to come on TV. He'd read the thing so often he pretty much had it memorized, but he enjoyed each fresh look at it just the same. Even more than the printed words he loved the picture, how the kids looked so excited and his tail was just freakin' amazing, nobody could look at that picture and not realize it. Right now he had the tail laid out on the bed, and when he turned in he'd move it to the couch. He'd decided it was best to keep the tail stretched out full length so it didn't start getting kinks in it like a curled-up rubber hose or something. After the party on Saturday he'd have to start thinking about how to store it again, but that was a bunch of days away and Plunk was a living in the now kind of guy.

There were maybe ten minutes left until kickoff, Browns versus Saints and neither really one of Plunk's favorite teams, but it was football. He'd just decided to go ahead and get up for a beer when somebody knocked on the door. Plunk figured it was probably Eddie, who didn't watch that many Monday night games over at Plunk's because Monday was Eddie's bowling night with guys he worked with at the Miller plant—they had a team in a league. But sometimes Eddie decided not to, and Plunk figured it was one of those times until he opened the door and a woman was standing there. It took him a second to realize who it was, the know-it-all from an apartment across the way.

"Hi," she said kind of tentatively, pushing her glasses up the bridge of her nose. "I hope you're not busy."

"Well, the game's coming on," Plunk replied, then realized that probably sounded kind of rude, which he tried never to be. "What can I do for you … " and there was a little pause while Plunk tried to remember her name, it was on the tip of his goddamn tongue.

"Darlene," she said, sounding patient but sad, like people forgot her name all the time. "Darlene Quaverley. From the apartment over there."

"Yeah, Darlene," Plunk said. "I know. What can I do for you?"

She flapped some stuff in her hand.

"There was a story about you in the paper," she said. "I didn't know if you'd seen it."

"Yeah, I did," Plunk said, and there was a moment of silence, Darlene obviously waiting to be invited in and Plunk finally thought to step aside and gesture for her to come ahead.

"There's the couch," Plunk said and Darlene sat down, obviously noticing the crumpled sack of potato chips on it, and also the empty foil TV dinner tray that was still on the card table. Plunk didn't mind stuff laying around for a while. Darlene kind of moved the potato chip sack out of her way, she could have sat farther to one side of the couch and not had to move the bag at all, but it was right where she was dropping her butt down. She tried to move the bag without making a big deal out of it, which made a big deal out of it and annoyed Plunk somewhat.

"So what's up?" Plunk asked again, dropping into the red chair with the spring that stuck in your back. "To what do I owe the honor of your visit?" He meant that to sound funny but even to Plunk it came out sarcastic.

"Well," Darlene said, squirming on the couch as though trying to find a comfortable spot. Wayward springs were poking her, too. "I saw the story about you in the paper and how you were telling about leopard geckos. I thought maybe somebody might ask you more questions, so I got on the computer and printed you out some articles on them." She reached across and handed Plunk the manila envelope she'd been holding, and he opened it. Inside were a bunch of pages with pictures and facts about leopard geckos.

"Real nice," Plunk said.

"There's a lot of information about them, what they eat and

things," Darlene said. "Maybe you looked it up already, I don't know."

Plunk said, "Nah, I haven't got around to it yet," which was true. It was also true that he never looked anything up on computers because computers kind of scared him. He was always worried about hitting a wrong key and wiping out the Internet or something. Every day at work, Jessika had to remind him how to log in on his desk laptop and then type in the password he always forgot (*dallascowboys-rule*) to check his emails. Plunk took one sheet at random out of the manila envelope from Darlene. The printout began, "Leopard geckos are found in dry areas. They prefer rocky desert and semi-arid grassland over open stretches of sand. They're crepuscular and nocturnal, spending the daytime in rock crevices or burrows."

"That's real interesting," Plunk said, even though he had no idea what "crepuscular" and several other things meant. "I appreciate your trouble."

"It wasn't hard," Darlene said, twitching a little back and forth like she couldn't make up her mind whether to lean back on the couch or not. She was wearing a black sweater and pants and Plunk could see some old crumbs from the couch, potato chip and cookie and so forth, sticking to her clothes. She noticed them too and tried furtively to brush them off.

"I work in the library so I can look up anything I want to," Darlene continued. "There's reference books and magazines besides the internet. If you want more I can find it for you."

"This is plenty," Plunk assured her, and because he felt more conversation was required to seem polite and appreciative he added, "You're a librarian?"

Darlene shook her head.

"I'm a librarian's assistant. I don't have my certification. Yet. But I'm going to Tarrant County College at night to get it."

"That's real good," Plunk said. "Librarian's a good job." And it seemed to him that it was, getting to sit around and read all day if that was what you liked to do. Plunk didn't, he had no books in his apartment and in fact hadn't read a book since he graduated high school.

"It's all right," Darlene replied. "But when I do get certified it's just something I'll be doing to pay the bills until my own books come out. I'm really an author. I'm also taking writing courses and I'm going to write bestselling novels like Colleen Hoover and Nora Roberts and Sandra Brown. I've been working on the draft of one for a year and I've finished almost two chapters. They're really good."

"Hey," Plunk said, trying to sound impressed. He hadn't heard of the writers Darlene mentioned, but then he didn't know the names of any writers. He steered the conversation back to more comfortable ground. "How long you been working at the library?"

"Five years," Darlene said. "You're supposed to be able to get your librarian certification in two, but I've been sidetracked with taking writing classes and also the writing itself. Being a librarian's not my ultimate destiny. One of my professors at Tarrant County College, he once had a novel published in New York. So when he says I've got potential, he knows what he's talking about."

"I guess he does," Plunk said. He peeked at his watch, because he knew the game was coming on. "Say, I appreciate you bringing me this stuff about the geckos. It'll come in real handy."

Darlene didn't immediately take the hint.

"If we get on your computer I can show you some actual leopard gecko sites," she said. "People keep them as pets."

"Ah, I don't have a computer here," Plunk said. "Don't feel like I need one." Which was true. Plunk could get all the sports scores on ESPN, and news on Fox.

"Okay," Darlene said. "Well. I better let you go. If you get any more questions about leopard geckos let me know. Though I guess since Halloween's over you won't be wearing that tail anymore and nobody will ask you about it."

"Not true," Plunk said proudly. "My boss wants me to come to his kid's sixth birthday party on Saturday and wear the tail. He says they'll go nuts over it, just like everybody on Halloween did. So I'm keeping it out. It's a special tail."

Darlene arched her eyebrows in surprise, and the motion caused her glasses to slide back down her nose. She pushed them up with a practiced gesture and said, "Well, that must make you happy. Because it sure seems like you loved wearing that tail."

"Yeah," Plunk said. "I got it right back in the bedroom. Did you get a good look at it in the parking lot the other day? 'Cause if you want, I could bring it out for you to see now."

Darlene seemed pleased.

"If it's not too much trouble," she said.

"Nah, not at all," Plunk assured her, and it only took him a minute to go get the tail, which he strapped on so he could show Darlene how he'd rigged the retractable leash to pull the tail tip up and down.

"You're really clever," she said, and that pleased Plunk because it wasn't a word people generally used to describe him. So he ended up offering Darlene a beer if she wanted, and she took one but just had a few small sips, woman-style, no gulping it down like men do, and Plunk found himself talking about the whole experimental process, the wire and the string and the duct tape and the visit to the store to buy the three different leashes. Darlene seemed very interested and made the helpful suggestion that he ought to get a pair of yellow work gloves to wear on Saturday so it would sort of look like he had lizard claws instead of human hands. That led, and afterward Plunk wasn't quite sure how, to the suggestion that she come with him to the birthday party on Saturday to help with the tail or whatever, maybe have a little question-and-answer session on leopard geckos for the kids, though Plunk knew any real kid, at least any six-year-old boys, would care less about something like that. But if there were little girls at the party maybe they'd like it, so what the hell.

Darlene ended up staying for almost an hour, and when Plunk turned on the game after she left he'd already missed all of the first quarter and most of the second. He sat on the couch with the tail stretched out beside him and idly wondered when the last time was a woman had been in his apartment.

13.

"What the hell, Plunk, you got you a *date*!" Larry B. hollered. It was Tuesday lunchtime and Plunk, Larry B., and Red had piled into the cab of Red's beat-up old F100 to go out for burgers. Mostly they brought their lunches, they didn't make enough to eat out every day, but earlier that morning Plunk happened to mention Darlene's visit and of course his buddies just had to make more of it than there really was, though maybe Plunk had emphasized how pleased she'd seemed when he said she could go with him on Saturday.

"It's not a date," Plunk insisted, though in a sort of speculative tone that implied it might be one after all. "She just wants to come help me with my tail." That sounded just suggestive enough, and all three of them howled with laughter. "Screw you dirty-minded guys," Plunk added. "You know what I mean."

"What's important is, she knows what you mean!" Red said. "You say she's one of those quiet ones. They're hell on wheels in the dark."

"Now, I never said she's quiet, cause she isn't," Plunk said. "She talks all the damn time. I said she acts like she's smart. She works in the library."

Larry B. and Red, roommates who shared a taste for adult movies, turned out to have recently seen a show involving a librarian who liked hands-on research of a sexy nature. They described it in some detail until Red pulled his truck into the parking lot of the hamburger place he liked so much.

"Hey, this is the place that girlfriend of yours works," Plunk said. "Or ex-girlfriend. Susan? Didn't you say you weren't going out with her again?"

"I think her name's Suzanne. She kept getting weird on me," Red said. "All about where we'd go the next time. And wanting to be a hairdresser. Life's too short."

"You got laid, though," Larry B. pointed out. "So it wasn't all bad."

"Won't it bother you seeing her, knowing she's waiting to get asked out again and all?" Plunk asked.

"Nah," Red grunted. "The burgers here are great, and it's not like I even told her afterwards I'd call. So I'm gonna keep coming. It's all right."

Which it turned out to be. The burger place wasn't real big, and when they got their table the waitress Red went out with came right over and acted fine.

"You guys look hungry," she said, and Plunk noticed her name tag read "Suzette."

"What's good today besides you?" Red asked, which Plunk thought might not have been the best thing to say, but Suzette laughed it right off.

"I guess some stuff's too good for you, but the cheddar burger's on special for $9.95 with fries," she said. So they each ordered one and also beers: Even though Austin didn't really like anybody drinking on the job, one wouldn't hurt. The weather was shitty anyway, intermittent cold rain, so lots of the site crews had already called it a day and the three of them might as well just not bother making calls the rest of the afternoon. Suzette came by every so often to ask if they needed anything else, and Plunk felt like she was maybe hoping Red would show a little interest in another date, but he didn't and she finally slapped down the check a little harder on the table than absolutely necessary and went to the other side of the room, where she stayed. She didn't glare over at Red or anything, just talked to the other waitress with studied nonchalance. They split the bill and Plunk and Larry B. each left a dollar tip. Red left two dollars, which Plunk thought might have been the result of a guilty conscience. Also, Suzette actually looked not too bad and Plunk wondered whether Red was being real smart giving up sex with her just because afterward he had to listen some about her sore feet and dreams of hairdressing.

Which got him thinking that way for a minute about Darlene, though she wasn't at all sexy with her glasses and ponytail. Maybe her body was good, or at least okay. Plunk couldn't remember.

But Larry B. and Red joshed him some more about his date on the way back to work, and he had to admit to himself that he sort of enjoyed it. They were so much younger and sometimes they had dates to talk about when they came over on Sundays to watch football, Red especially. Plunk had sort of given up on dating after Annie. For a couple years there were occasional short, clumsy periods involving women, but after that nothing. He wasn't real good at dealing with females and he realized it. Everybody else did, too. Sometimes people knew girls they wanted to introduce to their single guy friends, but never to Plunk. So he subscribed to a couple TV streaming services, ones that had movies and series with sexy things in them. Plunk didn't believe in watching out-and-out porn, that was dirty, but if you had Netflix or Apple and some of their shows had naked stuff, it was all right to go ahead and watch it and maybe do whatever. That pretty much comprised his sex life.

So since Annie he'd hadn't had any significant romance. At first he thought he would again sometime soon, and then he thought he would eventually, and finally he just kind of got used to being alone that way. Some single guys he knew talked about going into Fort Worth or all the way over to Dallas for hookers, but that would have made Plunk uncomfortable. It was better to do without.

But sometimes he wished he had something to brag about like Red and Larry B. did, stories to tell that were probably exaggerated but maybe not, everybody hollering and hooting like guys do. Maybe Darlene wasn't much to look at and Saturday wasn't a date, but it was still something that involved Plunk and a woman for his friends to kid him about. That made him feel better about Darlene, who he'd previously dismissed as a know-it-all the few times he'd met her. She seemed to like the tail—well, who wouldn't? And she'd gotten that research crap for him, which was thoughtful though unnecessary. The idea about the yellow work gloves was good. What the hell.

Plunk saw Darlene twice more that week. On Wednesday they passed in the parking lot when they were both getting home from work. Plunk noticed she drove one of those little Japanese cars, he never could remember the name. It was scratched up and dented some, didn't look anything like new. She waved and said she was looking forward to Saturday. Plunk wondered why she said it so loud. There were some other people in the parking lot and they probably overheard. Then on Thursday night she knocked on his door just as he was finishing up dinner, a grilled cheese sandwich from the microwave. The smell of cooked cheese hung in the air as he let her in. She handed him a bag with a pair of yellow work gloves in it.

"I thought you might get too busy this week to pick them up, so I went out at lunch," Darlene explained. "These were on sale at Home Depot."

"How much? I'll pay you back," Plunk said, but Darlene shook her head.

"It's okay. Look, I went ahead and put black spots on the backs with magic marker. To match the tail." Plunk looked, and she had, wide irregularly-shaped spots. They looked pretty good, and he told her so. He offered her a beer and she said sorry but she had to get to class, it was Thursday and all. As she left Plunk tried to take a furtive look at her body, just to get an idea, but she had on a baggy sweater and he couldn't tell anything. Not that he was going to make a move, but it would have been good to have some details for Red and Larry B. if they mentioned her again. Which he thought they would, because they'd kept on joking about his Saturday date.

So Plunk and Darlene agreed they'd leave for the party around one on Saturday,—it wasn't a long drive to Keller, but they didn't want to get there late and keep the kids waiting. Darlene asked what should she wear, was it a dressy party, and Plunk said he was sure it was just a bunch of kids running around and hollering, she should wear whatever she wanted.

Friday at work Jessika gave Plunk directions to Austin's house, a map she printed out from the computer. He knew that most cars nowadays had that GPS stuff and a voice coming out of it that told you when and where to make turns, but his Ranger was so old that it didn't have one. And of course Plunk realized that you could use a computer to get you directions complete with a map. Jessika knew he didn't know how to do that, so she did it for him. The map she gave him said it was 26.3 miles from Plunk's apartment in Crowley to Austin's place in Keller, and the trip would take forty-two minutes because there was always heavy traffic on that part of the highway. Plunk didn't usually appreciate computers but this directions stuff was useful.

In the afternoon Austin popped his head out of his office to remind Plunk he needed to be there right at two on Saturday, and Plunk promised he would. Larry B., who was sitting nearby, yelled to Austin that Plunk was bringing a date, which got Jessika's attention because she always liked gossip about love lives unless it was speculation about her own. Jessika wanted to know who the girl was and Plunk started explaining it wasn't a girl, it was just Darlene from the apartments and it wasn't a date, but it was kind of nice to have attention paid to even a made-up love life and he didn't end up denying he had a girlfriend. It wasn't like Darlene was ever going to know.

Austin said real nicely that he looked forward to meeting "the lady" and she would be able to sit and have some wine with his wife and her friends while the kids had their party on the lawn. Plunk wondered about that because in his childhood experience, all the mothers usually had to be right there keeping party-crazed kids from wrecking stuff, but whatever.

"I'll be there at two," he promised.

Most of Friday night Plunk stood in front of the mirror with the tail strapped on, practicing pushing the button on the leash while wearing his new gecko gloves. Darlene had really done a helluva job drawing the black spots.

14.

Plunk was up early on Saturday, wiping the tail with damp paper towels until every inch of gold and black beauty was glistening. He checked the tip to make sure it was still perfectly pointy, and also the belts, which weren't looking very good. The holes you stuck the little metal tongues through were getting pulled out of shape, and it seemed to Plunk like the stitching holding the belts to the vinyl outer skin was loosening. Obviously he would have to get that fixed, he wasn't sure where or how, but right now he couldn't do anything because the party was in a couple of hours.

Just to be on the safe side he strapped the tail on to make sure the belts wouldn't break right off. He was just wearing his jockeys, which is how he slept, so the feeling of the tail pulled tight against his ass was even a little more intense than usual. Plunk walked to the mirror, maybe sashayed was a better description because wearing it felt so good, and for the full effect, hell, why not?, he got the leash handle and used it to pull the tail tip up and down a few times. Actually, more than a few, because there was a knock on his door and he looked at his watch and it was almost eleven. It was like time stood still for him when he wore the tail.

Plunk thought it must be Darlene coming over early or something, so he took off the tail and pulled on a T-shirt and jeans before opening the door. But it was Eddie instead.

"Hey, buddy, TCU-Baylor kickoff in five!" Eddie said. "Can't miss that one, can we? TCU wins, and they're probably gonna be conference champs!"

Eddie sometimes came over to watch college games on Saturdays as well as the pro games on Sundays. Plunk didn't mind. It was company, and he was going to watch the games anyway. There wasn't any set schedule for Eddie to drop in, just whenever he wanted. Usually they'd pass in the parking lot during the week and Eddie'd say this game or that was going to be on and Plunk would say come on over, but now Plunk realized he hadn't seen Eddie since Sunday and so hadn't mentioned anything to him about having to go to Austin's kid's party and all. Come to think of it, Plunk hadn't even remembered the TCU-Baylor game at all, weird for him because of how his weekends were devoted to TV sports. But this week he'd mostly been thinking of the party and wearing the tail.

"C'mon in, but I may not be able to watch all the game with you," Plunk said, mostly talking to Eddie's back because the dickwad swept right by, flipping on the TV and making himself at home like he always did. "I got this thing I need to go do."

"What's that?" Eddie asked.

"Kid's party, my boss's son. You know, Austin. He wants me to come to the party and wear the tail."

"That's great," Eddie said, all distracted because he was already locked in on the game telecast, where the announcers were saying just before kickoff that this was the biggest game for TCU and Baylor in years, for once somebody else besides Texas Tech or Oklahoma State had a real chance to win the conference title. "You see that story about you in the *Observer*?"

"Yeah, I kept you a copy if you want it," Plunk said, but Eddie had concluded his interest in anything else but the game and didn't reply. Plunk got one of the copies out anyway and laid it on the counter in the kitchen so it would be there for Eddie later on.

They watched the game for an hour, Eddie hollering at the screen and getting all excited because TCU stayed a touchdown ahead, and Plunk paying attention sometimes and more often thinking about the tail and the party. At halftime it was about 12:30 and Plunk left Eddie on the couch drinking a beer while he went into the bedroom to get changed. The tail in all its recently-polished glory gleamed on the bed while Plunk put on the black jeans and yellow sweatshirt he'd washed earlier in the week at the laundromat. Then he pulled on black socks, a new touch, and the black tennies. He inspected the tennies for dust spots, saw a few, pulled them off and went into the kitchen to get a paper towel to wipe the dust off.

"You're gonna miss the second half kickoff," Eddie warned.

"That's okay," Plunk said. "I got to be leaving soon."

"Can I stay here 'til the game's over?" Eddie asked. "Your TV's so much better than my shitty one."

"Sure," Plunk said. "Just lock the door on your way out and leave me a couple beers. I want to watch Miami-Florida State tonight."

"Seven p.m., right?" Eddie said. "I might come back for that one. No hot date tonight. You mind?"

"Fine with me," Plunk said. "I gotta finish getting dressed now."

"Sound like a damn girl," Eddie cracked and got back to watching the game.

Plunk wiped off the tennies and laced them on. He knew he couldn't wear the tail while he was driving, the angle of the tail strapped to his ass made it impossible to sit down, but he worried it might somehow get messed up during the trip. So he looked around until he found a big old beach towel, all the fuzz worn off but better than nothing, and he was experimenting with how to wrap it around most of the tail, it wouldn't fit around all of it, when there was another knock on the door. He checked his watch: 1 p.m. Darlene!

Plunk realized all in one fast horrible moment that something bad might be about to happen. He hadn't told Eddie anything about Darlene going with him to the party, and wouldn't you know it but Eddie hollered, "I'll get the door," and hustled over to open it, there must have been a commercial on TV. Plunk rushed out of the bedroom just as Eddie did a doubletake on seeing Darlene standing there.

"Yeah?" Eddie said, and Darlene looked less than pleased to see him too.

"I'm here for Plunk and the party," she said, and as quick as he could Plunk elbowed Eddie out of the way and said, "Yeah, good, come on in."

"What the?" Eddie asked, and Plunk cut him off before he could say any more.

"Darlene's coming with me to Austin's kid's party to help out," Plunk explained. The three of them stood in the living room. Eddie had forgotten the game in his surprise at seeing Darlene. He looked puzzled and she looked annoyed, like Plunk was doing something wrong having his friend over. Plunk noticed she was wearing a sweater and slacks again, dark-colored, but she also had on some kind of dangly earrings that looked like they weighed a ton. Her earlobes were all pulled down.

"What kind of help you need, Plunk?" Eddie said mockingly. "Tail too heavy to carry all by yourself?"

"I'm going to help Plunk answer questions about leopard geckos," Darlene said in a snotty kind of voice, drawing herself up stiffly. "When the children want to know."

"If this is a birthday party, all they'll want is cake," Eddie said. "Shit, buddy, you needed somebody to help, you could've asked me."

"Well, Darlene said she would," Plunk said, feeling all weird and kind of mad at both of them because of it.

"Do you have your gloves?" Darlene asked, acting all of a sudden like Eddie wasn't even there. "We need to be going if we want to get there on time."

"Gloves?" Eddie asked, and Plunk quickly said, "Yeah, gloves," and went back in the bedroom to get them and of course the tail also. He got it up in the crook of his arm—he'd learned by now how to balance the weight when he had to carry it that way—and came back to find Eddie and Darlene just sort of glaring at each other, not speaking at all.

"I got everything," Plunk said. "Eddie, enjoy the rest of the game. Lock up when you leave. See you later."

"Miami-Florida State at seven?" Eddie asked.

"Right," Plunk said, and thought he saw some kind of shadow briefly pass across Darlene's eyes. "Okay, we got to go." He led Darlene out into the parking lot, pulling the apartment door closed behind them.

"My Ranger's right over there," he told Darlene. "Kind of beat-up, but it'll get us there and back."

"That man is rude," Darlene declared, obviously disinterested in transportation details. "He's horrible."

"Who, Eddie?" Plunk said, trying to keep it light. "Yeah, he's a piece a work. Don't mind him. He was watchin' football and got interrupted."

"Well, he doesn't have to act so rude," she said. "Good manners don't cost anything."

"I guess they don't," Plunk agreed. "Okay, here's my keys. Can you unlock the door so I can put the tail in? Can't lay it loose in the truck bed. It might bounce out."

Darlene took the keys and quit bitching about Eddie, which was a relief. She helped Plunk settle the tail in one of the pickup cab's two back fold-down seats, even suggesting they have parts of the beach towel underneath the tail so it wouldn't get scratched up any. The ends of the tail drooped toward the floor; even for human passengers there was hardly any shoulder or leg room, the space being so cramped. But Darlene made sure the tail was properly positioned on its seat and not too smushed. Plunk appreciated her concern.

15.

Austin was always saying how business was so bad, but it had to be good most of the time because his house in Keller was like a freakin' castle, it was so big. At first Plunk thought he had to be at the wrong place, this one had a driveway that all by itself looked to be a mile long, and there was a white picket fence enclosing a front yard the size of a football field. But he checked the address on the map Jessika had printed out for him and it matched, and Darlene pointed out there was a van in front with a "Too-Fun Tex" sign painted on the side. A smallish horse trailer was hitched to the back of the van. The van itself was kind of old, but the sign paint was apparently new because it was still shiny. Plunk had thought the cowboy clown called himself

Two-Gun Tex, but maybe he'd misunderstood.

"Smell the country air," Darlene sighed as they pulled up in the driveway past the truck. It was a pretty day for early November in North Texas, cool in the fifties but the sun was out and that made it seem a little warmer. "Your boss is so lucky to live out here."

"Yeah," Plunk muttered. The size of Austin's house was throwing him off a little. He'd never before in his life been invited to a place like this. "Well, it's ten 'til two. We better get this tail inside."

He unbuckled the seat belts and gathered up the tail, still keeping the beach towel wrapped around it. Darlene very helpfully got the gloves, and also another manila envelope she'd brought with her. In it were copies of the leopard gecko facts she'd brought to Plunk earlier, just in case, she said, if they needed to verify anything when one of the kids asked a hard question. Plunk could hear kids hollering faintly somewhere back behind the big house.

Darlene rang the doorbell since Plunk had his arms full with the tail. A very pretty woman answered and said, "Yes?" in a polite kind of way before looking past Darlene and seeing Plunk, or rather the long, thin tail tip protruding from under the towel.

"You're from Austin's staff at work," she said, sounding much friendlier. "We appreciate you giving up some of your Saturday for Timmy."

Plunk figured Timmy was Austin's kid who was having the birthday. He didn't know for sure. Austin kept a framed picture of a boy on his desk but never actually identified him by name, at least to Plunk.

"Well," the pretty woman added, "won't you both come in? I'm Leanne, Austin's wife."

"This is Darlene," Plunk said. "She came along to help me."

"How nice," Leanne said. "Right this way."

She led them down a long hall. Plunk looked into the rooms opening off of it and couldn't believe anybody ever sat or did anything else in them, they were so perfect-looking and clean.

"I thought you might want to put on your costume where the children couldn't see you," Leanne said over her shoulder. "In case there are any secrets involved."

"Okay," Plunk said. He wondered how big the house really was, because it was taking *minutes* to get wherever they were going in it. Behind him he could hear Darlene occasionally emitting tiny gasps; Plunk guessed she was reacting to the fancy furniture or something. They passed a staircase but stayed on the bottom floor, and finally Leanne said Plunk might want to change here in this guest bedroom, which all by itself was bigger than Plunk's whole apartment.

"While we're waiting for Plunk, is that correct?" Leanne said, and Plunk nodded to confirm that was his name, "perhaps Darlene might want to join me and my girlfriends for some wine out on the back deck. Unless she's needed to help put your tail on. It's very big, isn't it?"

"Yeah, it is," Plunk said, noticing the gleam of panic in Darlene's eyes behind her thick glasses. The thought of drinking wine with Leanne and her friends seemed to scare her. "Go on, Darlene. I'll get the tail on and catch up."

"I don't want to bother you," Darlene said to Leanne. "You've got to watch the children with the party and everything."

Leanne laughed, a high tinkly sound.

"We're paying that cowboy clown a lot of money to entertain the kids," she said. "I guess I can relax and have some wine." She didn't say it in a particularly snotty way, just matter-of-fact. Darlene still hesitated, so Leanne took her by the arm and led her out of the room, telling Plunk to just come out to the back when he was ready before pulling the door closed behind her.

Plunk took a deep breath. He couldn't blame Darlene for feeling nervous, because he was too. The house was really too fancy for people like him to be there. Plunk always believed everybody was created equal, it said so in the Constitution, but still you lived the way that was natural for you and there were different levels for different people. It was okay that Austin turned out to be way richer than Plunk had thought, he owned his own company and good for him if he was making lots of money from it after all. That was what America and

Texas in particular were all about. But Plunk still felt funny in such a big house with so many rooms.

Then he strapped on the tail and some of the nervousness went away. The pressure of the tail on the base of his spine was comforting as always. There was the added pleasure of wearing the uniform of yellow sweatshirt and black jeans, of pulling on the decorated work gloves. The closest thing to it Plunk could remember was Little League when a game was obviously lost and the coach would let Plunk play catcher, which meant putting on shin guards and chest protector and face mask, kind of like a knight getting into his armor. Plunk hooked up the retractable leash to the tip of the tail and gave a few experimental tugs to make certain it would flop up and down just right.

Keeping the tail tip pulled up high so he wouldn't knock over any vases or anything, Plunk went down the hall a little further. It led into this big wide kitchen with what looked like a whole wall of windows opening up on back deck and beyond that a backyard that went on for freakin' ever. There were tables covered by umbrellas out on the deck and Leanne and about a dozen other pretty women sat by them with glasses of wine. Darlene was there too, leaning forward awkwardly, and frankly looking a little dowdy in her ponytail and dark baggy sweater and slacks. The other women had on sweaters and slacks, too, but theirs were all colors and tighter, and where Darlene had on the dangly earrings that pulled down her earlobes all the other women had sparkly roundish earrings, probably diamonds, and Plunk didn't know why he'd notice something like that. Darlene was also the only one with a ponytail.

Beyond the seated women was a milling pack of men in sweaters, not sweatshirts, and slacks, not jeans. They held drinks in their hands, real drinks by the look of them even though it was only two in the afternoon, and they smiled and looked relaxed and broke up with rich men's comfortable, deep laughter that sure sounded different than the screechy braying Plunk and the guys emitted when they hung out watching football at the apartment on Sundays. He saw Austin, and also Kevin and Broc from work.

And beyond the men, down on the rolling, expansive lawn of the backyard, some two dozen neatly dressed children yelled and scurried, and they had a lot to yell about. There was a pony on the lawn, a kind of raggedy-looking brown one with a grubby white mane, and a man dressed like a cowboy trying to help riders up into the saddle. The man had on clown makeup, which figured from what Plunk had heard about him, but wasn't wearing holsters with bubble-making guns or toy guns of any sort, which Plunk had expected. Only a couple of kids were lined up to get on the horse. The rest of them chased each other around and screamed really loud. The cowboy clown kept trying to get them to come over to the pony, but they ignored him. Plunk stood in the wide kitchen and watched. He noticed on a table on his right there was a fancy birthday cake with "Happy 6th Timmy" on it along with a lot of decorations, and on yet another table—how many tables did they *have* in this kitchen?—there was a mountain of wrapped gifts, more presents in one place than Plunk had ever seen before, even in the movies.

It threw him more than a little. There was too much of everything, hallway and lawn and fancy people and cake and presents. A birthday party with a clown and a pony. Plunk wasn't mad or jealous, just uncomfortable. He probably stood there uncertainly for five minutes before Austin broke loose from the men on the deck and came back into the kitchen.

"Leanne said you were here," Austin said. "You've got the tail on? You're ready?"

"I don't know if those kids out there need me," Plunk said. "They already got a pony and the cowboy. He shot off his bubble guns yet?"

Austin waved an arm dismissively.

"The pony's got fleas and the clown doesn't have any guns, at least that I've seen. The kids wouldn't care anyway. I think every friend of Timmy's who's had a birthday party this year had this guy there. I told Leanne he was old stuff, nothing fun about him. But she didn't listen, no surprise, she never does. That's why it's great you're here. I showed Timmy your picture from the paper and he thought it was cool. None of his other friends had a tail guy at their parties."

"I don't know," Plunk said doubtfully. He really just wanted to take his tail and go. Also he wanted to get Darlene, who didn't seem to be talking to any of the women on the deck. She looked pretty miserable up there.

"It'll be great, Plunk," Austin said. "Now let's get to it. I told the kids you were coming."

Plunk reached behind him and touched the tail, like a child in need of reassurance reaching for its mother's hand. He rubbed his fingers along the vinyl. Nobody else had a tail like his. He'd had his picture in the paper.

"What the hell," he mumbled to himself, and then, "Okay," somewhat louder. Austin opened the door for him and Plunk stepped out onto the deck, leash grip in hand and tail tip waving high.

16.

The women saw him first, all of them smiling and pointing, and Darlene jumped up like she couldn't wait to get away from them and said to Plunk, "Are you ready?" A couple of the women, obviously mothers of the kids on the lawn, pulled their cell phones out and aimed them at Plunk. One of them exclaimed, "It's so *big*," and the rest giggled like they'd heard a dirty joke. The men, the dads, were right behind them, and Broc from work said, "Good going, Plunk," which was nice since Plunk hadn't actually done anything yet.

"Thank God you're out here, the kids are bored out of their minds," Leanne said. They didn't look bored to Plunk, though they clearly weren't interested in the cowboy clown. They were running around yelling like kids at birthday parties mostly do. But Leanne hollered out, "He's here, Timmy," like an announcement, and all the kids turned and looked and one of them, a little blond boy, came racing up to the deck while all the other kids sort of stayed back.

"Timmy, this is Mr. Landy," Austin said, and Plunk had to give it to the kid, he had good manners and stuck out his hand. Plunk shook it, noticing as he did Darlene was so close behind him that his elbow almost poked her in the ribs.

"Hey, Timmy," Plunk said genially. "Happy birthday." Then there was a long moment when everybody just sort of stood there, until Darlene hissed in Plunk's ear, "Take him down on the lawn," and that seemed like as good an idea as any so Plunk did, holding the leash grip in one gloved hand and Timmy's hand in the other.

"Is that your real tail?" Timmy asked in the openly curious way a kid would, just kind of innocently wondering, and Plunk told him no. When they got to the bottom of the steps he showed Timmy the belts holding the tail in place. Timmy said he thought the belts were breaking and Plunk replied yeah, he had to get that fixed. At that point the other kids started gathering around, just like the trick-or-treaters on Halloween had. Plunk showed them how the tail could go up and down, and told them they could touch it but not yank on it. They minded very well, Darlene sort of got them lined up to take turns, and while they looked and touched Plunk saw over their heads that the cowboy and the pony both were watching and looking kind of sad.

"There's plenty of room for pony rides," the cowboy said in a loud voice.

"The children are busy," Leanne told him.

"Where'd you get the tail?" one of the kids asked, so Plunk told about the costume shop, which they didn't seem to care about.

"Do you know what *kind* of tail it is?" Darlene asked the kids, and of course they didn't. One said, "Spotted," and Darlene told her that was very good, in fact it was colored and spotted like a leopard's tail and that's why this particular reptile was called a leopard gecko. Plunk didn't know why, maybe it was because they really were bored with pony rides and clowns, but the kids acted like this was interesting. He hadn't realized Darlene was going to be the one to tell about leopard geckos if it became necessary, but she did look up all that stuff and Plunk thought she explained it pretty well.

"Now, these leopard geckos are *crepuscular*," Darlene went on.

"Can any of you tell me what that means?" Plunk was glad she asked the kids and not him, because it would have looked bad for him not to know. It turned out "crepuscular" meant the leopard geckos liked to come out in twilight rather than full daylight, and Darlene threw in a bunch more stuff about where they usually lived and how their eyes were different from most other lizards. When she told how you could keep them as pets several of the kids yelled they wanted one, and when Darlene added they had to be fed live crickets and lived maybe thirty years sometimes one of the mothers made all the other parents laugh by saying then *her* kid wasn't getting one, he'd have to settle for the lizard-tail man instead.

Darlene must have studied her lizard stuff hard, because she kept going for several minutes and even Plunk found some of it sort of interesting, like how leopard geckos can actually let their tails be pulled off if they needed to run away fast.

"Is that where your tail came from?" a kid asked Plunk, and Plunk reminded him no, it came from the costume shop.

"A real leopard gecko tail would be too small. It wouldn't even cover my a–, I mean my bu–, uh, my *behind*," Plunk said, struggling for the appropriate word. He didn't really talk directly to kids that much and his child vocabulary was rusty.

"I think there's supposed to be cake now," the cowboy interrupted all huffy-like, and when the kids dutifully went up the stairs to the deck (most lingering for last touches of the tail) Plunk saw that Leanne was glowering at the cowboy's wide back.

"This is so good, something educational as well as entertaining," Leanne said to Darlene, who looked a lot happier than before.

"Well, that's what we intended," Darlene said, and Plunk felt this little start in his chest, because who said anything about educational, or "we" for that matter?

The three of them walked up the steps after the kids. Plunk had let the tail all the way down again to enjoy the sloofy sound of it dragging across the thick pillowy grass before pulling it up to prevent scratching from the wood steps. The kids were all inside the kitchen, and as Leanne began supervising the cutting and passing out of cake, the cowboy went out front, got in his van, and backed it and the horse trailer down the driveway to the edge of the backyard. He led the pony into the trailer, then began picking bits of brightly colored stuff off the grass.

"We won't be using that man again," Leanne said to Darlene. "You two are so much better. The kids said the pony smelled funny anyway."

"A lot of children are afraid of horses, and also clowns," Darlene said. "The tail seems much friendlier." She tipped her head toward the cowboy. "I think we've made him mad."

"Like I care," Leanne said. She went back to sit with her friends on the deck while the kids ate cake. Darlene hesitated, then followed Leanne outside. Plunk thought about asking for some cake, but the kids were shoving their plates of it at each other and things were getting messy, so he wandered down to where the cowboy was obviously getting ready to get in his van and go without saying goodbye or anything. Plunk felt bad about how things at the party turned out for the poor guy. He said to him, "Hey, kids—you never know how they're gonna act. You got a real nice pony there."

The cowboy grunted. Up close, his clown makeup was put on all uneven, globbed on in some places, barely smeared on in others. His bright blue cowboy hat had dark sweat stains around the crown and brim. "It's the parents," he said. "They look at you like you're trash, the kids pick up on that."

"Ah, well, you're Two-Gun Tex," Plunk said, trying to cheer the guy up. "Next party, the kids'll love you again. Besides the pony, shooting bubbles from pistols and all."

"My ass," the cowboy said. "Two months ago I had to stop with the bubble guns. They worked great. I'd shoot the bubbles from my guns and pass out squirt guns full of bubble soap and everybody'd let loose at everybody else and all the kids loved it. Then some mother complained that I was doing gun violence or some shit and some more mothers started saying it. Bubbles from squirt guns are violent?

What kind of idiots say that?"

"Pretty dumb," Plunk agreed. "Hard to believe anybody from Texas would even think it."

"Just the damn way things are going in this whole country, you know?" Tex fumed. "Somebody doesn't like something normal, they bitch about it, and then the normal thing is all of a sudden wrong. I been doing this kids' party stuff for years, no complaints, kids love shooting bubbles from squirt guns. But a few mothers bitch, and I start getting asked not to do the bubble gun part of the show because some lame brain moms got offended. So I tried changing—not Two-Gun Tex anymore. Too-Fun Tex instead. Cost me a hundred and fifty bucks to get the new name painted over the old one on the side of the van."

"New name looks good there," Plunk said, trying to keep things positive. He hated sad stuff.

"Too-Fun Tex, my ass. I try to provide fun for the money, but I got no fun left in the show," Tex said. "Without the squirt guns, all I got is the pony, which is like sitting on some big fat pillow, what's really fun about that? And I learned how to make balloon animals, but I do them for the kids, give them to them, and they just pop 'em." He dug in his pocket and extracted a handful of colorful balloon bits. "And now they always expect me to pick up the balloon scraps after. Screw it. I'm done."

"No, you're not," Plunk said. "Guy like you, wants everybody to have fun and all, you can do this forever. It's maybe slow now, but it'll pick up again."

"The hell it will. One minute everything's fine, then it's over. My time's run out. You wait, it'll happen to you." He gestured at Plunk's tail. "That's not gonna be hot stuff forever. Enjoy it while it lasts, you poor bastard."

After Too-Fun Tex's van and trailer disappeared around the corner, Plunk walked back to the birthday party. He felt unsettled until all the dads wandered over to get a better look at the tail. They were pretty complimentary, and one of them said he knew a leather shop in Cleburne that could probably fix the belts, maybe put on new, stronger ones. He didn't know the address but he did know the name, Cleburne Leatherworks, which Darlene wrote down.

"The guy there does great work on golf bags," he told Plunk. "A little pricey, but it's worth it to get it done right."

"Sounds good," Plunk said, though "pricey" didn't. If these people thought something cost a lot then it was probably more than Plunk had to spend.

Kevin from work brought Plunk over a drink.

"I bet you can use this," he said. Plunk took a sip and it was liquor, not beer like he preferred, but what the hell? He drank a little and thought that Kevin usually didn't pay much attention to him at work, it was nice he'd do it here when Plunk really didn't know anybody except him and Broc and Austin and Darlene. Plunk had hoped Jessika might be there, too, but she wasn't.

"Kids liked the tail," Kevin went on. "My daughter's the one in the pink dress in there. Meredith. By the table with the presents."

"Lots of presents," Plunk said, just to have something to say. The liquor burned the back of his throat in a nice way. Darlene went over with the women and their glasses of wine; she was talking now, everybody acting friendly to her. This was turning out okay.

"Here's the thing," Kevin said. "All these kids are in the same class at school, and they all get invited to each other's parties. One every weekend, it seems like. They get so many presents they get tired of opening them. And that Tex guy with his pony. Must have seen him three, maybe four times."

"Well, probably not anymore," Plunk said. "He told me he might stop."

He and Kevin sipped their drinks and Kevin had just mentioned how it had been a bitch of a week at work when his little girl came running out of the deck, icing smeared on her face and the front of the pink dress.

"Hillary threw up right in the room, Daddy," Meredith said. "I don't like the smell, so I came out here." She looked at Plunk and his tail. “What’s your name?” she asked.

“Plunk. Mr. Landy,” Kevin said.

“No, he’s not,” she said, looking up at Plunk, then back down at the tail. “I want his fun name. Who *are* you?”

“Your dad said,” Plunk answered.

“No,” Meredith insisted. “*That’s* not your name.”

“Meredith,” Kevin said in a fatherly warning way.

“It’s okay,” said Plunk. “All right, who am I?”

Meredith screwed up her face, thinking furiously. She picked some bits of icing off the front of her dress and put them in her mouth.

“*Tail Man*!” she crowed. “You’re Tail Man!”

And Plunk knew right away that’s exactly who he was.

17.

Plunk and Darlene ended up not getting away from Austin’s house until close to five. Right up until then, the kids kept coming up for additional touches of the tail, and their mothers took more pictures.

“It’s been such a pleasure having someone here that the kids actually enjoyed,” Leanne said. “I’ll tell you, that Tex is nothing but yesterday. He might as well try his luck in Waco or someplace common like that, where they have to take whatever they can get. And he charges so much.”

“How much?” Darlene asked a beat too quickly.

“Oh, I think it’s three-fifty to run the party,” Leanne said, “That plus seventy-five more for the horse. He doesn’t own it. He rents it from some stable. And we had to order the cake from the bakery ourselves. Well, he’s not getting any more money from me, or from my friends here, either. We’ve agreed on that.” Timmy started hollering far across the lawn. His mother sighed and added, “What now? It’s always something with them, you know?”

“Kids,” Darlene said sympathetically, and as soon as Leanne had walked a few steps away she leaned over and whispered to Plunk,

"Did you *hear* that?"

"What, her kid yelling?"

"No," said Darlene. "How much Too-Fun Tex charges."

"None of our business," Plunk said, looking down at the belts holding on his tail and hoping they wouldn't bust right here at the party. He'd been wearing the tail for three hours and it still felt great, that special sensation.

"Well, it is our business," Darlene said, and Plunk wondered why but not enough to request further explanation. He posed for pictures with some more kids. Darlene was pulled aside by a couple of the mothers; it was nice she was socializing a little. Plunk himself had never realized what a nice guy Kevin was, though he wondered if Kevin would still be friendly on Monday back at work, he'd never paid much attention to Plunk before except to say, "Plunk Landy—wardrobe by Target," which was in fact mostly true.

Just before five the sun went behind some low clouds and it got pretty chilly. The moms and dads tossed off their last drinks and called for their kids to come on, it was getting late. Austin and Leanne grabbed Timmy and made him thank each of his friends for their individual gifts, though there had been so many Plunk didn't think the kid could really keep it straight who gave what. As the last families left, Darlene told Plunk it was probably time for him to go in and take off the tail, which he really didn't feel like doing since it might be a long time before he got to wear it out in public again. But he couldn't drive wearing it, and it had been fun being Tail Man at the party. Plunk felt hopeful that Tail Man might become a Halloween tradition in Crowley, maybe people wouldn't get tired of that like they did Warrior Mascot.

Darlene stayed out on the deck with Austin and Leanne while Plunk went in and took the tail off. He looked it over pretty good and the belts seemed like they might tear off any minute. Darlene had the name of the place in Cleburne where it could get fixed. Plunk hoped he had enough money in the bank to cover it. He couldn't stand thinking of his tail being stuck away in damaged condition while he had to save up the repair money.

Plunk wrapped up the tail in the beach towel, stuffed the yellow work gloves in his back pocket, and went back out on the deck. Darlene seemed to be getting along with Austin and Leanne okay. Though it was getting dark early, North Texas in November and all, Plunk could still see Darlene's cheeks were flushed, he guessed from the wine she'd been drinking.

"It was so nice of you to come for Timmy," Leanne said. She was a little too friendly sounding, the way rich people are when they thank regular people for doing something for them. Trying to act like everybody's equal but not quite pulling it off. "It meant so much to him. He's inside playing with some of his new things, but I'm sure he'll write you a thank-you note."

"That's okay," Plunk said, and it was. He was ready to leave. If he was late getting back for the Miami-Florida State game Eddie would really give him shit.

Leanne had some last things to say to Darlene, so Austin walked Plunk out to his car, chatting casually about the Cowboys and golf just like Plunk was his pal along the lines of Kevin and Broc.

"We ought to get you out on the course sometime," Austin said. Plunk knew he was just being polite, but it was nice of him to say all the same. "And that tail is great. Made Timmy feel special, having you at his party before any of the other kids had their chance."

Plunk didn't exactly understand what Austin meant by that, but what the hell. As Darlene got into the front seat, Plunk finished settling the tail on one of the Ranger's fold-down seats, and then he straightened up and shook Austin's outstretched hand. Something else confusing: A piece of wadded paper was left in Plunk's palm when the handshake was over.

"Really appreciate it," Austin said, winking, and turned and led his wife down the long front walk back to the house.

Plunk got into the car and only then looked at the paper. In the fading light it took him a moment to realize it was a folded-up hundred-dollar bill, Ben Franklin's face right there.

He showed the bill to Darlene and said, "Shit, I gotta give this back to Austin. I never said anything about getting paid to come today."

"You shouldn't give it back, and they got you cheap," Darlene said. "More than four hundred to Tex, and the kids didn't even care about the pony and balloon animals. I told Gretchen, Hillary's mother, that we'd need to get three hundred for you to do her birthday party in two weeks."

"Three?" Plunk said wonderingly. "Hundred?"

"That's lots cheaper than Tex, and the kids like you better," Darlene said. "She couldn't say yes fast enough. We're all set if you say it's okay. Two of the other mothers wanted you for their kids, too. Their parties are a ways off. We ought to think of other things in between, keep people talking about Tail Man."

"Hang on," Plunk said, feeling confused and having some trouble navigating the dark narrow roads leading out of Keller onto I-35. "You want me to go to another kid's party wearing the tail. And get paid."

"Why not?" Darlene said. "You like wearing the tail. Why wait until next Halloween? Have fun and make some money at the same time."

"Three hundred's a lot just to let kids at a party look at the tail and touch it a little," Plunk said.

"I'm thinking about that," Darlene said. "We could also do some question-and-answer like at Timmy's party. I'd handle that part, and you'd pose for pictures with all the kids and maybe we can figure out some kind of leopard gecko reptile ride. You think you could pull kids around while they're sitting on your tail if you get the belts fixed, maybe made stronger?"

"No," Plunk said, already imagining the tail being torn off his ass or even gouged by kids' heels. "Absolutely not."

"Well, we'll come up with something," Darlene said. "We've got two weeks."

Plunk was mad at her and grateful at the same time. The idea of charging to wear the tail at parties made him feel funny, but extra chances to wear the tail would be wonderful. Maybe Darlene was almost as smart as she acted like she was, and she could come up with some party games. Wearing the tail, and getting paid three hundred when he did?

"About the money," he said hesitantly, thinking he might tell her three hundred was too much, let's charge maybe one fifty or two.

"I know," Darlene blurted, misunderstanding. "It's your tail, you're Tail Man like the kids were just calling you. You're the star, but I can be really helpful to you. Let's say I get 25 percent for being your manager, making the bookings and doing the Q and A. You get 75. And for things like new belts for the tail, you pay for that right off the top before we split what's left, 75–25. Does that sound fair?"

Plunk couldn't tell whether it did or didn't. It was all so fast and overwhelming. He felt an almost physical ache at the base of his spine and wished he could pull off the road for a minute and strap the tail back on. It would soothe him, he knew. He nearly did it, but didn't want Darlene to think he was weird, which was what Annie started calling him after a while.

He thought about getting paid to wear the tail as the narrow side road finally fed into the better-lighted interstate. Funny how life had its surprises. Sometimes they even turned out to be good ones.

18.

Darlene said they ought to stop for dinner on the way back to Crowley.

"You know, to celebrate," she said. "Getting hired to be Tail Man at Hillary's party. And how well things went today at this one."

"Can't," Plunk said. "At seven I got to watch the football game with Eddie."

"We're going past Fort Worth, and there's a good Chinese buffet place," Darlene said. "It's not yet six. If we eat fast you could be back."

But Plunk still said no. He wouldn't have minded eating, even Chinese which wasn't his favorite, but he thought Darlene would want to talk a lot more and it might be halftime of Miami–Florida State before she stopped to take a breath. Plenty had happened during the afternoon and Plunk didn't feel like he needed any more conversation about it, just the uncomplicated pleasure of watching football on TV.

"Then we ought to have lunch tomorrow," Darlene said, and Plunk picked up that she was anxious though she was trying not to let it show. "To plan for the next party and everything."

"Sundays get tough for me," Plunk said. "In the mornings I go see my mother, and then in the afternoons the guys and I watch the Cowboys."

"You go see your mother on Sundays?" Darlene asked. "That's so sweet. Every Sunday?"

"Yeah," Plunk said. "She lives in this place with her friend Helen. A retirement place called Pleasant Valley."

"I know where that is," Darlene said. "I'd like to go with you and meet her. I'm sure she's nice."

"She is," Plunk agreed. "Maybe sometime if you want." He was worried Darlene might say tomorrow was when she wanted to, and she did start to say something but stopped. Not that Plunk didn't appreciate all Darlene had done for him lately. Still, he had his regular routine.

Yet he didn't want to hurt her feelings and in a way he was beginning to like her, so he added, "We could go eat some night next week. Spend this hundred I got."

"Well, maybe," Darlene said. "Tuesday and Thursday nights I have class."

"For your library license?"

"Librarian certification. It's not like a driver's license. But right now my class is about writing, like I told you. The book I'm writing. Which is what I usually work on all the other week nights."

"Okay, then," Plunk said. "I guess dinner's out. We can talk about the next party whenever you get a minute."

Darlene pushed her glasses back up her nose.

"I could put the book off for one night," she conceded. "If you want."

"Sure," Plunk said, not exactly sure why she sounded like somebody who'd gotten what she wanted after all.

"Wednesday?" said Darlene.

"Sure, why not?" Plunk replied. Wednesday there wasn't any football on TV that he remembered.

When they got back to The Jacksonian it was maybe half past six. Darlene held the apartment door open while Plunk carried in the tail. He put it on the couch and they stood there looking down at it.

"We probably ought to take it to that leather place in Cleburne," Darlene said. "To get it fixed before Hillary's party."

"I will," Plunk said. "Thanks for helping today and everything."

"I had fun," Darlene said, and they stood around a minute more.

Plunk wondered why she didn't just say good night, and then thought he knew.

"You'll get some of this hundred," he said. "Like our deal with the 25 and 75. I got no change, but I'll get some and give you yours."

"Oh, no," Darlene said. "We don't do that until Hillary's. It was nice just to come out and help."

"I insist," Plunk said in a fake masterly voice and Darlene laughed. She actually had a pretty cute laugh.

"Use the money for dinner Wednesday," she said, and just then there was a knock on the door and they both knew it was Eddie.

"Well," Plunk said. He went to the door and let Eddie in. Eddie and Darlene sort of nodded at each other.

"I'll be going," she said to Plunk. "See you Wednesday night. Seven?"

"Yeah, seven," Plunk said, seeing Eddie's eyes narrow and wishing Darlene hadn't said anything. "Thanks again for everything today."

"I loved it," Darlene said brightly. "Enjoy your football game."

"What a bitch," Eddie said as soon as the door closed behind her. "And you're taking her out Wednesday? Jesus."

"Her name's not Jesus, it's Darlene," Plunk said, trying to keep things light. "I'm not really taking her out, it's just having dinner to talk about this deal she made for me and the tail." He told Eddie about Timmy's party and the kids loving the tail and other mothers wanting Tail Man at their birthday parties. Eddie didn't seem real interested until Plunk mentioned the three hundred, and how Austin slipped him a hundred as he was leaving. Then Eddie whistled and sort of reverently touched the hundred with Ben Franklin's picture on it.

He was a lot less impressed when Plunk told about Darlene and the 75–25 split.

"You need a helper, I can do it," he said. "I wouldn't charge so much, either. She's trying to make money off you."

"Not really," Plunk said. "It was her idea, anyway."

"It's *your* tail," Eddie said. "She just talks all the time and tries to sound smart."

Plunk couldn't argue with Eddie about that one. Fortunately, the game came on, and Eddie had brought a cold six-pack. Plunk moved the tail from the couch to the bed, and Eddie sat on the couch and so did Plunk, beers on the floor in front of them. The game itself didn't turn out to be much, Florida State had it won early on, but there were some big plays to holler about. Because he'd had a drink during the afternoon, a guy who didn't usually touch the hard stuff, the beers during the game maybe affected Plunk a little more than usual and he felt really loose by the time the game was over around eleven.

"Can't believe you're going out with her," Eddie griped as he slouched toward the door. It was the first mention of Darlene since the game began. "Plunk and his know-it-all girlfriend."

"She's not my girlfriend," Plunk protested, the beer making "she's" sound more like "sheesh."

"Maybe not yet, but she's working on it," Eddie said. "Wait and see. Better, don't. On Wednesday tell her thanks, but Eddie's going to be my assistant instead."

"Ah, I'm not gonna do that," Plunk said. "You can come help too, though. Pay you something."

"All that money, you better," Eddie said. "Okay. Noon tomorrow for the Cowboys?"

"Same as always," Plunk agreed. Eddie left and Plunk transferred a couple beers from his bladder to the toilet, then went to the bedroom to turn in. The tail was there on the bed, spread out long and beautiful. Plunk just loved it. He ran his hand along it and buzzed as he felt he still noticed there were some sticky spots left by icing-grimed hands. So he wet a paper towel and wiped the tail down until it was all clean again.

"You and me in a couple weeks," Plunk said, not caring how crazy it was to talk to a fake leopard gecko tail. There was only the tail and him in the room, who was going to tell? "Forget waiting 'til next Halloween." Of course the tail didn't say anything back but Plunk thought it somehow looked pleased.

"And we're getting those lousy belts fixed," Plunk promised. He started to move the tail to the couch, but when he picked it up it just seemed natural to strap it back on. And once it was on he sure didn't want to take it off.

"Ah, I'm tired," Plunk said. He lay down on the bed on his stomach even though besides the tail he was still wearing all his clothes. He was too far gone to attach the retractable leash to the tail's tip. So the tail sort of sagged back down between Plunk's ankles, very awkward-feeling. Plunk shifted onto his side and now the weight of the tail rested on the bed too, plenty of room because it was the double bed Plunk once shared with Annie; she didn't want to take it when she left.

Tail Man fell asleep in seconds with the light still on.

19.

Plunk woke up on Sunday with a headache, no surprise, and also to find one of the tail's three belts had broken loose during the night. It was the one that went around the left inside of his crotch, and it had ripped off right where the strap attached to the tail.

This bothered him more than the hangover. His tail was flawed, damn well *injured*, and it was Sunday and Darlene had the address of the leather place in Cleburne, which wouldn't be open on Sunday anyway. Reluctantly, Plunk unbuckled the other two belts and laid the tail back down on the bed. Maybe the belt wouldn't have broken if he hadn't gone to sleep wearing the tail. He'd have to be more careful with it.

He'd slept later than usual and it was already 10:30. Mom would be waiting for him at Pleasant Valley. He rushed out, not even grabbing something for breakfast, and was both relieved and sorry that when he got to her room she didn't seem to have noticed he wasn't on time. They had their usual talk, about what she'd been eating and what he'd been eating and the card games she'd played. Mom didn't mention Annie once, but when Plunk was leaving one of the aides on weekend duty handed him a note she said had been left for him by Mrs. Jance, the administrator who'd said they ought to start thinking of moving Mom to twenty-four-hour care. The note said exactly what Plunk expected, that Ida was showing increasing signs of significant mental confusion and it was important that Mr. Landy come in for a meeting at his earliest convenience.

"Shit," Plunk muttered. But he loved his mother and asked for a pen and paper so he could leave Mrs. Jance another note promising he'd call her first thing Monday morning.

He got back to the apartment just before Eddie and Red and Larry B. showed up with beer and microwave popcorn as usual, as well as a couple bags of corn chips Larry B. said had been left over at a party he'd been to the night before. The Cowboys game was actually going to be the second one on because they were playing Seattle out on the West Coast, so during the first game none of them particularly cared about they talked some about their Saturdays. Eddie said Plunk "and his woman" weren't back from Keller until the Florida State–Miami game was already almost over, what were they doing on those back country roads to make them so late, and because Plunk had his headache and was also worried about his Mom he called Eddie a lying bastard with a little too much emphasis. That made everybody uncomfortable, and then the Cowboys got blown out, which was also depressing, and everybody was glad when the game was over and Plunk's three guests could leave.

Monday Plunk didn't have the headache but he still had his Mom problem. As soon as he got into the office he called Mrs. Jance, who wasn't going to be in until later and since Plunk had to go make sales calls he said he'd try to call her back. Austin had a rule about using cell phones for personal business on company time, so Plunk couldn't phone her from the road. The morning's sales calls were mostly a waste of time. It was getting on toward winter and that meant a lot of outdoor construction was over until spring. Kevin and Broc with their bigger accounts had companies to call on that did a lot of indoor stuff, but not many of Plunk's regulars did. He always had a lot less money to live on from November through April, May if it was a particularly long winter. Darlene had better get Tail Man a lot of birthday parties, he thought, especially if there were extra costs moving Mom to twenty-four-hour care.

Plunk was in such a rare crappy mood that he didn't want to be around people. Usually at lunchtime he would have grabbed something and gone back to eat at the office with Larry B. and Red and Jessika if they didn't pile into Red's truck and go out someplace instead. But this time Plunk decided to grab a burger by himself, and when he looked around where he was the best nearest place was the burger joint where Red's waitress worked, the one he wasn't going to ask out anymore. It might be awkward seeing her. Hopefully one of the other waitresses would get him.

But sure enough, Red's castoff was the one who came up to Plunk at his solitary table and asked what he'd have. He told her a plain hamburger, mustard and American cheese and a couple thin slices of onion, Coke and no fries. Plunk figured she'd walk off to get his order placed, but instead she grinned and said, "Is that enough lunch for a celebrity?"

"I guess," Plunk grumbled. He looked at her name tag again and added, "Why you ragging on me, Suzette?"

"Hey, you're the famous Plunk Landy with the tail," she said.

That made Plunk curious.

"How do you know about that?" he asked. "Did my butthead friends tell you or something?"

Suzette smiled a little wider, and Plunk thought again that she was too close to pretty for somebody like Red to dump.

"I live in Crowley too and I read that paper they got," she said. "Big picture of you with those kids on Halloween. Your name was in the story and everything."

Bummed as he was, Plunk couldn't help but feel pleased.

"Yeah, must've been a slow day for news," he said. "Now I'm on the bottom of everybody's bird cage."

"Not mine," Suzette said. "I cut the picture out and it's on our bulletin board over there, the one where we show our celebrity customers." She gestured and damned if it wasn't true. There was Plunk's picture tacked up alongside a couple others. There was a fireman getting an award, and a woman with a big bowling trophy, and also a baseball card from years ago. The ballplayer looked familiar.

Suzette saw Plunk staring at the baseball card, trying to remember.

"Skunk Yawn, played with the Rangers for a while and then was their first base coach for two years," she said. "He didn't actually play much, only when somebody else was hurt, but everybody knew him because of his hair, that mullet. Plus how he got his nickname, when he thought he was petting a stray cat." And then Plunk remembered.

On those rare occasions when Skunk got in the game, fans always yelled things like, "Ya went to the blind barber again," also, "I can smell ya from here." All in fun, of course.

Then Suzette surprised Plunk by saying, "Skunk and me went out a couple times. So I kept his baseball card."

"Seen him lately?" Plunk asked. He himself had never actually met someone who played in the major leagues.

"Not for a while," Suzette said. "But I dated him, so I put the card up. Like your picture."

Being on the bulletin board was a big thing for Plunk, so he ate his hamburger and went back to Campbell Bolt & Screw feeling a little better. He called Mrs. Jance and she was there. She said it was better to talk in person and while there wasn't actually any emergency with Ida they really ought to make plans. Plunk explained how he had to make sales calls all during the week, and Mrs. Jance said she could meet with him at Pleasant Valley on Saturday morning, no problem. Plunk asked if nine was too early. They settled on that and Plunk was glad. He wouldn't have told Mrs. Jance, but he wanted to get to Cleburne as soon as he could on Saturday to take the tail to the leather shop, wherever it was. Mom came first, of course, but he also was responsible for the tail.

And from there it got even a little better, because Austin stuck his head out of his office and called, "Hey, Tail Man!" and then told everybody how great Plunk had been at the party on Saturday. Kevin said a couple nice things, too, and Austin added that Plunk's girlfriend seemed nice. This gave everybody a chance to kid Plunk about Darlene for a few minutes. He didn't mind, and though there was the Mom problem in addition to the tail's broken belt, Plunk still felt pretty much like himself by the time he drove home, grinning because his Tail Man picture was on a restaurant bulletin board.

20.

It snowed on Wednesday night, early for the first significant accumulation of the winter. The calendar said winter didn't officially start until December, which meant the calendar didn't live in North Texas. But it was a nice fluffy snow, not the mostly ice stuff that was nasty, and dangerous besides. Plunk had no problem driving with Darlene to the Chinese buffet place in Fort Worth. That's where she said she really wanted to go. Plunk had suggested a café on Main Street in Crowley and promised she'd like the chicken-fried steak they served, but Darlene wanted the Chinese in Fort Worth. When her folks came up from where they'd retired in Florida to visit, that's where they would go eat, she said, and that made it kind of her "special place." Plunk didn't much like Chinese food because it often looked like barf, but he felt he owed it to Darlene to take her to eat wherever she wanted, and a little Chinese food probably wouldn't kill him.

"You come from Florida?" he asked as they circled the block looking for a place to park. Fort Worth's population kept going up and that made parking places hard to find.

"No, that's where my aunt and her husband live," Darlene said. "We'd go visit them every summer, they're in Fort Myers, and Mother fell in love with the beach there. When Daddy took early retirement from the county two years ago, they moved to Fort Myers."

"So you're from here?" Plunk said, trying to keep polite conversation going while he found a parking place, geez, it was tough with all the traffic and falling snow.

"Born and raised," she said. "Proud graduate of South Crowley High."

"Go Warriors!" Plunk said.

"You mean, go Tornadoes."

"Well, when I went there we were called the Warriors, and I was the mascot," Plunk said, maneuvering his Ranger into a tight parking slot between two SUVs. "You remember when we were the Warriors."

"Actually, I don't," said Darlene, trying hard to open her door without banging it into the side of the towering SUV on the right. "I don't think I even knew it wasn't always the Tornadoes."

"When did you graduate?" Plunk asked.

"Oh, a long time ago, thirteen years now," Darlene said, inching between the cars to join Plunk on the sidewalk. "I'm thirty-one," she added in a much lower voice.

It about made Plunk's head spin. He'd thought Darlene was older than that, maybe even older than him instead of eleven years younger. She sure looked a lot more than thirty-one with her prim pursed mouth and everything.

"Chinese food," Plunk said to get the subject changed. "Right here around the corner."

The place was bigger than Plunk had expected, his few experiences with Chinese buffets involving tiny dives with gluey-tasting crap. But this one had several different steam tables and all kinds of stuff, which it ought to for $18.99 a piece for the buffet, beverages not included. At least Plunk had the hundred bucks from Austin. He just hadn't realized he was going to be spending so much of it on dinner. He'd hoped there would be plenty left over to pay for getting the belt on the tail fixed, but maybe not.

They filled their plates, Darlene making several suggestions, and he agreed to most but absolutely wouldn't touch what she called *moo she* because it truly looked like vomit. He didn't tell her that, of course.

When they sat down Darlene took off her coat and Plunk saw she was wearing a bright red sweater instead of a dark color, also a long skirt that came about to her shins. Why she wore that instead of her usual slacks on a cold night when the wind must really be swirling up on her, Plunk couldn't understand. But what the hell, none of his business what she wore. They ate and Darlene talked. She talked about working as a librarian assistant, you weren't supposed to check out the latest titles coming in before the public got its chance, but part of her job was to help catalog new arrivals and so she just took one home every now and then if it looked especially interesting. She read so fast she could get it back the next day, two tops.

"Sounds pretty good," Plunk said, though he himself hadn't touched, let alone read, a book in forever. That's what they made you do in school.

"And the pay's not bad, twelve-fifty an hour," Darlene added. "If I get my certification I'll get bumped to eighteen, but more and more I don't think that will happen. I'll finish my book and sell it and then I can just write and not have to work someplace anymore."

"Writing pays that much?" Plunk asked.

"New York publishers pay a lot for books, I think a minimum of a hundred thousand or something," Darlene said. "Then I'm estimating that the author gets about another ten dollars for every copy sold. I could, of course, self-publish, and then I wouldn't have any interference from an editor. I'd also have the freedom to promote my work however I pleased. But there's lots of conflicting information about self-publishing on the Internet, and besides I'm a traditionalist. The New York publishers provide a lot of financial security to authors. My teacher at the junior college tells me not to worry about the money, just focus on the writing craft. He had a novel published in New York, you know."

"If he got all that money, why's he here teaching at the junior college?"

"Authors like to share their knowledge," Darlene said a bit huffily. "He's just trying to give back. I will too after my book is published. I'll do what he does, inspire others."

Plunk made the mistake of asking Darlene what her book was about, and she took almost ten minutes telling him. A gifted young woman, she said, an aspiring author, lived in a small North Texas town where she worked as a high school librarian during the day and crafted a brilliant novel at night. Then there was a series of murders ("Gruesome, but not explicit") and the young woman solved the killings with the help of her handsome new boyfriend, this mysterious man who'd come to town and taken a job teaching English at the same high school.

"After my book's published I'm sure they'll make it into a movie," Darlene said. "So I'm all excited. And I'll have to move, probably. To New York or else Los Angeles, depending. Those are the artistic centers of the country, don't you think?"

"I think I wouldn't live in either one," Plunk said. "Weird places, is what they are. Full of pushy people who hate everything regular."

"Why do you say that?" Darlene asked. "Did you have some kind of bad experiences there?"

"Oh, I never been," Plunk said. "But I've heard a lot. No need to actually go."

"Where do you go?" Darlene asked. "When you travel, I mean. Where was your last trip?"

Plunk poked his fork around on his plate, trying to find some meat among all the vegetables and crud that Chinese people evidently loved so much. "Couple months ago, me and Eddie drove out to that new Buc-ees on the interstate south of Dallas. Heard a lot about it, wanted to see for ourselves. Big place, sold all kinds of stuff, and the bathrooms were just as clean as their billboards say."

"No, not like that," Darlene said. "I mean, real trips. Actual travel."

"Okay," Plunk said. "Dallas, which isn't a real trip, or I guess you could call going to Dallas a trip to Hell. Houston a couple of times. Abilene once when Austin wanted all of us from work to go to a trade show there. My Pop's family was down in Stephenville, so we went there sometimes."

"But where out of state?"

"You mean, out of Texas? Never."

"Never?" Darlene said, sounding kind of surprised. "Not even once?"

"Nope. No reason to. Everything I like's right here."

"Don't you want to see different things, experience them?"

"I got all the experience I want. It's normal here. Do you go on trips? Where?"

Darlene smiled. "Oh, I've been lots of places. Biloxi, when my family drove to Florida for visits with my aunt and uncle and cousins. Fort Myers, of course. Oklahoma City, so many nice places to eat. Branson. That's in Missouri. The Osmonds had a wonderful show there, and also a fiddler from Japan though he mostly played American tunes. We were supposed to go to Arizona once, we'd see the Grand Canyon, but my sister got sick just before we were supposed to leave, just a little cold or something but she carried on like she always does and my parents decided we'd stay home. Still, all those trips."

"But none to New York or LA?" Plunk asked.

"No, but that just means all the excitement there is just waiting for me," Darlene said. "It's going to be wonderful. You'd like it, too."

Plunk didn't think so but chose not to say it. He switched the subject back to Darlene's book, which he felt sure she'd be glad to talk about more.

"You got just a couple chapters finished, you said," Plunk pointed out. "How much longer 'til you're done?"

"It's going to go pretty fast now," Darlene said, taking a bite of her disgusting-looking moo she. She wrapped the stuff in what she called a pancake and ate it. "At the library right before Halloween we got an advance copy of Dr. Jennifer Nice's new book in, and I took it home and it was just inspiring. Like all her books."

"Dr. who?" Plunk asked.

"Dr. Jennifer Nice. The one who had that bestseller *Face the Facts: Make Life Fair Even When It Isn't.* Everybody read it."

"Not me."

"Well, you should," Darlene said. "She tells you how not to let problems get you down, even when the problem is caused by somebody else. You learn what makes the other person do the wrong thing, and then you use what you learned to find an acceptable solution instead of staying mad at the one who was wrong, which isn't productive. Everybody should read Dr. Nice. She sells about a billion copies every time she has a new one in the stores. Which she will in January. It's called *Set Them, Get Them: Why Goals Are Better Than Dreams, and*

How to Achieve Them."

"Long name for a book," Plunk said.

"But it's so good," Darlene said, leaning forward and pushing her glasses back up her nose. "What Dr. Nice says in it, everybody has things they aspire to, but if you don't have specific plans to accomplish them then they're just dreams. Nobody achieves dreams, they're imaginary. But goals are what you achieve by having planned-out achievable steps, and you go a step at a time until one day the goal's accomplished."

"Huh," Plunk said.

"Like with my novel," Darlene continued, obviously not noticing Plunk's eyes glazing over. "Before I just piddled with the first couple chapters over and over. But now thanks to Dr. Nice's book I have a plan where I write two pages almost every night, so that in say maybe four months I'll have actually finished the book."

"That's your goal," Plunk said, trying to sound interested.

"No, that's just part way to the goal. Writing every night and finishing the book are steps. Then there are more, which I've listed and look at every day like Dr. Nice says to. I finish the novel. I get an agent. The agent sells the book. The book gets published. Everybody buys it, it's a bestseller. I become a full-time writer. Goal achieved."

"Sounds easy," Plunk said.

"Dr. Nice makes it easy. That's why everybody loves her books. You need to read *Set Them, Get Them* when it comes out. It might change your life, too."

"That's okay," Plunk said. "I mean, you just told me what's in it."

"No, you should read the book so you can specifically set your goals," Darlene said, eyes shining with evangelical fervor. "It's never too late. I mean, what do you really want to do with your life?"

"I want to get my tail fixed," Plunk said, and thankfully Darlene got distracted onto that. He told her about the broken belt and she said they ought to take the tail to the leather place in Cleburne on Saturday, she could call ahead and make an appointment. Plunk said not to bother, he'd do it himself, but she insisted they were partners and on Saturday they would go to Cleburne together. It seemed rude to disagree.

"I got one other thing to do before that, so maybe you meet me in the apartment parking lot at 10:30 that morning, around there," he said. "I don't know how long this first thing at nine's gonna take, but probably not too much."

Darlene wanted to know what the first thing was, and he ended up telling her about his mother and what Mrs. Jance thought. Which resulted in Darlene saying she'd go with him to Pleasant Valley, too, and when he said he wouldn't want to put her out she said it wasn't a problem and besides, if she came along and he didn't have to go back by The Jacksonian to pick her up afterward he'd get to Cleburne quicker. That meant a better chance the tail could get fixed right on the spot. He didn't want to have to leave the tail at the leather place, did he? Plunk certainly didn't, so he said fine.

Darlene insisted they get fortune cookies on their way out. Her fortune read, "The longest journey begins with the shortest step," which she said reflected the main lesson in Dr. Nice's great new book. Plunk's was, "Prepare your heart for romance."

"That's an interesting one," Darlene said.

21.

Mrs. Jance was waiting in her office when Plunk and Darlene got to Pleasant Valley on Saturday. Plunk felt strange being there but not coming to see Mom. Since it was nine he thought she would already have had breakfast. Maybe she was playing cards with Helen.

"Mr. Landy," Mrs. Jance said, standing up behind her desk and reaching out to shake hands. "Thank you so much for coming."

"Yeah, sure," Plunk said. "Mom and all."

"I understand," Mrs. Jance said. She turned to Darlene. "And hello as well. You are?"

"This is Darlene. Quaverley," Plunk said, pissed that he hadn't thought to make an introduction. He liked to think he had pretty good manners.

"A pleasure to meet you," Mrs. Jance said. "And your relationship to Ida?"

Darlene shot a quick look at Plunk.

"A friend of the family," she said.

"Of course," Mrs. Jance said. "Please, sit down." She offered coffee and they both said no thanks. So Mrs. Jance got down to business.

Ida, she said, was just the loveliest lady, a real favorite with both staff and other residents. She was never in any way deliberately difficult, which unfortunately was not true of many other residents with somewhat declining abilities. However, it had become evident to everyone, surely including her son Mr. Landy, that dear Ida was suffering from increased intellectual dysfunction, the signs of which indicated a form of dementia.

"She's getting senile," Plunk said, to cut the stream of big words short.

"Senile is rather generic," Mrs. Jance said. "There are many different forms of dementia."

"Like Alzheimer's but not always," Darlene said, and Mrs. Jance smiled and nodded and said that was absolutely correct. From then on she looked at Darlene as much as she did at Plunk.

At any rate, Mrs. Jance continued, Ida now had difficulty functioning as a minimal care resident. She forgot where she was supposed to be, her eating habits were becoming messy, and there had been a few unfortunate incidents involving bodily functions. These things were not unusual for residents who were afflicted with the onset of dementia. Unfortunately, the situation was progressive and inevitably became worse, never better. And so Mrs. Jance recommended that Ida move to the constant care wing, where there would be more staff available at all times.

"Which does bring us to financial issues," she said.

"Tell me," Plunk said, his heart sinking. He knew this wasn't going to be good.

Constant care for a patient involved much more staff time, Mrs. Jance explained, and of course staffers had to be paid. Mrs. Landy's Social Security and her husband's pension would continue to cover basic room and board. But there was an additional $600 a month charge for constant care. Was Mr. Landy in a position to handle that?

It was his Mom. So of course Plunk said he could, though at that particular moment he wasn't sure how. Plus he hurt for Mom, getting crazy and all. Looking down, Plunk was surprised to see Darlene had taken his hand. He hadn't noticed.

"Well, then," Mrs. Jance said. "Why don't we start the paperwork and perhaps we can attend to the details sometime this week? Because we all would certainly like to see Ida made as comfortable as possible, and she will be much happier in constant care."

"She likes her friend Helen," Plunk said, taking his hand back from Darlene, but careful not to yank it away. "That might be a problem, moving out of the room with her."

"We have experience with things like that," Mrs. Jance assured him. She turned to Darlene. "What a pleasure to meet you, Ms. Quaverley," she added. "I do hope you'll be a regular visitor to Ida and all of us here at Pleasant Valley."

"I will," Darlene promised.

"Geez, six hundred a month," Plunk said bleakly as he and Darlene got into his Ranger. The tail was draped along both back fold-down seats, Plunk had found a good angle for doing that, there was hardly any room between them to begin with, and he reached back to touch the tail for a minute before putting the pickup in gear and heading for Cleburne. "I'm gonna have to sell a lot more stuff for Austin to manage that."

Darlene patted his knee.

"We've got the Tail Man business now, remember," she said. "You'll be able to do it."

"I hope so," Plunk said. "Poor Mom."

"It's going to be fine," Darlene said.

Plunk hoped so, but this sure seemed like a time when just saying something was going to be okay might not work. Even before this new expense for Mom, money was tight for Plunk. Monthly rent and utilities took a big bite out of his income. Gas was a big deal, too. Austin didn't pay mileage—every once in a while, Plunk or one of the other guys would ask him to, and Austin's reply was always, "If you want to give up your weekly draw, fine, I'll give you mileage." But Plunk's sales to customers were always up and down, often down, meaning his 5 percent commission frequently didn't come to much. The $500 weekly draw at least gave him some guaranteed income, not that there was ever much to spare. He tried to think of what he could cut back on. He already had the minimal car insurance required to keep his Ranger eligible to pass yearly inspection, and no health insurance at all—Austin only provided that for Jessika, which was fair because everybody understood that the company would collapse without her around to keep everything organized. Not having much money usually wasn't a problem. Plunk really only wanted a couple special things, stuff any regular Texas guy coveted—a factory-fresh Ford F150 with all the extras, and a fancy gun, or even any gun. Plunk priced F150s and guns regularly, and even the used ones, cars and guns alike, cost way too much. He'd long ago accepted that these fine things would be forever beyond his reach, much like Vikki Brooks the cheerleader from back in his high school days. Things you imagined having but knew deep down you never would get. Plunk liked his life okay, even with its few basic extras. Now he'd have to give up some of those. The TV streaming services came to mind. He wouldn't like losing his sexy movies, but if that's what it took for Mom, he would. Cancelling Netflix and Apple would still leave him hundreds of dollars short of six hundred. What else did he have to give up? All he could think of was beer, and there the line had to be drawn. But Darlene might be right. Maybe Tail Man would come to the rescue. He'd think about that instead of the bad stuff.

The drive to Cleburne took a while, what with Saturday morning traffic. Plunk felt jittery the whole time, partly because of Mom and the extra money he was going to need every month, but also because he always listened to the radio when he drove, mostly the oldies station. That was his custom. But Darlene liked to talk in the car, never one silent moment allowed, and all the way she kept up a constant chatter, about her job and her novel and this younger sister she didn't get along with who wanted them to fly down to Florida for Thanksgiving with their parents. Darlene said she loved her parents if not her sister, but going to Florida for Thanksgiving would mean at least three and maybe even four or five days of not working on her novel. Dr. Nice, she was certain, would advise her to stay home and stick to achieving her goal, what did Plunk think?

"Whatever you want to do," Plunk said vaguely.

"What are you going to do for Thanksgiving?" Darlene asked. "I mean, will you be with your mother? Or … friends?"

"I guess," Plunk said. "That's a couple weeks away. They do a thing where Mom lives. I'll just see. Where's that leather place, anyway?"

Darlene had looked up Cleburne Leather's address on her computer and then printed out a map since Plunk's old pickup had no GPS. She'd called the guy there earlier in the week and he was expecting them at 10:30 or 10:45.

"You sure he said he could fix the tail while we wait?" Plunk said.

"He said maybe, depending on the amount of work involved. We turn off right up here."

They found the place, a little shop in a strip mall. It smelled great, with vests and boots and golf bags and even a couple saddles slung up on shelves. There was a door to the back where they apparently did the fixing, and when Plunk and Darlene opened the front door a buzzer went off and a wizened old guy came out from the back to greet them. Plunk showed him the tail and where the belt had broken loose.

"Good quality," the guy said, poking the tail here and there with his finger. "Industrial-grade rubber on the inside, I bet."

"I like it," Plunk said with the pride of a father just informed his kid was the best athlete on the team. "Can you fix the belt?"

"Easy," the old guy said. "But you ought to think about me putting three genuine leather belts on it, replace this plastic trash. See, the belts are supposed to look like leather but they aren't. You keep these on, they'll just keep tearing. Tail like this deserves better than that."

It made sense to Plunk. Just holding the tail, talking about it, made the problems with Mom settle in the back of his mind.

"If you can do it while we wait," he said.

"I guess," the old guy said. "Put off a couple other jobs. But you don't get a tail to work on every day. Say, you ought to have me run a good permanent stitch along this seam that goes from one end to the other. Way it is now, that could split, too, you drop the thing on something hard like a sidewalk. Wouldn't want that, I know."

"I wouldn't," Plunk agreed.

Darlene had been uncharacteristically quiet, but now she butted in.

"What kind of cost are we looking at?" she asked. "We need to know how much before you start on this. You could just say anything after you finished."

Plunk thought that was kind of rude but the old guy didn't seem offended.

"Okay, lemme think here," he said. "Three belts, all leather. Got some that should work just fine. Cost of them on their own plus stitching them on. And the long seam stitch. Run you, I guess, one-ninety for materials and machine use. Plus fifty for my time."

"I think that's too much," Darlene said.

"You could go someplace else," the old guy said, not sounding mad but sort of entertained. "They wouldn't do as good a job, though. Deserves the best, a tail like this."

"Yes, but still," Darlene said, holding up a warning hand to Plunk as he was about to blurt okay, do it for the hundred ninety plus your fifty.

The old guy rubbed his chin.

"Never had a chance to work on a tail," he conceded. "I'll throw in my time for nothing. One-ninety. You okay with that?" He was asking Darlene rather than Plunk, whose tail it was.

"While we're waiting," Darlene cautioned.

"While you wait," the old guy said.

It took him about forty-five minutes. When he was done and brought the tail back out, Plunk's heart leaped because it looked so good, and also the new belts had that rich leather smell. The old guy had Plunk try it on, the new belts around his waist and both thighs. Damned if it didn't feel even better, a little snugger; these leather belts were a shade wider than the old cheap ones. Plunk really hated taking the tail off so he could get out his credit card and pay, a hundred and ninety bucks was a lot but what the hell, he'd have tuna sandwiches or grilled cheese for dinner the next couple weeks, not those microwavable dinners that cost a lot more. On the ride back home he and Darlene talked about the birthday party next Saturday and ideas for leopard gecko games, and he only realized later with a guilty start that he'd forgotten all about Mom for a while.

22.

Sunday Plunk visited Mom, being careful not to say anything about her moving rooms because Mrs. Jance had suggested he shouldn't. Then he watched the Cowboys game as usual with Red and Larry B. and Eddie, sometimes thinking about the game, which the Cowboys won for a change, and more often Mom and every once in a while about the tail, which was back in the bedroom with its fine new belts. Monday work went okay, close to two thousand dollars in sales, but one customer told Plunk he might as well stop coming by 'til April or so because he didn't have any more projects lined up until then, winter weather and all.

Tuesday afternoon Mrs. Jance from Pleasant Valley called Plunk at his office to say the paperwork was ready if Mr. Landy wanted to come by to sign everything. Once that was done, dear Ida would be moved to her new room in the constant care wing. Plunk took the call while at his messy desk, filling out paperwork on the day's very few sales. Austin liked everybody to stay at their desks until at least five and it was only a little before three, but Plunk told Jessika about Mom and she said just go ahead, if Austin asked she'd explain. Jessika was nice that way, always glad to help.

So Plunk drove to Pleasant Valley and signed the papers Mrs. Jance had for him, most of them long and filled with complicated stuff. But one was very easy to understand. It said that Plunk was liable for six hundred dollars a month more, and as he took a second to stare at it before signing. Mrs. Jance said that by the way, Mr. Landy needed to give her a check for the first month, pro-rated of course, it already being nearly mid-November.

"Where does the time go?" Mrs. Jance asked, and Plunk thought it went the same place as his money, gone forever. He happened to have his checkbook, he'd sort of figured he'd need it, and Mrs. Jance said three hundred would be right and he wrote the check. It wasn't going to bounce, but there wasn't much left in his account with more than half the month to go. Plunk wondered if he and Darlene would get paid right after the birthday party on Saturday was over. He sure hoped so.

Once all the papers were signed and Mrs. Jance had her check, she said it was time to help Ida move to her new room. Plunk thought that was a signal for him to go get Mom, but Mrs. Jance said it was better to let staff manage things, they had experience and sometimes it was rather traumatic for residents. She told Plunk he should come back for his usual Sunday visit but if he didn't mind not before, giving dear Ida a few days to get settled.

So Plunk drove back to his apartment, feeling low about Mom, worried about paying the extra money every month and badly in need of comforting from his tail. Soon as he was inside he got the tail and strapped it on, this was something he usually did now when he was home by himself. He didn't want anyone to know about it because they wouldn't understand. But what harm did it do? He liked wearing the tail.

He also wanted a beer just then, the hard day with work and signing papers about Mom and all. Plunk liked to pop a beer and plop on the couch to watch ESPN, whatever was on was okay as long as it was sports, but when he had the tail on he couldn't sit down. So he walked around the apartment for about ten minutes while wearing the tail, comforted as always by the weight of it, the *feel*, and then still wearing it he went to the fridge and got his beer.

Holding the beer in one hand he undid the tail's two thigh belts with the other, thinking to then walk the rest of the way to the bedroom, put the beer can on the night stand, and use both hands to unbuckle the bigger, wider waist belt. But on the way the tail smacked against the side of the fridge, there really wasn't much room in the little apartment, and because the thigh belts were undone this knocked the tail from its resting place on Plunk's ass to the side of his right hip. His first reaction was shit, he hoped the tail wasn't scratched up or anything, but then the tail just sort of hung down to his side and he thought about it for a minute.

Beer still in hand, tail hanging at his side rather than straight back behind him, Plunk maneuvered carefully to his living room. He bent down, put the beer can on the carpet, and sat on the left side of the couch, picking up the tail and settling it on the couch beside him, there was enough room on his right. The waist belt held the tail close; he felt it against his hip rather than his ass. That was different, but still okay. Plunk grabbed the remote, snapped on the widescreen, picked up his beer, leaned back and took a good long cold pull from the can. ESPN was showing highlights from the weekend's big college games. Plunk took another sip, holding the can in his left hand while he reached over and rested his right hand on the tail. For the first time all day he felt at peace.

That lasted maybe twenty minutes until there was a knock on the door. He jumped up, the tail sagging from his hip.

"Be right there!" he hollered, not knowing if whoever it was would hear, and hurried to the bedroom, where he undid the waist belt and put the tail on the bed. He wasn't ashamed of wearing it around the place or anything, it was just something he somehow felt ought to be private.

Plunk hustled back to the door and opened it. There was Darlene, looking a little puzzled.

"What took you so long?" she asked.

"Bathroom," Plunk said, and Darlene nodded like she really didn't need to hear any more.

"I wondered how your mother did today," she said, coming in and pulling off her wooly mittens. It was cold out. "She was supposed to get moved, right?"

"Yeah, she did," Plunk said. "You want a beer?"

"Not right now," Darlene said. "It's not even six."

"But it's already getting dark," Plunk said, not wanting her to think he was some kind of alcoholic.

"That's okay," Darlene said. "Was your Mom fine with everything?"

"I dunno," Plunk admitted. Darlene had by this time been over to his apartment enough that she didn't wait to be invited to sit down. She sat on the couch, off to one side rather than the middle, which Plunk realized meant she wanted him to sit on the couch, too. He did.

"Mrs. Jance said sometimes people got upset about moving, so I should wait to see Mom until Sunday like usual," he said. "I hope she didn't cry or anything. I don't remember Mom ever crying much." Imagining that, he really wished he was still wearing the tail.

"She probably didn't," Darlene said. "I'll go with you on Sunday, in case she's unhappy or mixed up. Women feel more comfortable talking to other women about these things."

"Yeah," Plunk said noncommittally. "So what can I do for you right now?"

"It's about the birthday party on Saturday," she said, jamming a finger against her glasses frames to get them back up her nose. "Four days and all."

"That's right," Plunk said. "I guess with Mom I wasn't really thinking about it much."

"We've got the games thing," Darlene reminded him. "Two hours for three hundred is the deal. I talked to Gretchen today, just getting directions, and she asked about the games."

"Gretchen?" Plunk asked.

"Hillary's mother. It's Hillary's seventh birthday party. They live in Westlake, not Keller, though Hillary and Leanne's little boy Timmy go to the same private school. Westlake's not too far from Keller, you know."

Plunk didn't need the geography lesson. It was part of his job at Campbell Bolt & Screw to drive around all over the place, and he almost said so sharply to Darlene because he was upset about Mom and now also realized he had no idea what kind of games to play at the party.

"I know where it is," he said, trying not to sound mad. But Darlene still picked up on it, and sort of understood, because she said right away not to worry about the games, she'd figured it out.

"In fact, I mentioned them to Gretchen and she was excited," Darlene said. "Remember Leanne said Tail Man was entertaining and educational both. That's what I was going for."

"Okay," Plunk said, relieved at not having to think up games himself. "So what we gonna do?"

Darlene told about looking through websites on the library computer and finding this big color picture of a leopard gecko with its long tail dangling behind, and how she printed out the picture and then carefully cut the gecko out, trimming right along its sides and head. Then she laminated the gecko body, cut off the tail at the root and made lots of copies of the tail, which she also laminated.

"I went to Target and got a dart board, pulled the wire off and attached the gecko body to the board," she said. "Then I got straight pins, and at the party the kids can play Pin the Tail on the Gecko."

"Hey, that's great!" Plunk said admiringly. "I'd never've thought of that."

Darlene beamed.

"So we've got Tail Man himself, and the question and answer I do, and Pin the Tail on the Gecko," she said. "Real good, but we needed something more. Two hours is a long time to keep kids busy."

At which point Darlene described her other party game. Hillary's mom had agreed to go out and buy a roll of long, narrow, light-colored plastic trash bags, plus strong twine and black magic markers and from a packaging store a bunch of those white styrofome peanuts people put inside boxes when they ship fragile things. As a crafts game, the kids would make their own gecko tails, and then if the weather was nice they could have some races in the backyard wearing the tails.

"You're a genius," Plunk said. He almost said "goddamn genius" but stopped himself in time. Girls didn't like that kind of language.

"I try," Darlene said, obviously pretty proud of herself.

They talked about the party some more and also Darlene going with Plunk to see his Mom on Sunday, it just seemed now like of course Darlene would come, how could Plunk not let her after her great party games ideas? She seemed to hope Plunk might suggest they go out to eat or something right then, but after the check he'd written to Pleasant Valley, he was already eating sandwiches for supper for the rest of the month, so that was out. Finally Darlene said she had to go, Dr. Nice would be expecting her to get to work on the novel, and as soon as the door closed behind her Plunk went right into the bedroom to put the tail back on. He popped a fresh beer, dropped on the couch, settled the tail to his right and watched more ESPN. Plunk was in a great mood now, and realized the tail added to good times just like it bucked him up whenever he felt crappy. What a tail!

23.

"What's *he* doing here?" Darlene demanded Saturday morning in the apartment parking lot. She was referring to Eddie, who came out right behind Plunk when Darlene knocked on the door Saturday at noon.

"Ah, I told him he could help today," Plunk said. "He can carry things or whatever."

In fact, Plunk was carrying the tail out to the car himself. He didn't like other people touching it unless it was around his waist where he knew it was safe. Eddie didn't actually have anything to carry. He just smirked at Darlene like he'd won and she'd lost because he was getting to come along.

"We're partners and you should have asked me," Darlene said, getting pretty hot about it. "There's really no need for him to come."

"You never know," Plunk said. "There might be something he could do. Look, we gotta be going if the party's at one."

"I got shotgun," Eddie said, jumping in the front seat of the pickup cab while Plunk was still putting the tail in the back. Darlene glared, but Eddie was already buckling his seat belt on, so she had to get in the back and sit on one of the unpadded fold-down seats while the tail was on the other one, its pointy end across her lap. Plunk hadn't thought about seating arrangements. It would have been polite, hell, *smart*, for Eddie to let Darlene ride in the front where it was much more comfortable, since she was so pissed about him coming. But no, Eddie had to act like a butthead and now there would be tension Plunk didn't need.

"Let him sit where he wants," Plunk whispered to her. "You can sit in front on the way back. Do you want him to hold those bags?"

Darlene had a couple plastic grocery store bags with stuff in them, Plunk assumed the items for Pin the Tail on the Gecko.

"He'd just do something stupid with them," Darlene grumbled, and Plunk thought that she was right, Eddie probably would.

So they drove most of the way to Westlake in hostile silence, which at least had the advantage of Plunk not having to listen to Darlene chatter. But when they were getting close she said, "Gretchen told me she thought they'd do cake and presents in between our things. So we get there, you go put on the tail, we have the first pictures and tail-touching, then Pin the Tail on the Gecko. Gretchen brings in the cake, Hillary opens her presents, and then we have the Q&A, the tail-making time, and hopefully yard races. It's pretty cold but maybe it won't rain. And that'll be the two hours."

Before Plunk could say "Okay," Eddie butted in.

"Maybe he wants to have the races first and the pin the tail last," Eddie said in his wise guy kind of way. "You're not the boss."

"And you're not in this partnership," Darlene snapped. "Why don't you just be quiet."

"I'm here because he asked me," Eddie said. "He had a choice, you wouldn't even be in the truck."

Darlene started to say something back, but Plunk interrupted. He felt funny having to act like the grownup.

"You two knock it off," he said. "I got a mother in constant care and I need the money, so don't screw this up with griping. Where's this house, Darlene? Eddie, stop messing with her."

"I got us this job," Darlene said in a soft hurt voice. "I thought of the games, too."

"I know you did, and they're good ones," Plunk soothed.

"You asked me to come help," Eddie said, not wanting to be left out.

"You sorta asked yourself, but that's okay," Plunk said. "Just don't fight with her. We don't need that. Everybody get along."

"Are we doing everything in the order I wanted?" Darlene said. "I need to know."

"Sure we are," Plunk said. "Just like you want."

And they did, and it worked out fine. The house wasn't nearly as big as Austin's, not as many rooms and a lot smaller backyard, but still pretty nice. There were about the same number of kids as at Austin's but maybe a few more girls and fewer boys. Plunk had to put the tail on in Hillary's bedroom, all pink and little-girly, which was strange. Eddie went in with him and offered to help with the buckles. Plunk knocked his hand away. While they were in there Darlene explained to the kids what they were going to do and when, so when Plunk came out the girls and boys mobbed him and it was fun. Eddie of all people told the kids to line up and not yank or anything.

"So wonderful of you to come," Gretchen told him. "Hillary's been excited ever since Timmy's party that Tail Man was coming to her house. We had to send out more invitations because she told everybody at school."

Pin the Tail on the Gecko was wonderful, Eddie without being asked took on the job of blindfolding the kids and twirling them around. Darlene appointed herself judge, and Gretchen provided little prizes for the winner. After the cake was brought out and while Hillary opened presents in the den, Plunk, Darlene, and Eddie went over to the dining room table to look at the materials for tail-making.

"Oh, she got the wrong kind of garbage bags," Darlene moaned. "These are real dark-colored. The spots the kids draw won't show up."

"We passed a grocery store on the way in," Eddie said. "Plunk, you give me your keys and I'll run over and get light-colored."

"See? We did need him to help," Plunk whispered to Darlene as Eddie raced off.

"He'll probably come back with even darker ones," she predicted, but in fact Eddie bought light-colored like he was supposed to. After Darlene's Q&A, which only lasted a couple minutes because the kids were so excited, the tail-making was a big hit. Plunk sort of stood in the middle of it all like a model, and when everybody had a tail they went into the yard for races, it was still cold but no rain. Eddie again was very helpful with organizing and keeping everybody lined up. Even Darlene had to admit it.

So by the end of the two hours Tail Man was everybody's hero. Like at Timmy's party Plunk posed for photos, many he thought with the same kids who'd been at that first one, Timmy of course included. Leanne was in the bunch of mothers at the party, and they had mostly stayed a room or two away with glasses of wine and some cheese and fruit for snacks. Leanne did make a point of saying hi to Plunk and Darlene. There hadn't been many fathers, just Hillary's and a couple others, but when the backyard tail races were over the dads came up to chat. One asked if Plunk had a minute for a private word and pulled him off into the kitchen.

"I'm Dick Billings, Tail Man," he said, and Plunk was pleased to be addressed that way. "Love your act. Listen to those kids screaming in the back. They had fun today."

"Glad they did," Plunk said. He felt sweaty. He had a couple T-shirts on under his yellow Tail Man sweatshirt so he'd be warm enough outside. But inside it was a little too much.

"So I want to ask you," Billings said. He was taller than Plunk with the wide shoulders of a guy who worked out a lot. "Do you just do kids' parties?"

"Well, my friend Darlene out there handles everything," Plunk said, unsure of what the guy was getting at.

"Thing is, I've got an event next Sunday afternoon," Billings said. "Charity deal for Fort Worth Cook Children's Hospital. I'm on the board. We do a celebrity golf tournament every year the Sunday before Thanksgiving."

"Oh," Plunk said, for something to say. He still had the tail on, and he reached back to touch it because he was confused.

"I know, stupid to have a golf thing right at the beginning of winter," Billings said as though Plunk had pointed this fact out. "But that's when they want it. Good time for publicity and all, get those contributions in before people start thinking they need every cent for Christmas. We get golfers from around here to kick in five hundred each to play eighteen holes with a celebrity partner, businesses donate items like airline tickets and yard crews for a year, and we have a silent auction. Clear maybe fifty thousand, and it all helps. Lots of sick kids needing help."

"That's bad, all those sick kids," Plunk said.

Billings sipped from the drink he was holding.

"Look," he said. "I know it's short notice. But we're having some of our celebrities bail, the assholes. DeMarcus Pruitt, who used to play for the Mavericks and not even that well. Golden Throat Jacobs from that twenty-four-hour sports radio station, he says his wife's got to have surgery. Congressman Argent's still going to be there, and Bonnie Woody from *Daybreak Metroplex* on TV. Some scrub players from the Rangers, it's their offseason and a few of them live around here. But I need somebody else. Could you play?"

"I don't actually play golf," Plunk said. "And I guess I'm not a celebrity, either."

Billings shook his head.

"Don't worry about any of that," he said. "I can lend you some clubs. And if you wear the tail people will feel like that's something. We got a lot of kids who come with their parents, and if the weather's okay some of the less sick kids from the hospital itself. You can pose for pictures with them and everything."

"But golf," Plunk said. "I've never played it, even once."

"Not a problem," Billings said. "I'll bring my extra set of clubs. Nobody cares if the celebrities play well, anyway. Will you do it? One p.m. next Sunday afternoon at Benbrook Country Club near Southwest Fort Worth? Just park in the celebrity lot, there'll be a sign. Somebody'll bring you over and give you your tee time, introduce you to the rest of your foursome. Done by five, I swear."

Plunk hesitated. Golf, and also missing the Cowboys game?

"The Cowboys are playing the Sunday night game," Billings said as though he'd read Plunk's mind. "You with us? Ought to be lots of media, you'd get some publicity for your party stuff. I can't pay because it's for charity, but you'd meet lots of people who'd maybe hire you for things. So do I have Tail Man? Can we advertise you'll be there, be one of our celebrities?"

"Sure," Plunk said, dazzled by the concept of Tail Man as a celebrity. He went outside to tell Darlene. She was excited, too, and even talked decently to Eddie on the ride back to Crowley.

24.

Plunk knew Darlene wanted to be his girlfriend. He would have even if that butthead Eddie hadn't kept telling him Saturday night while they watched Texas play LSU on Plunk's widescreen.

"You let her, she's gonna put a dog collar on you and you'll have to ask her permission to go outside and pee," Eddie predicted. "Wait and see, she's the kind who won't want you to watch football with your friends."

Which was truer than Eddie knew. When they got back to Crowley after Hillary's party, Darlene pulled Plunk aside to say they should have dinner, talk about the charity golf event. Plunk replied he'd told Eddie they'd watch the game, and Darlene made a face and told him business ought to come first. Then she said they could have lunch after going to see his Mom the next day, and Plunk had to tell her Eddie and the other guys were coming over to watch the Cowboys then. Darlene gave this big sigh and Plunk agreed they'd have dinner after that, she was making him feel guilty for having fun with the guys and that was one of the things women always did.

"She just wants to talk about the golf thing," Plunk told Eddie, who waved his hand dismissively and replied, "Oh, yeah, I bet."

There had also been the money thing. Hillary's mom paid Darlene the three hundred in cash right after the party was over, plus another twenty-five as a bonus because it had gone so well. In the apartment parking lot Darlene took out the money right in front of Eddie and counted most of it into Plunk's hand.

"Two twenty-five of the three hundred for you, seventy-five for me," she said. "That's our agreement, three-quarters to you. Now the bonus twenty-five, I think we divide, too."

Even Darlene had to take a minute figuring out how to divide up twenty-five in a 75–25 split, and as she hesitated Plunk saw Eddie watching.

"We need to give Eddie the extra," he suggested. "For coming and helping."

Darlene's eyebrows arched so far up that her glasses slid all the way down to the very tip of her nose.

"He volunteered, I thought," she said.

Eddie started to splutter something angry and Plunk jumped in.

"We all go work, we all make something," he said. "Give him the twenty-five."

"Technically, a quarter of it's mine," she said. "That's, um, six twenty-five."

"I'll give you the six twenty-five out of my share," Plunk said.

"No, it's all right," Darlene said, and shoved a few bills at Eddie, who sarcastically said, "Thank you very much," before telling Plunk he'd see him at the apartment in a few. That was when Darlene brought up dinner and Plunk said he couldn't, followed by his explanation of why lunch the next day wouldn't work either.

But Darlene didn't give up until she had the promise of Sunday dinner, and now on Sunday morning as they walked from the apartments to Pleasant Valley she was doing the shoulder bump thing. It was what women did to make men realize they were interested without having to risk coming right out and saying it. Plunk hadn't experienced shoulder bumps much, but they were unmistakable. His first time for one was a big high school party, plenty of his sophomore classmates there and beer because the host's parents thought it was better they got drunk where the grownups could at least keep track of them, knowing the kids were going to drink anyway. Plunk was wandering around the backyard, slapping people on the back and trying to get them to laugh, when Margie from the pep squad started walking along beside him and her shoulder started bumping into him some, not like drunk and staggering but just these nudges, touches, and he understood. Margie was not a pretty girl, she was kind of fat if Plunk was honest about it. But she was a girl and she was interested, the first time he'd known for a fact a girl was, and they ended up in a corner doing a few things. Margie was the first girl Plunk asked to go steady and she agreed, though after two weeks she also became the first to suggest the just being friends thing.

Every once in a while after that Plunk would be walking with a girl, wondering if she was interested, and if she bumped her shoulder into him accidentally on purpose he knew she was. It didn't happen a lot. And now Darlene was doing it. Plunk wondered if women sat around together and worked out these signals. They all seemed to know them, to use the same ones. When it came to romance women were a lot better organized than men.

"I hope your mother's settled in," Darlene said. Because it was chilly she'd expected Plunk to say they'd drive over rather than make the fifteen-minute walk, but Plunk told her walking was better and she hadn't argued. As usual Darlene was all bundled up in a heavy shapeless coat. Plunk had on his Cowboys jacket, getting pretty worn but he loved it. The wind blew in from the north and his ears were very cold, but he thought wearing hats that covered your ears was sissy.

"I guess," Plunk said hopefully. "She liked her old room."

"The staff there has lots of experience with things like this," Darlene said. "Thank you for letting me come this morning." Her shoulder gently bumped into Plunk's arm. "It means a lot."

"Yeah," Plunk muttered. His mind was racing. It had been nearly three weeks since Darlene had first come over with the copy of the *Observer* and the leopard gecko information. Now they were business partners and she was shoulder-bumping him while they walked. If he didn't act interested back, if he didn't make a move, what if she got mad and wouldn't have anything more to do with the Tail Man thing? How would he get Tail Man jobs? He loved them, and also there was the extra money he had to have to pay for Mom's care. So many things to worry about, and Plunk's whole life was built around not worrying if at all possible.

"Where do you want to go for dinner?" he asked, just to keep the conversation going.

"Somewhere quiet," Darlene said. "Where we can talk." She knew of a place in North Fort Worth that was supposed to be good, seafood was the specialty.

"Cost much?" Plunk inquired. Already he was worrying about the six hundred Pleasant Valley would be expecting from him right on the first of December, not all that far away.

"I don't think so," Darlene said. "I've never actually been there myself, but one of the librarians told me about it. She brings her lunch to work every day, so I don't think she's really extravagant."

"It's not that I'm cheap," Plunk felt compelled to explain. "It's just with Mom, money's kind of tight."

"It's so wonderful you care about your mother like that," Darlene said. There was another shoulder bump, maybe the fourth or fifth. "You're a very caring person."

"I guess," Plunk said. He could feel the trap closing. It wasn't that he didn't like Darlene. She wasn't ugly or anything. He still didn't know what her body was like, she kept it so covered up. He was scared if he ever tried to kiss her he might knock off her glasses.

They got to Pleasant Valley and Plunk had to go to the desk to ask which room Mom was in. The constant care ward wasn't a real cheerful place. He noticed right away some old people sitting in the hall propped up in wheelchairs, their mouths hanging open and usually stuff dripping down their chins in long thin strings. Mom was in her new room, this one even a little smaller than her other one, but the pictures and knickknacks were up on the dresser. Whoever the new roommate was, she wasn't there. Plunk hoped it wasn't one of the wheelchair women in the hall.

But Mom was sitting in her chair, and so Plunk introduced Darlene and sat with her on Mom's bed. Darlene said she was pleased to meet her and Mom said Helen hadn't slept in her bed last night. That gave Plunk a chance to explain to Mom about changing rooms, of course he didn't say it was because she was getting crazy. He told her the people at Pleasant Valley thought she'd like something different.

From there on it was more or less a typical Sunday visit. Of course Mom mentioned the name Plunk hoped she wouldn't, but only once, and Plunk thought maybe Darlene didn't even pick up on it. And Darlene did just great, acting all interested when Mom talked about meals she'd recently eaten and how the blanket on this bed kept pulling loose and her feet got cold. When they got up to go Plunk gave Mom a hug. Darlene hugged her too.

"You want us to take you to the TV room maybe, Mom?" Plunk asked, and Mom said she'd just sit where she was for a while until Helen came back. When Plunk and Darlene were in the hall, one of the aides pulled them aside to say Mrs. Landy was adjusting, it was taking some time, but nobody needed to worry because everything was going as well as could be expected.

Plunk felt a little better after that, but on the walk back to the apartments he noticed Darlene wasn't shoulder-bumping anymore. She still talked nicely, about Mom and the room being very clean and well-lighted if a little cramped, but there was something tense too and Plunk wondered what it was, until they got to The Jacksonian. That's when Darlene asked suddenly, sharply, "Who's Annie?"

25.

Over dinner he told her, or at least most of it. The seafood place in North Fort Worth was dark with a candle lit in the middle of their table. The reflection of the flames flickered on the lenses of Darlene's glasses, and Plunk looked at the reflection when he talked rather than the eyes behind the lenses.

Plunk explained that a bunch of years ago he was working at Wal-Mart, and that he'd been promoted from the warehouse to sporting goods and liked it. He got to talk to lots of customers, and even if he wasn't any good at sports himself he knew about a lot of the equipment, what size bat a dad should buy for his Little Leaguer or which basketballs would bounce longest before wearing out. He was still living with his folks five years out of high school but had started thinking about his own place; he had some buddies who also worked at Wal-Mart, and they were talking about going in on an apartment together.

One day he noticed this new girl working in ladies' wear, she was kind of ordinary-looking but had a nice smile and seemed just that little bit familiar. Right after that they happened to be in the break room at the same time and started talking. Her name was Annie Fortescu and it turned out she'd been in South Crowley High three years behind Plunk. Now he started to remember, when Warrior Mascot led cheers as a senior, there was this freshman girl in pep squad who yelled louder than anybody, and it was Annie.

"But you didn't start dating her in high school?" Darlene asked.

"Ah, no," Plunk said. "Being Warrior Mascot took up lots of time."

Anyway, Plunk continued, he and Annie went out for cokes after work. She said how she'd been in junior college a couple years but it wasn't for her, she hated studying. Her folks said she had to get a job if she wasn't in school so she got on at Wal-Mart. Annie was fun to talk to. She liked sports, which helped, and also Halloween, she'd seen Plunk a couple times in his Warrior Mascot costume helping kids with their trick-or-treating. Best thing, she said it was retarded that the school had switched from Warriors to Tornadoes, Warriors was so much better.

So Plunk and Annie started dating. He liked her and was worried she'd end up telling him they ought to be friends, but she didn't. Plunk knew enough not to tell Darlene about him and Annie having sex like the fourth time they went out. After that it was sort of understood marriage was coming. He was twenty-three. She was twenty. If you kept going out and having sex when you were that old, you got married. It was what regular people did. Plunk's folks liked Annie, he thought her folks liked him, her father was a self-employed accountant and didn't talk much but her mom was great.

So they got married, a nice little ceremony. Plunk liked the idea of a wife. Annie didn't mind if he watched sports on TV, and for the first time he was having regular sex, maybe nothing fancy like in the movies but still pretty nice. They had their jobs at Wal-Mart and a little apartment Annie fixed up with stuff she bought at garage sales on Saturdays while Plunk and his buddies were watching football or whatever.

"I thought life was pretty good," Plunk told Darlene.

"What exactly went wrong?" she asked, so interested that she stopped taking bites of her baked flounder. A chunk of fish dangled from the tines of her fork.

Maybe a year into the marriage, Annie all of a sudden started asking Plunk these questions. When did he think they should buy a house? To do that, they needed more money, so what did Plunk want to do for a career? He couldn't work in Wal-Mart selling softballs all his life. To which Plunk replied why couldn't he, and what was so great about a house? They had plenty of time, so stop worrying about that stuff.

But Annie didn't. In most ways she kept on being a good wife, she let him watch his TV sports and she'd mostly still have sex when he wanted, though maybe that part was already cooling down. But when an assistant manager position opened up at work and Plunk wouldn't apply for it—you had to work Sunday afternoons, and there was football on TV then—they had their first big fight and she sulked for weeks.

Which led to the really big fight. On Halloween he dressed up like Mulder from *X-Files* because people said the Warrior Mascot thing had gotten old. He spent an hour getting the X taped on the back of the suit coat just right, and in the middle of it Annie said they'd be a lot better off if he worked as hard at getting promoted at work as he did on his stupid Halloween costume. Plunk lost his temper, which usually never happened, and yelled that this was what he did on Halloween, she knew that, and then she yelled back, and it was the first but not the last time she accused him of being weird.

They stayed married another couple years, but all that time Plunk could sense it was going bad. Annie wasn't actually mean to him. But she would talk now about houses and nicer cars and even that her dad was thinking of expanding his accounting practice, Plunk maybe ought to go to junior college and learn accounting. Which he had no interest in. When she asked him what he planned to do with his life he told her honestly that he was already doing it. Annie asked what else he wanted and he said what else was there? Annie said that scraping by as a store clerk, living in a crappy little apartment, watching sports on TV, and dressing up every Halloween wasn't a life at all. It was time for him to grow up.

What worried Plunk when he got to this part of the story was that Darlene started nodding like she couldn't agree more.

"I told her, I am who I am," he said to Darlene.

"I understand," she said, but Plunk wondered.

He told Darlene there wasn't much else to say about Annie. While he was watching ballgames on TV she started going out with friends, and one day she came back right in the middle of a Cowboys-49ers game and said they needed to talk. Plunk was a great guy, she said, he was kind and friendly and everything, but she wanted a different life and he was never going to change. So she was going to leave, she'd stay with one of her old high school friends in Arlington while she looked for a job there, and Plunk should get a lawyer because she had one and the lawyers would work everything out.

"Did you ask her to stay?" Darlene asked. "How did it make you feel?"

"I dunno," Plunk said, though he actually did know and just wasn't willing to admit it to Darlene. What happened was, he started telling Annie he was sorry, he understood and would be different, don't go, but he was also trying to watch the game because the Cowboys were driving for a tying touchdown. Annie noticed him doing it and that was that. It was only afterward, when the game was over and she was gone and Plunk was alone in bed for that first night that he wished he'd gotten up and turned the game off, but it was too late.

"Anyway, we got divorced," Plunk said. "End of story."

"Are you still in touch?" Darlene wanted to know. "Do you talk to her?"

"Nah. We went into court and the divorce was final, she said she hated doing this to me but she had to. I said it was okay and wished her luck. That was it."

"You never saw her again?" Darlene asked, and Plunk couldn't understand why she thought this detail was important.

"Nope," he said. "She took some of the stuff from the apartment but left the bed. I still have it."

"Oh," said Darlene.

"So that's enough of that," Plunk declared. "Your food's cold."

Darlene went back to picking at her fish, but Plunk could tell she was still thinking about Annie. So he distracted her by talking about the golf thing coming up, and that helped.

"I think we need to get Tail Man business cards printed up," Darlene said. "Something to hand out to everybody. You know, my phone number to call for bookings."

"Wouldn't it take too long to get them done?" Plunk asked.

"No, there's a place right down the street from the library that does business cards in an hour," Darlene said. "They can put pictures on them and everything. I thought maybe yellow and black ink on white paper, the leopard gecko colors."

"Sounds good," Plunk said. He had to hand it to Darlene. She knew how to arrange things.

They drove back to Crowley and Darlene was quieter than usual. After a while she said, "Have you had many girlfriends since?"

"Since what?" Plunk said, playing dumb.

"You know, since Annie."

"Not really," Plunk replied. "I guess some." He knew that wasn't true, but it sounded better.

"I've had boyfriends," Darlene volunteered, like she'd been waiting for him to ask her. "Guys. But nothing serious."

"Not much time for that, with work and going to school and writing your book and everything," Plunk said, trying to be nice.

"Exactly," said Darlene. Then she was quiet for another few minutes.

When they got back to The Jacksonian, Plunk parked the car and walked Darlene over to her door, which he hadn't done before. When they got there she turned her face up. Plunk leaned down and they kissed, not one of those graceful kisses though. Their noses kind of collided and Darlene's glasses were jiggled.

"Oh," she said, but not in a mad way, and they got their faces tilted right and their lips came together. It was a cold night and Plunk thought Darlene's lips were very warm.

After she went inside Plunk went back to his own apartment and was soon sitting on the couch telling the tail all about it.

26.

The sign in the Benbrook Country Club parking lot really did say "Celebrities." Eddie saw it first and pointed.

"You oughta ask them to let you take it home later on," Eddie suggested to Plunk. "Helluva souvenir."

"That would be unprofessional," Darlene said. This time she was sitting in the front passenger seat because besides being Tail Man's manager she was also his girlfriend. Nothing official about that had been agreed to between Plunk and Darlene, but it was understood. So Eddie had to sit in the back with the tail.

"We need to impress people today," Darlene continued, fiddling with the small oblong box of business cards in her lap. "So everybody act mature."

"Not much mature about a man dragging a tail on his ass," Eddie said. Darlene glared; Eddie knew exactly how to push her buttons.

"We get to park right by the front," Plunk said to distract them. "Shit, look at all the expensive cars." His battered old Ranger didn't fit in with all the fancy Lincolns and foreign jobs.

A woman with a clipboard came up as they were getting the tail out of the back seat. She asked for a name, and Plunk told her his.

"I don't see you, Mr. Landreth," she said.

"Try Tail Man," Darlene suggested, and the woman looked at the list and said it was right there at the top.

"The celebrities are invited to use the main locker room," the woman said. "After you've changed, your friends can meet you at the putting green over there, where everyone will be assigned their foursomes and tee-off holes and times." She gestured, and Plunk saw there were a bunch of people milling around a flat grassy area, many blinking in the afternoon sun. It was a nice day, no clouds at all.

"See you over there in a minute," Plunk said, grabbing the tail. He really didn't need to go into the locker room to change—all he had to do was buckle on the tail and he was ready to go—but he wanted to go inside anyway just to experience the specialness of it all, Plunk Freakin' Landy going where only celebrities were allowed. Darlene and Eddie nodded, any lingering hostility between them swept aside by the intimidating surroundings. Like Plunk, neither of them had ever been to a country club before.

There were maybe a dozen guys in the main locker room, and Plunk recognized Dick Billings.

"Glad you could make it, Tail Man!" Billings said. He smelled of cigars and also of lunchtime gin. "Shake hands with Javy Perez of the Rangers!"

Now, this was a thrill. Plunk loved football more than baseball, but he still loved baseball a lot. Javy Perez was a backup catcher, not an All-Star or anything, but he was still the first major leaguer Plunk had ever met and here he was sticking out his hand and grinning.

"Why they call you Tail Man?" Perez asked, and Billings gestured at the tail in Plunk's arms.

"Damndest thing you've ever seen," Billings said, and that made everybody else look and in a minute all these other celebrities, including two other scrub Rangers players and also the weatherman from Channel 8 were gathered around Plunk like he was the biggest star of them all. He had to put the tail on and show everybody how he could pull the tip up and down.

"Got my extra clubs by the putting green, Tail Man," Billings said when everybody had their look at the tail and backed off some. "Matched Ben Hogans, ought to suit you pretty well."

"Like I said, I never played golf before," Plunk reminded him. "I think I'm gonna be shitty."

"Nobody will care," Billings assured him. "They just want to play with celebrities and get write-offs for their registration fees."

Billings was in a sweater and slacks and wore golf shoes with tiny little spikes on the bottom, but Plunk didn't have any of those, just his black tennies. He also was wearing the black jeans and the yellow sweatshirt, which was showing signs of fading and he really needed a new one. But he still felt pretty good about the way he looked, because the tail was waving proudly, and when he went over with Billings to the practice green everybody looked at him, not at the baseball players and other famous people.

"I've already given out at least a dozen cards," Darlene gushed. "*He's* given out a few, but mostly he's been pestering *her*." She gestured over to where Eddie was gazing worshipfully at a very pretty young woman, hair blonder than maybe nature intended and dressed in this attractive outfit of slacks and sweater. She looked different dressed that way than Darlene.

Billings saw where Plunk was looking and said, "Hey, Tail Man, let's have some introductions." He pulled Plunk over right between the woman and Eddie like Eddie didn't even exist. "Bonnie, you got to meet Tail Man. Tail Man, you for sure watch Bonnie Woody on *Daybreak Metroplex*."

"Sure," Plunk said. It was a lie. When Plunk watched TV in the morning it was ESPN, or once in a while Fox News. "Nice to meetcha." And it was. Bonnie Woody was so friendly, didn't act like a big shot at all, and when she smiled her teeth were so white Plunk couldn't believe it.

"Tail Man," she said, the words sounding like musical notes. "I see why they call you that. What's it made of?" and without asking she reached out to stroke the tail. Plunk sure didn't mind.

"Vinyl," he said, and tried to think of something else to say, but couldn't.

"Why do you wear it?" Bonnie asked, and Plunk had to stop and think a minute. While he did, Darlene answered for him.

"We do children's parties and things," she said. "Educational entertainment. Here's a card." She handed one to Bonnie. It was an impressive card, Plunk thought, yellow with a couple black spots and in black raised letters it read *TAIL MAN: Parties, Shows, Personal Appearances*. In slightly smaller letters underneath it continued *For Bookings, Contact Darlene Quaverley*, and then it had Darlene's phone number and e-mail address: literarylass@aol.com. When he first saw it, Eddie said that sucked, it ought to have Plunk's name and contact information, not hers, because he was Tail Man and she wasn't. But Darlene said she was the one who set up the appearances, so of course it had to have her phone number and e-mail. Plunk backed her up, though he thought to himself it would have been nice to see his information on the card, too.

"Well," said Bonnie, looking at the card. "That's interesting." She stuck the card in her pocket. "I feel silly being out here," she said mostly to Plunk and Billings, though Darlene was there too. Eddie was still hanging nearby, but on the edge rather than in the group itself. "I don't play much golf, so I'm going to be terrible. But it's for a good cause."

"Ah, you're probably a great golfer," Plunk blurted, and she rewarded him with a mega-watt smile.

"I just hope I don't have to play with anybody very good," Bonnie said. "That would be so embarrassing."

"I've never played golf at all," Plunk confessed, suddenly finding conversation coming easily. "I may not be able to even hit the ball."

"But you've got your wonderful tail," Bonnie said. "Just look at how everyone's staring."

Which they were. It made Plunk happy.

"I bet they're really looking at you," he told Bonnie, wanting to sound modest, and Darlene said kind of snippily that no, they were looking at him.

"It's getting on one o'clock," Billings said. "Guess we ought to get our clubs and join our foursomes. Everybody ready?"

Plunk said he was, though he really wasn't. He preferred the pleasure of the tail being looked at to the certain humiliation of proving golf was just one more sport he couldn't play for shit. But he followed Billings to the putting green, Darlene and Eddie trailing along behind. Bonnie Woody was joined by a guy lugging a TV camera. Billings told Plunk they were planning to shoot something called "B-roll" for the next morning's *Daybreak Metroplex*.

"Publicity for the hospital, plus it makes them look like they care about the community," Billings said. "So it helps us and their show, too."

Billings led Plunk to a spot just on the side of the green. There were two bags of golf clubs lying there, and Billings pointed to one. Plunk knew that meant they were his loaner clubs and nodded. There was also a long line of golf carts by the putting green, and in the middle of the green was a man standing by a big chart.

"Your pairings are here, and your starting hole assignments," the man said. "We've got eighteen foursomes, so each starts at a different hole. Look for your name and your starting hole. One mulligan on the first, that's it. This is a best ball competition, so pick up whenever you're out of contention. Handicap strokes are indicated on the tee yardage signs."

"What?" Darlene hissed in Plunk's ear.

"You got me," he said. The guy could have been speaking Chinese for all Plunk knew.

But he understood he was supposed to look for his name on the chart. There it was in big black letters, Tail Man, and underneath were three smaller names he couldn't quite make out and also the number sixteen.

"I guess I start on the sixteenth hole, wherever that is," Plunk said to Darlene, and as he did a familiar voice hollered, "Tail Man! Plunk!" It was Austin.

"Damn near had to bribe Dick Billings to put me in your group," Austin said. "Pretty great having one of my people here as a celebrity. Leanne's over there with Timmy, he loves seeing his friend Tail Man again." Plunk looked over where Austin was pointing, and there were Leanne and Timmy. Timmy was waving. Plunk waved back.

"Where's this sixteenth hole?" Plunk asked, trying to sling the borrowed bag of clubs over his shoulder. It was *heavy*.

"You don't carry those," Austin said. He snapped his fingers at a cluster of guys in identical dark green jump suits and two of them hustled over. "That's what caddies are for." He gestured to Plunk's bag and also one at the ground by his feet. "Load those up and let's get going," he ordered. The two men wordlessly picked up the clubs and carried them over by one of the golf carts.

Austin motioned for Plunk to follow him. He got behind the wheel of the golf cart. Plunk climbed into the seat beside him, figuring that was what he was supposed to do.

"Let's ride, partner," Austin said, and off they went, Darlene and Eddie left on the putting green behind them.

27.

It seemed to Plunk that Austin was more impressive on the golf course than at Campbell Bolt & Screw. At work, he kept himself closed in his office and when he putted balls into the metal glass it seemed sort of silly. But at the country club, dressed in his golf outfit, he was much more relaxed and happy-looking, like he was where he belonged.

"We're gonna kill 'em, just kill 'em," he assured Plunk as their golf cart careened toward the sixteenth hole. "I was hitting them great on the practice range, and we get to count you as a thirty-six handicap since you never played before. Hell, you bogey a hole and we still pick up a stroke."

"Sure," Plunk said. He'd watched just enough golf on TV when no real sport was on to know what bogies and handicaps were. "Best ball" and "mulligan" were still foreign terms.

Plunk had loosened the tail so it could be twisted to the side of the cart, and the tip dangled out there pretty good. He worried it might get snagged in a bush or something. He'd have to be careful.

"Here we are," Austin said. They pulled up to a tee where two other men were waiting. They looked exactly opposite, one very tall and gangly and the other short and squatty.

"Bill Berger," the squatty one said. "Internal specialist at All Saints Children's."

"Phil Mears," said the tall one. "But call me Stretch, everybody does."

"Stretch's Lone Star Chevrolet," Austin said. "Course I know you. The TV commercials, Plunk," and Plunk knew them. Stretch Mears had lots of ads for his car lot on during ESPN shows, mostly the weekend morning ones about fishing. He always promised to *stretch* financing to fit any budget.

Austin introduced himself and Plunk, "better known as Tail Man." Bill and Stretch admired the tail, which Plunk buckled back on all the way as soon as he was out of the cart. He explained how he'd never played before and nobody seemed to mind. Stretch said he'd been playing thirty-five years and it still always looked like he'd never picked up a club.

"Guess we better get to it," he added. "Got to get all eighteen in by four-thirty, they said. Caddies just got the bags here."

Austin explained to Plunk that the sixteenth hole was par three, just 185 yards. Plunk looked from the tee to the green where a flag waved in the breeze, showing where the hole was. It seemed pretty far—185 yards was almost two football fields long.

"Use your three wood, Plunk," Austin suggested. Plunk knew the different numbered clubs from his days selling sporting goods, so he took the three wood out of the bag and waited while Bill, Stretch, and Austin teed off first. The first two hit balls that went off to the side of the green. Austin's ball landed not that far from the flag and he whooped.

Plunk teed up his ball and stood over it. He was more aware than usual of the weight of the tail behind him; it seemed to keep him from leaning over the ball comfortably.

"Swing easy," Austin said, and Plunk tried, but only the very back edge of his club ticked the ball, which rolled a couple feet away.

"Mulligan," Stretch and Bill said in unison. Austin explained that meant he got to try again.

"You guys sure got a sorry celebrity," Plunk said, trying to keep it light and sort of apologize at the same time. He swung at a second ball and topped it maybe twenty yards ahead.

"It'll get better," Austin said, but it didn't. They fell into a pattern. The other guys would hit their shots, some of them long and soaring and straight. Plunk would arrange his tail behind him, trying to position its tip at various levels to see if anything helped the balance issues, swing and hit his ball in any one of many directions, except never where he was actually aiming. Sometimes he missed the ball altogether. Plunk would have been really embarrassed except for what was happening around them.

There were lots of people at the club for the event, four or five hundred at least. Just about everybody playing had brought family or friends. There were others, mostly men, with stacks of photos they kept hollering for the pro athletes to sign. And there were tons of kids, some of them Plunk thought had come from the hospital itself, patches over their eyes from surgery or maybe in wheelchairs pushed by their parents. As Plunk's foursome played its round, at every hole more and more people began following them until they numbered in the high dozens, and it was because of the tail. People shouted out suggestions when Plunk raised or lowered it before shots. In between holes kids asked to touch it and some people wanted to take pictures. Nobody seemed to care that Plunk was playing so lousy. In fact, they started cheering every time he swung a club, it seemed like loudest for the shots that were worst.

"We got a gallery," Austin said. "Feels like it's the damn Masters or something." He and Plunk's other two partners started mugging for the crowd, bowing deeply after good shots, shrugging after bad ones.

About halfway through the round, Dick Billings came chugging up in a golf cart, interrupting his own game to see what was going on.

"This is great!" he said. "Everybody having fun, getting their money's worth. You're the star, Tail Man!" And Plunk knew he was. He saw Darlene and Eddie passing out the business cards. Everybody seemed to want one. The tail gleamed in the bright November sunlight.

Every once in a while Plunk's group would cross paths with another foursome. Once it was Bonnie Woody's. She was with three women players, all of them older than her and not nearly as pretty, Plunk thought.

"Look at you," she said. "All these people." Some of Plunk's fans recognized her. They said things like, "Hey, Bonnie," and she would look over at them and smile like they'd just made her whole day. But Plunk noticed that after Bonnie's foursome moved on, none of the people who'd called out to her left his group to go follow hers.

On the next hole, Stretch asked to ride with Plunk as they went forward to where their drives had landed. His was way down the middle of the fairway. Plunk's had disappeared into a clump of high grass far off to the left.

"Forget it," Plunk suggested. "It'll take too long to find it."

"Might was well look," Stretch said cheerfully. He rolled the cart up to the grassy area. They got out and poked around gingerly, using the handle end of their clubs. Even in November, Texas still had its snakes.

"Say," Stretch said, "I see how you're pulling this crowd. You do parties, you say?"

"Yeah," Plunk said, wondering how long they'd have to look before the ball was officially lost. "For kids and things."

"Austin says you wowed everybody at his son's birthday," Stretch said. "Ah, here you go." He pulled aside some of the high grass and there was Plunk's ball.

Plunk pulled up his tail tip so it wouldn't catch in the grass. Then he took out a pitching wedge and swiped at the ball. It popped straight up and fell right back down in the grass maybe two feet from where it was to begin with. Everybody watching hollered and cheered like Plunk had actually nailed it.

"I guess you can pick up," Stretch said. They got back in the cart and whizzed toward where his ball waited in the fairway. "Say, you think you could do a meet-and-greet at the lot for me?"

"Huh," said Plunk, not understanding and not wanting to admit it.

"Not this next Saturday, too many people gone the whole weekend for Thanksgiving," Stretch said. "But say ten in the morning to two in the afternoon the Saturday after that, first one in December, just be on the display floor and keep kids busy while their folks look at cars. You think?"

"Sure," Plunk said. "I could do that."

"Maybe get my guy to film you in a spot beforehand," Stretch said. "Advertise your appearance in advance on TV. What'd you charge me for four hours?"

"You got to talk to my manager," Plunk said. "Darlene. The one with the business cards."

"I'll do that as soon as we're finished here," Stretch said. He stood over his ball and whacked it right up onto the green, closer to the flag than Austin's or Bill's. "I was gonna ask one of the Rangers, but nobody's following them around here like they are you. 'Stretch Presents Tail Man at Lone Star'. Ought to be pretty good."

"Ought to," Plunk agreed. People started clapping when the golf cart reached the green. Being a celebrity was even better than he'd imagined, and it was something that he'd imagined it a lot.

28.

Plunk especially enjoyed the tenth hole he played. He took a six on the par four, but he didn't have to pick up his ball. Twice he even hit it pretty straight. Austin explained to him how his double bogey was actually a par when you factored in the thirty-six handicap. The foursome itself, Austin said as they climbed into the cart and Plunk rearranged his tail, wasn't really in contention to win—"The rest of us can't putt today for shit"—but the next hole they were coming to would be the fun one, the car one.

"Car one?" Plunk asked, and then the cart came over a low hill and there was the biggest crowd Plunk had seen all day, bigger even than the group following Tail Man and his partners.

"Stretch Mears put up a new Tahoe for the kids' hospital if anybody makes a hole in one here," Austin said. He pointed to a bright red truck parked maybe ten yards to the side of the green. "Par three over water, tough hole, but not impossible. It's one thirty-seven to the green, just an easy seven or eight iron."

"But all the people," Plunk said, wondering.

Austin grinned.

"They're here because this is where they've got the photographers from the big papers, *Dallas Morning News* and *Fort Worth Star-Telegram*, and the little local weeklies too. The big papers always need photos for their sports sections. So they shoot all the ballplayers and celebrities hitting off the tee, makes for a good picture. And see over there, it's the *Daybreak Metroplex* guy with the TV camera. So people think if they stand around the green, maybe they'll get on TV or their photo in the paper. It's a big deal to them. You understand."

Plunk certainly did. He thought he could pick out Linda Prescott, the stringer for *The Crowley Observer*, standing by the green with some other people who were also probably reporters. There was also a man in a suit who stood right in front of the Tahoe. Austin said that was US Congressman Rod Argent.

"He'll hand over the keys to the hospital board chairman if anybody actually wins the thing for them," Austin said. "Politicians. Now, *they'll* do anything for publicity."

They got out of the cart and joined their two partners. Plunk cinched his waist and leg belts a little tighter. He didn't want the tail sagging unattractively with so many people watching.

"One of you boys gonna cost me a car?" Stretch asked, grinning. Looking past him, Plunk could see Darlene and Eddie down by the side of the green, looking up at the tee box. Leanne and Timmy Campbell were standing there, too. Up by the tee itself about a half-dozen photographers crouched, with the TV guy standing up behind them, his camera on his shoulder.

The same guy who'd been out on the putting green earlier telling people how to find playing partners and starting tee numbers now stood with a microphone at the tee, announcing the name of each player as he or she stepped up to drive.

"One of the nation's leading internists from the staff of Cook Children's Hospital, Dr. Bill Berger," he said, and Bill stepped up and whacked his drive, which bounced on the green and rolled far away from the flagstick in the hole.

"Owner of Campbell Bolt & Screw, based in Fort Worth but serving all of Tarrant County, Austin Campbell."

Austin's shot wasn't a hole in one, but it still ended up only a dozen feet or so away from the cup. Some people clapped and Austin waggled his club in the air to acknowledge the applause.

"The man who has offered to donate this beautiful Chevrolet Tahoe to Cook Children's Hospital if anyone makes a hole in one. The owner of Stretch's Lone Star Chevrolet, Phil 'Stretch' Mears!"

Stretch hit his ball into the lake in front of the green. There were some friendly hoots from the crowd.

"And now the celebrity who has taken this competition by storm." The guy peeked at something in his hand. Plunk guessed it was one of Darlene's business cards.

"From the community of Crowley, available for parties and other events. I suppose he's part man, part leopard gecko. The entertainer everyone knows as … Tail Man!"

The cheering gave Plunk goose bumps. Tail resting on the grass behind him, he teed up his ball. The photographers were snapping pictures. The *click-click-click* was kind of distracting, and even more so was the TV camera guy maneuvering for a better angle. He might get on TV!

He was about to draw back his club when Austin hissed, "Wait, you got a driver! That's way too much club. You need an iron!" Plunk had been so distracted by the crowd that he'd pulled the wrong club out of his bag.

But he knew it didn't make any difference, because he wasn't going to hit the ball solid anyway. So he ignored Austin and made a show out of getting his tail settled behind him just right. Everybody laughed, and Plunk thought maybe a tail-settling picture might find its way into a couple of the papers even if he swung and missed the ball completely, which he thought he would.

Instead, he hit it hard, just not quite straight. The ball took off on a low line toward the side of the green, traveling at near light speed and causing everybody there to screech and duck. Plunk distinctly saw the congressman dive to the ground, covering his head with his arms. The ball whizzed right over him and ricocheted off the side of the Tahoe with a metallic *thunk*. Then it rebounded back onto the green and rolled straight toward the cup.

That made the screeches morph into *ooohs* as everyone watched the ball roll and roll, and then there was a collective sad sigh as it stopped just a few inches away from the hole.

"Goddamn, Tail Man," Stretch said. "You just about did it."

Now there were more cheers, and a thundering round of applause. Plunk, stunned, climbed into the golf cart beside Austin. When they reached the green somebody—Plunk later learned it was Eddie—started chanting "Tail Man! Tail Man!" and everybody else picked up on it. The photographers, who'd run down to take pictures of the humongous dent in the Tahoe, sprinted over to snap shots as Plunk rearranged his tail and stepped onto the green to see for himself how his ball rested less than a foot from the pin. Somehow he knew exactly what to say.

"Missed it by *that* much!" Plunk yelped, cribbing a line from some old TV show or other, but nobody cared about his lack of originality. There was more laughter, and then Plunk felt somebody coming up behind him. Putter in hand, Stretch reached right past him and nudged Plunk's ball the last few inches into the cup.

"I believe we got ourselves a hole in one here!" he announced. "Whaddaya say?" There was a thunderous ovation.

"Hey, Congressman!" Stretch yelled. "Come over here and give the keys to the folks from Cook Children's Hospital!"

Congressman Argent ignored the grass stains on his nice suit and white shirt. Grinning, he came over to shake Plunk's hand, turning Plunk a little to face all the photographers as they snapped away. Plunk's tail rested nicely on the grass at their feet.

There were some short speeches, from the congressman and Stretch and somebody who apparently was the hospital's board chairman. Plunk was asked to pose for the photographers with some of the kids who were patients there. When he did, he noticed the congressman also leaned in to the pictures, though Plunk couldn't recall the photographers asking him to.

The reporters asked a few questions. Then Bonnie Woody pulled on his arm.

"Can we tape something for the program tomorrow?" she asked.

"I guess," Plunk said. He was too thrilled to be nervous. Something like this happening. All thanks to the tail, assisted by the Tahoe.

The TV camera guy got right up in their faces as Bonnie said to Plunk, "Tail Man from Crowley, that was quite a fabulous shot!" Her breath smelled sweet.

"Yeah," said Plunk. "I just got lucky, hitting the car and everything."

"But it worked out wonderfully well for the boys and girls being helped at Cook Children's Hospital," Bonnie suggested, tilting her microphone toward herself, then back at Plunk.

"Helping kids any way I can, that's what I'm all about," Plunk said. "Me and my tail."

"Let's have a quick word from Chevrolet dealer Stretch Mears, who donated the car won today by Tail Man for the hospital," Bonnie said.

Stretch hopped between them and said, "Tail Man's making an exclusive appearance at Stretch's Lone Star Chevrolet in Fort Worth on the first Saturday in December from 10 a.m. to 2 p.m. Come on out and meet him in person!"

"Well, I really think that's enough free advertising," Bonnie said, kind of laughing when she said it but not really. She pulled the microphone away from Stretch and the cameraman focused back on her.

"This is *Daybreak Metroplex*'s Bonnie Woody at the Cook Children's Hospital annual charity golf event," she said to the camera. "Where I certainly didn't make a hole in one, but at least I got to meet Tail Man."

29.

Monday morning Darlene and Eddie were in Plunk's apartment at six. That was when Darlene said *Daybreak Metroplex* came on. Plunk didn't know because he'd never seen it. Darlene said she was actually a regular viewer because they often had authors on the show.

Sure enough, right at the beginning they showed a tape of Bonnie Woody swinging a golf club, then switched to her sitting on a sofa beside a slick-looking guy.

"It's Monday morning and time to start another week," she said. "I'm Bonnie Woody."

"And I'm Tim Carter," the guy added. "From now until 9 a.m. we've got an awesome show lined up with several exciting guests, up-to-the-minute traffic and weather reports, and a look at Bonnie on the golf course, which I promise is something else."

"Not because of how I played yesterday at the Cook Children's

Hospital benefit tournament," Bonnie said. "But you won't believe it. Coming up you're going to see one of the most unique golf shots ever made by perhaps the most unique celebrity."

"She means *you*!" Eddie told Plunk. Darlene shushed him.

"That's later on in the show," Bonnie continued. Plunk thought she looked even prettier on TV than in person, if that was possible. "Right now, let's get a traffic report from Clara Herrera in the *Daybreak Metroplex* helicopter."

Plunk, Eddie, and Darlene fidgeted through the next couple hours. Bonnie and the Tim guy would periodically promise the golf stuff was coming, but then after each commercial there'd be weather or another traffic report or one of them interviewing somebody—a man from a local animal shelter, a woman promoting a weight-loss product.

"They got to put me on soon, the show's gonna be over," Plunk said, tearing his eyes away from the TV screen to look at his watch. "Maybe they forgot."

"They didn't forget," Darlene said. "It's the most important thing on the program, so they're saving it for last. Like dessert."

And finally with just five minutes left, there it was. Tim started kidding Bonnie about her lack of athletic ability and Bonnie said maybe that was true, but at least when she played golf she got to meet some of the most interesting people anywhere. She explained about the fundraiser for the kids' hospital and there were quick shots of some of the celebrity golfers, mostly the Rangers' players.

"But the real star of the show had something a little extra to offer," said Bonnie. "A huge crowd followed him all around the course. You might say they were *tailing* him."

Then Plunk's face filled up his whole TV screen. The camera panned back to show his torso, legs—and tail. Bonnie's voice explained this was Tail Man, a guy who performed at children's parties and all sorts of other events, teaching about lizards and nature. Then there was Plunk at the car hole, swinging his driver and nearly killing the congressman with the resulting line drive. There was a close-up of the dent on the side of the Tahoe. Finally there Plunk was with Bonnie, and he listened to himself saying that he and his tail were all about helping kids, then Stretch telling about Tail Man's scheduled appearance at his car lot. They finished with a shot of the tail sloofing over the grass. Then it switched back to the *Daybreak Metroplex* hosts on their couch.

"You don't see something like that every day," Tim said to Bonnie.

"That's true," she said. "Well, everybody, if you happen to see a man with a tail like a lizard, go say hello unless he's got a golf club in his hand. If he does, *duck*!"

Bonnie and Tim waved goodbye and the program was over. Plunk sat there and tingled. He'd never tingled before and would never have expected to. But he was, little electricky sensations up and down his spine and legs and arms.

"Shit," he said.

"Same here," Eddie seconded.

"Well," said Darlene. "That was certainly something."

When Plunk got to work, a little late but who cared, it seemed like everybody had seen him on *Daybreak Metroplex*. He hadn't realized it was so popular. Jessika pretended to want his autograph, Red and Larry B. said he was probably too important now to let them come over to watch football, and Austin bitched in a joking way that he'd actually hit the best shot on that car hole, but nobody wanted to interview *him*.

And the TV thing wasn't all of it. Plunk didn't subscribe to the big city newspapers—always full of bad news and besides you could get all the sports stuff on ESPN, and Fox was so helpful explaining what you should think about politics and crap like that. But Austin and Jessika both brought in the sports section of the big Dallas paper. There, right on the front page of the sports section, was a picture of Plunk following through on his swing at the car hole, tail upraised behind him in an especially eye-catching way. "Scorecard Tells the Tail: Hole in One!" read the headline, and Plunk thought that was just like the media, not getting it right. His ball hadn't gone in until Stretch shoved it. But he still tingled again.

It was a color photo and the tail looked great, all yellow and black against the green of the golf course and the blue of the cloudless winter sky. Everybody exclaimed over it, and Austin added that all the area weeklies had been there, too, he bet they'd also have pictures of Plunk and maybe even stories. All the Dallas paper had was what Austin called a caption underneath the picture.

"Tail Man, an entertainer from Crowley, stole the show at Sunday's charity golf event benefiting Cook Children's Hospital in Fort Worth. On the 8th hole of Benbrook Country Club, Tail Man won a new Tahoe truck for the hospital by ricocheting a shot off the car, which was parked to the side of the green, and rolling the ball in for a hole in one."

"I really didn't hit the ball in the hole," Plunk felt compelled to explain. "It sort of bounced off the car and almost went in. Guy who donated the car pushed it the rest of the way."

"It was still a good shot," Jessika said, and everybody wanted to take a closer look at the photo. They asked Plunk to describe in detail how he hit the shot and what happened afterward.

Plunk reveled in the attention, but attention wouldn't pay Mom's new expenses. So after the wave of congratulations subsided he got in his car to call on as many small customers as he could: With business slowed down for the winter he had to hustle to make decent commissions. Maybe it was just coincidence, but lots of the people he called on had seen the TV show and maybe the paper too. They all ordered stuff from him, though nothing major. It was like they thought they were obligated to buy something if a guy who'd just been on TV was making the sales call.

Around lunchtime Plunk went back to the office figuring he'd ask Red and Larry B. if they wanted to grab a sandwich or some enchiladas someplace. Neither one was there, sometimes if customer calls took them too far afield they just stayed out all lunch hour, so Plunk couldn't eat with them. He'd sort of hoped they'd insist on treating him to lunch because of his being on TV and in the newspaper. That way he'd save ten bucks or so and every cent helped with Mom's new bills. But no.

"Your friend Darlene, the one who says she's your manager, called," Jessika told him. "She says you need to call her right away."

Plunk did, and Darlene was excited.

"Fourteen!" she yelled into the phone so loud it hurt Plunk's ear. "We got fourteen!"

"Fourteen what?"

"Fourteen calls asking Tail Man to do parties. Mostly kids' birthdays, but a couple grown-up things. Yesterday I passed out all those cards, you know. Somebody from *Daybreak Metroplex* also called, I gave Bonnie our Tail Man card, remember. Anyway, he said he was an assistant producer and people had been calling, asking how to get in touch with us. I mean, you. So I said it was okay to give them my number. It's so amazing!"

"Fourteen, huh?" Plunk said, wishing he was better at math. But he still knew fourteen times three hundred, even less Darlene's 25 percent and something for Eddie, would pay Mom's extra for a long, long time.

"One woman wants to pay you to play a round of golf with her husband," Darlene said. "It's supposed to be his birthday present, something she said he'd never expect."

"Don't know about that one," Plunk said. "I nearly hit the congressman."

"Of course you'll do it," Darlene said. "You're getting paid to be Tail Man, not a good golfer."

She told Plunk she'd also talked to Stretch. He'd said he'd pay $450 for four hours at his lot a week from Saturday, but she'd reminded him Tail Man got $300 for two hours, so $600 was more appropriate. They compromised on $525.

"You're good," Plunk said, really meaning it. Darlene said they would sit down with the list of requests that night, look everything over and make sure there weren't two for the same time and date.

"A lot of these are for birthday parties around Christmas," she said. "I wonder how we can fiddle with the Tail Man costume to kind of reflect the holidays."

"You'll think of something," Plunk assured her. "You always do."

30.

Because Red and Larry B. weren't around, Plunk asked Jessika if she wanted to go to lunch. It seemed like he ought to be celebrating. Jessika said she'd brought her lunch, but she could put it in the little refrigerator they had there and eat it tomorrow. They got into Plunk's car and he asked what she wanted to eat. She said maybe a hamburger, she'd brought a salad because of her diet but what the heck. Jessika added that she couldn't wait to tell her boyfriend that she'd gone out to lunch with a celebrity like Tail Man. Plunk felt funny for a second, not that he'd invited Jessika to lunch planning to try anything. Plunk hated it when guys made sloppy moves on girls. Besides, he knew if he did try something, Jessika'd tell him she just wanted to be friends. She'd also recently had that birthday when she turned twenty-six, and Plunk had shoes older than her.

Since Jessika wanted a burger Plunk drove to the place where Suzette worked, the waitress Red loved and left. The burgers were good there, and Plunk thought Jessika might notice his *Crowley Observer* picture from Halloween tacked up on the bulletin board. She didn't, but only because the bigger one in color from that morning's Dallas paper was pinned right over it, the picture and the caption also.

"It's the star known as Tail Man," Suzette said as she came to take their order. "Big shot Plunk Landy. I bet you saw yourself on TV this morning. You're in the paper, too."

"I guess," Plunk said, trying to sound modest. "You got the picture up already?"

"Sure," Suzette said. "We want customers to know that celebrities eat here. Who's your friend?"

"This is Jessika," Plunk said. "She works with me."

"Must be a pretty interesting place," Suzette said to Jessika with just a trace of sarcasm. "Plunk Landy the Tail Man, and that asshole Red."

Plunk worried that might offend Jessika, since it always seemed like she and Red got along real well. But she giggled.

"You obviously know Red," she said to Suzette.

"Sure do. We went out a little. What a loser."

"He asked me out a few times," Jessika said. This was news to Plunk. Red had never mentioned it. "But I have a boyfriend, and also I could tell Red was one of those. Thinks he's a real player."

"Absolutely," Suzette said. "But you got to throw back lots of minnows before you catch the big trophy fish, you know? What can I get you?"

Plunk ordered the special, a bacon-chili burger, and Jessika asked for a plain burger with just some lettuce and tomato and maybe a little mustard on the side, no fries. When Suzette brought their plates Jessika left the top half of the bun off. She spread the mustard on top of the lettuce and ate the burger with a knife and fork. It seemed like a waste of a good half a bun but Plunk didn't say so.

He and Jessika talked a little about work and a lot about Tail Man. She said Darlene seemed really nice on the phone and how were things going with her? Plunk said fine, Darlene was cooking him dinner Tuesday night because she was leaving Wednesday morning to fly to Florida for Thanksgiving with her folks and wouldn't be back until Sunday. Suzette, who apparently had been standing right there and listening to everything, interrupted to ask if they wanted refills on their drinks and Jessika said no, in fact she needed the restroom if Suzette could tell her which way.

"Darlene your girlfriend?" Suzette asked as Jessika walked away.

"I suppose," he said. Having a girlfriend was something new in his recent life, and also his not-so-recent life. It took some getting used to. He'd always thought girlfriends were for high school, and he was after all forty-two. But "womanfriend" sounded stupid.

"So you're alone on Thanksgiving?" Suzette asked. "Me too. I hate that. But what can you do?"

"There's football on TV all day," Plunk said. "And my Mom's retirement home has this Thanksgiving thing in the morning, so I think I'll go there."

"Morning's early for turkey and gravy," Suzette said.

"It's okay," Plunk said. "They like you to come and then be gone so most of the staff can get home for their Thanksgivings. I'll watch the football."

"Well, enjoy it," Suzette said. Plunk once again thought she didn't look too bad, what was the matter with Red? Though this new information that Red had asked out Jessika only to be turned down was kind of interesting. Not that Plunk ever cared about other people's private lives, but Red was supposed to be a buddy and he was over to watch the Cowboys almost every Sunday. He talked about women a lot, but never a peep about Jessika. That might be something to kid him about down the road.

"Oh, Red," Jessika said on the drive back to work. "Isn't he something?"

"How so?" Plunk asked.

"He just is," Jessika said. "A lot of men are like that."

"Like what?"

"Wannabe players, lead girls on for fun and maybe get a little something," she said. "You know."

Plunk didn't, but they were pulling into the parking lot and the conversation was over. When they went in Austin said there was a message from Plunk's lady friend. Plunk said yeah, Jessika had already given it to him, but Austin said if he hadn't gotten it in the last ten minutes then it was a new message.

Plunk went to his desk and called Darlene, who said she didn't like bothering him at work but she'd had eight more calls.

"That makes twenty-two, but three of these new ones were from teachers who want Tail Man to talk to their classes," she said. "Elementary school science teachers, like third or fourth grade."

"Sounds good," Plunk said. "More money."

"No, we can't charge for you to go to schools. Maybe we can do some when you're not so busy with ones that pay."

"You're tough," Plunk said.

"I just want this to work out for you," Darlene said defensively. "Your mother's bills and everything. Besides being Tail Man, which I know you like."

"I do," said Plunk. He glanced up. Austin was standing by his desk looking at him. "Hey, Darlene, I got to go. Talk to you tonight." He hung up and said to Austin, "You need me?"

"Yeah," said Austin. "Let's go in my office."

Plunk could tell this was a different kind of thing because Austin didn't start putting a golf ball across the carpet. Instead, he sat behind his desk and gestured for Plunk to sit in the chair in front.

"This Tail Man act you do," Austin said. "On TV, and in the paper, and the golf yesterday. You're getting a lot of attention."

"Seems like," Plunk said, wondering.

"When your lady friend called, I took it," Austin said. "Nobody else here. The phone rings, it could be a customer."

"I'm sorry she called me on company time," Plunk said, thinking that was the problem.

Austin waved his hand.

"No, not that," he said. "She mentioned all these Tail Man jobs they want you to do. Lot of money, I guess."

Plunk shrugged. What was a lot of money to him probably wasn't to Austin.

"So I'm wondering if you might be thinking of leaving," Austin continued. "Could be tempting, all the money and publicity. But you don't want to do anything too fast."

"No," Plunk said. What the hell?

"What I mean is, don't do that without talking to me," Austin said. "Might be some way for you to move up right here. Tail Man of Campbell Bolt & Screw. Maximize the benefits for everybody."

"Why not?" Plunk asked.

That seemed to satisfy Austin.

"I'm glad we talked," he said. "Maybe right after the holidays, beginning of January, we ought to make some plans. Be thinking about it."

"I will," Plunk promised.

Jessika winked at Plunk as he left Austin's office.

"I knew he was going to do that," she whispered. "Get everything out of him you can."

"I will," Plunk said again, though he still was puzzled.

31.

The word introspection wasn't in Plunk's vocabulary, and if it had been he still wouldn't have wanted anything to do with it. He figured one of the big problems in the world was that people thought about everything too much, whether they should do this or not do that. That kind of thinking was a waste of time when you could be watching football on TV or doing something else useful.

Yet there had been such big recent changes in his life that Plunk had no choice but to think about them. There was the Tail Man business and there was also Darlene. Before he found the tail in the costume shop his life had been settled for a long time into a comfortable routine, never much new in it but that was fine. He liked it. Maybe the way he lived wasn't for everybody, but it suited him. Mostly, what he wanted was to do what he enjoyed. Halloween was his special annual moment and he looked forward to it all year the way as a kid he'd once counted the days until Christmas.

With this new Tail Man thing it was suddenly like every day was Halloween, only better. He dressed up with the tail, went out, and people looked at him and had fun because of it. Plunk loved that part. He also got paid, almost more money for a couple tail-wearing events than he made in a whole week of selling for Campbell Bolt & Screw. The most unbelievable thing, his picture was in the papers and he was on TV, which meant he was not only helping people have fun but he was getting famous besides. Being famous outside the little town he lived in was unexpected, though he'd daydreamed about it some, and now that it was happening he had to admit he liked it a lot. Like that waitress Suzette putting up his picture in the burger place because she wanted customers to know celebrities ate there. People from all over the place seeing him on TV. The big time is what it was.

But there were also Tail Man downsides Plunk couldn't ignore. Besides the fun and fame and money, there was the time he'd be spending at the birthday parties and a week from Saturday at Stretch's car dealership and whatever else Darlene was lining up. She had this legal pad she kept making schedule notes on. Most of it was going to be on weekends, Plunk's usual time to hang out with the boys and watch sports on TV. Missing the Cowboys games was something that would have been unthinkable before. He'd always relied on routine to get through life, the comfort of not having to wonder exactly what he was going to be doing or who he'd be doing it with. If there was some downside to it—working for peanuts, no girlfriend, Halloween the biggest thing he ever had to look forward to—it was still acceptable, because it was both regular and familiar. He was living instead of thinking much. It seemed like the best way. Now being Tail Man was going to change all that. He was excited about the new things but couldn't help regretting the old life he was giving up in return. It had been so easy.

Plus there was Darlene. She complicated things even when she didn't mean to. Like her trip to Florida for Thanksgiving. She was flying down Wednesday morning, coming back Sunday night, her and her sister, the one she didn't like. Plunk was fine with that. He thought everybody ought to be with their families on Thanksgiving. But Darlene kept saying she wondered if she should go at all, what with the Tail Man calls and everything else, whatever "everything else" meant. She asked Plunk if he wanted her not to go, and of course he said she should, go have fun in Florida. This seemed to bother her. Then she said okay, she would fly down Wednesday and maybe switch her ticket so she could come back Friday morning or even Thanksgiving night after dinner with her folks if she could get a flight. Plunk asked what about her sister and Darlene said what about her? Katie could get back by herself, she was an alleged grown-up. Plunk told her to stay 'til Sunday, everything would be fine.

He actually wasn't sorry Darlene would be gone all those days. It would give him a chance to drink beer and watch lots of football with the guys. Eddie would be around, and Larry B. and Red both had family in the area so they might hang out some with Plunk, too. Starting with the appearance at Stretch's Lone Star Chevy dealership, it looked like Plunk's weekends were going to be one Tail Man thing after another. Thanksgiving weekend was going to be a chance to enjoy his old uncomplicated ways.

Darlene was also messing up his everyday routine of get home from work, have a quick meal, watch TV. After their first kiss, she right away expected them to spend time together besides going out on Tail Man jobs. He had non-Darlene time Tuesday and Thursday nights when she went to her writing class, and since she'd read that goals book by the doctor she tried to write a couple pages on her novel every night. Still, now she always came over, knocking on his door, wanting to talk about her day or whatever. They would sit on the couch after Plunk turned down the sound on ESPN. Darlene would talk—she loved to talk, and more than that, she loved to explain things, all sorts of stuff like she thought she was the teacher and Plunk was her class. She acted like she knew everything about politics and books and which actresses were starving themselves to death, the kinds of things Plunk didn't care about because what did any of it have to do with him? But Plunk always did his best to look interested. Darlene frequently said that she couldn't understand how he could live without reading newspapers or having a computer at home so he could check things on the internet. She said this all the time.

Plunk had yet to see her apartment, but that was about to change. Darlene insisted that he come over so she could cook him dinner Tuesday night since she was leaving for Florida on Wednesday. From the way she asked, smiling kind of shyly, even he could tell she didn't want him coming over to talk about Tail Man stuff. It was going to be romantic. And that made Plunk nervous.

Since that first clumsy kiss they'd shared a couple more over the next few days, just lips pressing together and tongues not included, plus a hug or two. Darlene didn't seem to be the kind of girl who wanted her clothes ripped off like some of them did in the Netflix and Apple shows. Her body was as much a mystery to Plunk as ever. If and when that would change, he didn't know and thought she didn't either.

Plunk sensed the invitation to Tuesday dinner was an important step forward to Darlene's way of thinking. She asked several times what he liked best to eat, and he said KFC and macaroni and cheese. She really wasn't much of a cook, she admitted, being more interested in writing and putting all her energy into that. Plunk said he'd be glad to eat whatever she put in front of him. He just liked food, period. She might be nervous about the meal, but he wasn't.

What he was nervous about was after the meal. He was forty-two and out of practice sex-wise, at least with somebody else involved. Darlene was a lot younger and he wasn't sure what she might be expecting. He didn't want to try too much or attempt too little. He couldn't discuss it with Eddie because if anything Eddie was less active romance-wise than Plunk. Maybe Eddie made fun of plain, know-it-all Darlene being Plunk's girlfriend, but at least Plunk had one now. Red and Larry B. were too young. They couldn't know what it felt like to be forty-two and not sure everything would work like it was supposed to when the time came. Men had it tougher than women that way. Women didn't have to worry about what they looked like naked. Oh, they might pretend they did, but Plunk was pretty sure they knew deep down as long as they had boobs of any size or shape men were going to want them. When it came to sex, women had no pressure on them. They could just lay there. The guy had to be able to do it. It had been so many years for Plunk, maybe one or two drunken fumblings with women he never saw again but nothing as part of an official couple since Annie walked out. What if he messed up completely? Why did he have to worry about this stuff when Darlene didn't? This was why Plunk had gotten comfortable with no woman in his life. It took all the romance-related worrying out of it.

Concern about Tuesday night dinner with Darlene kept Plunk from completely enjoying the Tail Man planning stuff with her on Monday. At one point, he told Darlene to just go write since she had been complaining she wouldn't be able to during her Florida trip. He gave her a kiss and a hug, and she said she hoped he was looking forward to dinner tomorrow night, and he said he was.

The minute Darlene was out the door, Plunk strapped on the tail. He did this every night now when he was alone in his apartment, sometimes wearing it just for a few minutes, more often a couple hours, sitting on the couch with it laid out beside him, drinking beer and watching ESPN and feeling safe, content. He liked to wear the tail when he was worried and when he was happy both. He didn't feel complete anymore without it. Tail Man, that was him.

He really wished he could wear the tail over to Darlene's for dinner. It would make him more confident about things. But he couldn't. She'd think it was weird.

32.

On Tuesday night Darlene had the door open almost before Plunk's knuckles were finished knocking on it. She had her hair up instead of in a ponytail and she was wearing a blue dress speckled with yellow flowers.

"Hello," she said. "Thanks for coming."

The semiformal greeting threw Plunk almost as much as her hair and dress.

"You look pretty good," he said, and Darlene blushed. She did look good, for Darlene. There wasn't anything she could do about the glasses or the way her mouth pursed when she wasn't smiling. Though she had her hair pulled up, it was kind of leaning to the right, which made her head look lopsided. But the dress was shorter and tighter than anything he'd so far seen her wearing, not short and tight like the things Jessika sometimes wore at work, just short and tight compared to Darlene's usual getup.

They stood awkwardly in the doorway for a couple seconds until Darlene said, "Well. Please come in."

Plunk did, and the first thing he noticed was the computer, set up on the coffee table in front of the couch. It was big and clunky, not like the smaller laptop ones they had at work. Darlene's apartment looked like it had the same layout his did, living room and kitchen and a short hall to the bedroom and bathroom. Unlike Plunk's living room where the widescreen had pride of place, Darlene's living room was dominated by the computer. He saw over to the side a TV so small it sat comfortably on what his mother used to call an "end table." No wonder Darlene wore glasses. She had to really strain her eyes trying to watch that measly thing.

She saw what he was looking at and said, "I really only watch *Daybreak Metroplex* in the morning while I'm having breakfast, and maybe the news at night. It's important to stay informed, don't you think? I don't have time for most television now, maybe just a few shows here and there to keep up with popular culture, which writers need to do. Mostly I work on my book, so that's why the computer's there. I'd like a bigger place so I could use an extra bedroom as my study."

Plunk associated "study" with all the reasons he'd hated going to school, so he let that one go. He saw that Darlene had a regular table to eat at, not like his card table. It was set with silverware and two candles that were already lit. Beyond the table there was a wooden bowl on the kitchen counter.

"Something smells good," he said hopefully. He couldn't actually smell anything, but Darlene had said they'd eat right when he got there so he assumed something had to be cooking.

"It's nothing fancy," she said a little defensively, he thought. "I've got one or two more things to do, so I thought maybe I'd give you a glass of wine and you could sit here while I do them. We can talk even though I'm in the kitchen."

That was obvious enough. It was a tiny apartment. The kitchen was practically on top of the couch.

Darlene brought Plunk a glass of red wine and he thanked her even though he never drank wine. It was girly. But he wasn't surprised Darlene didn't offer him beer, because women never had beer in their refrigerators. He made a little show of sipping the wine and going, "Mmmm, very good." Darlene nodded and went into the kitchen, where she rummaged around with things.

While she did, Plunk glanced around the apartment some more, and saw that the short narrow hall was lined with the kind of cheap fake wood bookcases sold in discount stores. He knew because he used to un-box them in the Wal-Mart warehouse. There were some in the living room, too. Every shelf was crammed with books, most of them paperbacks but also some hardcovers. He got up to look at the closest bookcase, leaving his glass of too-sweet wine on the coffee table by the computer. The books were by people named Sandra Brown and Anne Rice and lots and lots by Colleen Hoover. One of the Anne Rice books was called *Interview with the Vampire*. Plunk remembered seeing a couple episodes in a miniseries with the same title before getting bored. As he recalled, the vampires did too much talking and not enough biting. There were also a couple of books by Dr. Jennifer Nice, the one who told you what you were supposed to do with your life.

"You can borrow anything you want," Darlene called from the kitchen. "I mostly like women writers, you can tell. My sisters of the printed word. I study what they do so I can write better. Not that I'd plagiarize or anything. Just for the inspiration."

"Yeah," Plunk said. "You got lots of books."

"But never enough," Darlene said. "No matter how many you read, there's always so many good ones you haven't gotten to yet. But I try." She banged open the oven door and added, "Why don't you sit at the table. I think everything's ready. Go ahead and bring your wine."

Plunk did, wishing he could tell her he'd like some water to wash the sticky wine taste out of his mouth. But he knew that would hurt her feelings.

Darlene turned off the lights so there were only the flickering candles, then carried in two plates. She put one in front of Plunk and the other across from him, though not far because the table wasn't very big. Plunk looked down at his plate. There was a piece of chicken breast with the skin off, a big pile of salad made with strange-looking stuff, and a roll.

"I know you like chicken so I thought I'd serve that," Darlene said. "And salad because we'll be eating so much on Thanksgiving we ought to eat light now. I hope that's all right."

"Sure," Plunk said, wondering if he might at least get an extra roll. "Looks real good." He poked with his fork at an oddly-shaped thing in the heap of salad.

"Don't you love bell tomatoes?" Darlene asked, seeing what he was doing. "I couldn't believe they had some at the store this late in the year. Please, let's go ahead and eat."

Darlene did most of the talking during the meal, starting with how she'd keep her cell phone handy in Florida to monitor the Tail Man request calls. Counting a couple that day there were twenty-four possible paid appearances, plus the unpaid requests from teachers.

"A few of the paid ones are for right after January first, after the holidays, but some are for Christmas parties," she said. "Maybe we can think of something Christmassy for Tail Man to do."

She talked more, about not liking her sister and how her book was coming along and what her writing teacher had said in class last Thursday night. With this week off from classes because of Thanksgiving break she would have liked to spend some of the extra time working on her book, but she couldn't because she was going to Florida.

"It's such an inconvenient time to be taking a trip," she complained.

Plunk tried to eat slowly and keep Darlene talking, because when the meal was over whatever was going to happen would happen. He could tell Darlene was nervous too, though he couldn't imagine why.

She kept punctuating her talking with little giggles, and just took tiny bites of her food and left most of it on the plate. Then she waited, talking nonstop, of course, while Plunk drew out the process of eating every bite of the bland chicken breast and salad and the roll, which was warm from the oven and actually pretty good.

Finally when there wasn't a crumb left on his plate Darlene cleared her throat and said, "Well. Why don't I clean up later. We can take our wine into the living room." Plunk had been hoping for dessert. He could have dragged out eating a piece of cake or some ice cream for another fifteen minutes. But he got up and went with her over to the couch. They set their glasses of wine on the table beside the computer and sat down. Darlene's shoulder rested lightly against Plunk's.

"I really could come back sooner than Sunday," she said. "I wouldn't mind."

"Well, your folks," Plunk said. "It might hurt their feelings."

"You're so thoughtful," Darlene said. She squeezed his arm. "And you're having Thanksgiving dinner with your mother?"

"More like Thanksgiving lunch," Plunk said. "Eleven or eleven-thirty. Be over in maybe an hour."

"I'll call you on Thanksgiving," Darlene said. "What time?"

The last thing Plunk wanted was Darlene on the phone forever while he was trying to watch football, but that was one of those things you couldn't say.

"I'm not sure," he said. "Probably Eddie'll be over after I go see Mom. He doesn't have any family to be with."

Plunk hoped Darlene might show some sympathy for poor family-less Eddie, but she just grimaced.

"Eddie," she said, in a way that made the name sound like a cussword, or, as Plunk's Pop used to say, like a fart at a funeral. Plunk thought he better change the subject.

"I guess you can call me anytime," he said, and they sat there for a minute.

Darlene said in a softer voice, "I'm glad about us," and tilted her face toward him. Plunk knew this was it. He kissed her, easy at first. When he took his face away from hers Darlene was looking at him with this very serious expression. He wondered if she was going to take her glasses off or if he should do it for her. But the glasses stayed on. They kissed some more. She shifted so she was facing him more directly and they put their arms around each other. Tongues came a little bit into use. Plunk couldn't help feeling excited even though it was Darlene and not the hot women from the streaming services movies. At the same time he was scared about whether he was going to be any good at what was coming next, what if he couldn't do it well or even at all?

Then Darlene pulled away, though not like she was upset or anything, and said, "Can we do this gradually?"

Plunk wasn't sure what she meant, so he didn't say anything back.

"I don't think we should do everything at once," she said. It seemed to Plunk that she was asking rather than telling. "This is all so beautiful. We shouldn't rush it."

"No," Plunk said, wondering.

"I don't want you to think I'm a certain kind of woman," Darlene said. "Relationships should be built on respect."

Relief washed over Plunk. She wasn't saying let's be friends. As scared as he was about having sex, he feared the let's be friends thing more.

"Okay," he said.

"Are you mad at me?" Darlene said in a silly little voice.

Plunk shook his head.

"Nah, whatever you want is fine with me."

Darlene hugged him hard.

"I knew you'd understand," she said, sounding all relieved. "You're so special that way."

They kissed a couple more times and then Darlene started talking about packing and having to be at the airport at 6:30 in the morning, going through security and all. Her sister Katie was picking her up at 5:15. Plunk said he hoped she'd have a good time with her folks and

Darlene reminded him she'd call sometime on Thanksgiving.

"I'll miss you every minute," she said as he was leaving.

Plunk said he'd miss her, too. Then he went home and put on the tail.

33.

Plunk woke up just before nine on Thanksgiving morning. He ate a couple pop-tarts and watched the sports news on ESPN. It was a nice lazy morning. He didn't wear the tail, but it was reassuring to know he could if he felt like it.

A little before eleven he pulled on his Cowboys jacket and went out into the parking lot. There were very few cars there. Most of the apartment residents were off to spend the holidays with family. But Plunk knew Eddie wasn't. He didn't have any family, or at least never mentioned one. So Plunk knocked on Eddie's door and told him to get his ass over around one, they'd watch themselves a whole day and night of football. Eddie, knuckling stuff from the corners of his eyes like he'd just waked up, yawned and said he'd be there.

"Bring beer," Plunk reminded him.

"Don't I always?" Eddie asked. "Had to go out and get a couple six-packs last night. Most places are closed today. You got food?"

"Sandwiches," Plunk said. "Some sliced ham from the store. It's pretty good."

When Plunk got to Pleasant Valley a lot of people were there ahead of him, wanting to do the right thing and visit their fading old relatives and also get the visit over with ASAP so they could get back home and have their real Thanksgiving dinners. The Pleasant Valley staff was serving one, too, neutral-tasting turkey and gravy and mashed potatoes and green beans and pie. None of it tasted very good. There was a forced cheerfulness about the meal. The residents—you weren't supposed to call even the sickest ones "patients"—were gathered around tables in the big dining room with vacant seats beside them for family visitors. Ida Landy was down at the far end with the others from the constant care wing. Many of constant cares were in pajamas and robes, and fewer of them had anyone there for the meal.

Plunk started to go over to Mom, but then he saw her friend Helen. Helen's daughter and son-in-law and a grandchild were with her.

"Hey, Helen," Plunk said. "Lots of room down at the end. You guys come sit with Mom and me."

Helen glanced up.

"Oh, I've promised my new roommate Jean that we'd eat with her and her family," she said. "But tell Ida hello."

"Tell her yourself, she's right over there," Plunk said, pointing to where his mother sat listlessly staring straight ahead.

"Oh, I will," Helen promised, but she looked away from Plunk fast and it was obvious she didn't want to see him or Mom at all. He couldn't understand why. She and Mom had been friends for years.

Plunk went over and sat down beside Mom, asking how she was. She didn't have much to say. She kept patting her hair bun. He tried getting her interested in the food, because she always liked to talk about gravy especially, but it didn't work. One of the staff came by and said, "Now, you need to eat, Ida. Let me see you take a bite," and Mom dutifully stuck her fork in the mashed potatoes and shoveled a little in her mouth. It went that way for the next depressing half-hour. Most of the visitors ate fast; they were saying goodbye to their relations while Plunk was still trying to get Mom to taste her turkey. It scared him. She'd never been like that about food before.

"She's probably just tired," the staff woman said when Plunk asked her if Mom had a problem. "All the Thanksgiving excitement." Plunk looked around and didn't see anybody acting very excited.

"But Mom always likes to eat." Plunk said.

The woman smiled and touched his arm.

"Your mother's changing now, Mr. Landy," she said. "You have to expect things like this."

Plunk felt rotten walking home. For two cents he'd have told Eddie sorry, don't come over after all. The base of Plunk's spine ached for the comforting pressure of the tail. It would have helped so much, but he couldn't wear it around the apartment in front of Eddie. God knows what the butthead would say.

Yet as depressed as Plunk was about Mom, and as much as he wanted to be by himself to put on his tail, he couldn't bring himself to leave Eddie all alone on Thanksgiving. So when he got back to the apartment he gave the tail a quick pat and then set out the sandwich stuff—white bread, mustard, the sliced ham, a very soft tomato Plunk found in the deepest recesses of his refrigerator—on the card table along with a couple knives to slice the tomato and spread the mustard. He ripped off some paper towels for napkins. No glasses necessary. Eddie was bringing the beer and they'd drink it straight from the can.

When Eddie showed up he had a box of Ritz crackers as well as two six-packs of beer.

"These were in my cupboard," Eddie explained. "Forgot I had 'em."

The crackers were pretty stale, but they tasted okay with beer. Plunk put on the first football game, the Detroit Lions featured as always on Thanksgiving, this time playing the Chicago Bears. They'd already started. It was just after half time. After this game, there'd be the Cowboys and Tampa Bay. And after that, college football on ESPN, Oklahoma and Ole Miss. A full wonderful day and night of TV football.

Which ended up not being so wonderful. Beer was some of the problem. By the time the Lions and Bears made it to the fourth quarter, Plunk and Eddie were already each on their third can and it was clear two six-packs weren't going to be enough for the football marathon. Plunk told Eddie he ought to go get some more, and Eddie said he'd brought the first two and Plunk could get the next ones, he had all that Tail Man money. Plunk thought that was pretty shitty, since he was providing the food and the widescreen TV, but he got up anyway and put on his jacket. Then he had to drive to a couple different places before he found a 7-11 that was open, and he bought two more six-packs from a clerk who looked about as pleased as Plunk was to be in the store on Thanksgiving. When he got back to the apartment he'd missed two touchdowns and a field goal and that pissed him off some more.

Then Eddie wondered why there wasn't anything else to eat besides a ham sandwich and rotten tomato, and Plunk replied kind of sharply that the big-ass turkey was in the oven and ought to be done any minute. They drank beer in sullen silence for a while, and then there was about a half hour between the end of the Detroit game and the start of the one in Dallas and they had to talk again.

"Great goddamn Thanksgiving," Eddie observed, draining his sixth beer and crunching the empty can in his hand. He belched, a long wet one, and dropped the crumpled can on the floor beside the couch. It clinked against the others he'd previously deposited there. "I hate the holidays."

"Hey, we got football and we got beer," Plunk said. "Could be a lot worse."

"You're right," Eddie said, "It could be. That girlfriend of yours could be here."

Plunk normally didn't mind Eddie ragging on Darlene. It only seemed fair, the way she talked about him. But he was buzzy from the beer and kind of defensive on her behalf after the kissing on Tuesday.

"She's all right," Plunk said. "I guess she's in Florida now with her folks. Coming back Sunday. And all the weekends after this for a while, we're gonna have Tail Man stuff to do, so you two need to get along if you're gonna keep helping."

"You and Darlene better ask me before you agree to do those things," Eddie said. "I might not be available sometimes. What do they call them, schedule conflicts."

Plunk told Eddie not to give him any of that shit, they could do the Tail Man appearances just fine without him, and also it wasn't like Eddie had anything else to do on weekends except maybe sit around and play with himself. Eddie shot back that he'd rather play with himself than with Darlene.

"At least I got a woman to play with," Plunk said. The Cowboys and Tampa Bay were underway but he couldn't make himself shut up. "When's the last time any woman was ever interested in you?"

Eddie smirked and took a long pull of beer.

"I could tell you something," he said.

"So tell me."

"Maybe I shouldn't."

"Say what you've got to say."

Eddie seemed to be thinking things over. Finally he said, "It isn't like you were the first one she went for. She's come on to every guy in the complex. Women get desperate like that, they go after everybody. You're just the one who said yes."

Little red dots started to flash in front of Plunk's eyes.

"Bullshit," he spluttered.

"No bullshit," Eddie assured him. "Hell, she came after me I guess six months ago. Heard I worked at Miller Brewing and started trying to tell me all about the history of beer. Said she worked at the library and could copy some stories about brewing beer for me. Pathetic. That's why she's so shitty to me now, because I wasn't interested."

"You're a liar."

"I'm not and you know it."

Maybe Plunk knew it and maybe he didn't, but the beer had hold of him and Eddie both. They called each other names but stopped short of hitting, and Plunk told Eddie to get the hell out and Eddie said gladly, why waste his time with some pitiful asshole who was so hard up he'd settle for Dar-goddamn-lene. He slammed the door when he left, and Plunk locked it behind him.

He sat there steaming, drinking beer that suddenly didn't taste as good, making and eating a sandwich because he'd bought the sliced ham especially for Thanksgiving, and trying to watch the football game. He told himself Eddie was full of shit and just jealous because of Darlene and also because of Plunk's new fame as Tail Man. But for all he wanted to believe Eddie was making the Darlene stuff up, the line about working at the library and offering to copy things sounded a little too familiar. Was he hooked up with a woman so sorry even Eddie didn't want her?

"It doesn't matter," Plunk muttered, but he felt like it really did, and also he felt bad fighting with Eddie because the dickwad was probably his best friend. What if they never spoke again? He hated it when life got complicated.

Next thing Plunk knew, it was past eight and the Dallas game was long over. He must have dozed off from all the beer. His mouth was cottony and he was just thinking about going to put on the tail before he switched channels to what was left of the college game when there was a knock at the door. Eddie had obviously thought things over and wanted to apologize. Plunk would let him.

34.

Plunk fumbled with the lock, got the door open and it wasn't Eddie. Suzette from the burger place said, "Alone on Thanksgiving sucks. Can I come in?"

It was a cold, nasty night. Even standing in Plunk's doorway, the wind whipped her hair around pretty good. It still took another second for Plunk's slightly-drunken mind to grasp her being there. Suzette stood patiently and he finally said, "Yeah, sure."

She handed him a clipping, and also her coat. He put the coat on the kitchen counter.

"The weekly Weatherford paper had this about you at the golf thing," she said. "Came out yesterday, didn't know if you'd seen it."

He looked at another photo of himself, a slightly different angle than the picture in the Fort Worth and Dallas dailies. This one didn't show the entire tail but he still liked it.

"Hey, thanks," Plunk said. "Nice of you to bring it. Why aren't you eating turkey somewhere?"

Suzette shrugged.

"Like we were saying the other day, no place to be, no one to be with."

"What about your family? Parents?" Plunk said.

"I don't see them anymore. Do I get to sit down?"

"Anywhere," Plunk said, gesturing vaguely. Suzette sat on the couch. She took in the crumpled beer cars Eddie had dropped, also the empty Ritz Cracker box and the sandwich stuff on the card table.

"Thanksgiving feast," she said, with a nice little laugh. "I had a can of soup."

"You want a sandwich?" Plunk asked. "Sliced ham, pretty good stuff."

"I'm good," Suzette said. "But I bet you got some more beer around here."

This pleased Plunk—a woman who asked for beer!—but also puzzled him, because asking for a beer meant she wanted to stay a while rather than just dropping off the article and saying see you sometime. He got her beer and also one for himself and came back into the living room.

"Nice TV," Suzette said, looking at the widescreen. "Girlfriend's in Florida, right?"

"Yeah," Plunk said. He tipped his beer can in her direction. "Well, happy Thanksgiving."

"Same," she said. "Okay. Where's this famous tail?"

"You want to see the tail."

"Sure I do," she said. "I mean, it's cold out there. I didn't drive over here not to see the tail worn by the most famous man in Crowley."

"How'd you know where I live?" Plunk asked. It was hard to talk because his smile was so wide. The most famous man in Crowley? He liked the sound of that.

Suzette grinned back at him, not the exasperated grin some women get when they think a guy asked a stupid question, but a look of genuine amusement.

"My laptop said there's only one Plunk Landy living in Crowley," she said. "Easy to get the address. Come on, show me the tail."

The most famous man in Crowley got it from the bedroom, carrying it sort of spread out in his arms so Suzette would get the full effect. She got up from the couch and came over to where he stood. She stroked the tail, obviously admiring the smoothness of the vinyl. He showed her how you could poke it with a finger and the dented spot would pop right back up.

"Good solid rubber in there," Plunk explained. He attached the retractable leash and showed her how he could use it to pull the tail up and down.

"Pretty nice," she said. "So you going to put it on?"

After the day he'd had, Plunk didn't need much of an invitation. He strapped on the tail and immediately felt so much better.

"So that's Tail Man," Suzette said speculatively.

"I wear some other stuff too," Plunk said. "Yellow sweatshirt, black jeans, gloves that kind of look like lizard claws."

"But the tail's the big thing," she said. "What everybody wants to see." She touched the tail again and went back to the couch. Plunk watched her take another drink of beer. She didn't sip delicately like a girl. She took a nice swig.

He stood there with the tail on, not sure what to do next, and Suzette said, "You going to sit down and have your beer? It's no good if it gets warm."

"Sure," Plunk said. He went to the bedroom and took off the tail. He felt so odd, with this woman showing up unexpectedly and now staying besides, that he actually dropped the tail on the floor instead of laying it on the bed. He went back into the living room, sat on the chair with the spring poking into his back, and drank beer too.

The college game was still in progress on the widescreen and Suzette seemed to be watching it. Plunk tried to look at Suzette without her knowing. He guessed she was maybe early thirties, there were some little lines at her eyes and mouth, but still she looked fine. She had on a gray sweatshirt and jeans, tight jeans. Also Plunk kind of thought she didn't have a bra on under the sweatshirt. Suzette's sweatshirt was pretty bulky but Plunk still thought he might have detected some boob swaying.

And wondering about Suzette's bra or lack of one got something stirring in Plunk's pants, he'd been especially sensitive there since the kissing episode with Darlene. The beer helped him realize he'd have done just fine Tuesday night if Darlene had cooperated. He was forty-two goddamn years old. He didn't need to play by "will you still respect me tomorrow" high school girl rules. He bet she watched CNN. Plunk got aggravated with Darlene just thinking about it. He drank some more beer.

Over on the couch, Suzette stretched, a big one with arms extended all the way above her head, back arched so the front of her sweatshirt pointed directly at Plunk. He tried not to stare but it was impossible.

"Did I tell you I went out with Skunk Yawn, the Rangers' coach?" Suzette asked.

"I know you went out with Red," Plunk said, to be funny.

"Yeah, well. I've gone out with Skunk Yawn, and he played on the Rangers besides coaching them later on. He had his own baseball card."

"He did," Plunk agreed. "You put it up at work like my picture. But my picture's bigger."

Suzette sort of slid her fingers up and down her beer can.

"I went out with the guy who got Fireman of the Year in Burleson a couple years ago," she said. "Also somebody who got elected vice-president of the Southwest Fort Worth Young Republicans. They both had stories in the paper with pictures."

"Pretty good," Plunk said.

Suzette put her beer can on the floor and stood up.

"Tail Man," she said. "The famous Tail Man from Crowley. In the newspapers. On TV." She reached for Plunk's hand and pulled him to his feet.

"Hey," Plunk said. Maybe it was the beer, but he felt excited where he'd been nervous with Darlene.

Suzette led him toward the bedroom. She seemed to know exactly where it was, no big trick because the apartment was so small. Plunk's cell started ringing and he ignored it. If it was Eddie he could call back. Suzette pulled off her sweatshirt and Plunk had been right, she wasn't wearing a bra.

After a while she said, "Why don't you put on the tail."

35.

Plunk came to rather than woke up on Friday. It was late morning, just past eleven, a good four hours after he usually got up during the week to go to work. But there was no work today, Austin gave everybody the day after Thanksgiving off, and Plunk was glad of it because he was hungover in a particularly vicious way, the kind where the pain was right behind his eyes. And Suzette was still in his bed. She lay there snoring, blankets tugged up around her. She had her back turned to Plunk. The shoulder not covered by the blankets was smooth and pale.

Plunk badly needed to get up and pee, but the effort involved was considerable and so he just lay there despite the bursting sensation in his bladder. This was so new to him, and the killer hangover was the smallest part of it. He'd never had really crazy sex before, Annie wasn't into any of that. She liked it ordinary. If he deviated even slightly from the usual she told him not to do that. Suzette did things to him and had him do things to her he hadn't thought of before, or, if he'd thought of them, he'd never expected he'd actually ever get the chance to do them. A couple times she even got the tail involved.

Plunk tried to look without moving his aching head, and from the corner of his eye he could see the tail curled up on the floor by the bed as though it too was worn out from all the sex. He hoped the new leather belts hadn't broken from the strain.

Gingerly, because of both his head and not wanting to wake Suzette up—what would he say to her, what if she wanted to start doing it again?—Plunk eased out of bed and tiptoed into the bathroom. He closed the door behind him. He had to sit down to pee because when he tried it standing he wobbled too much and kept missing the bowl. When he finally had every drop gone he remained seated and rested his head in his hands.

Memory kicked in first at a glacial pace, then faster. The stuff he'd done with Suzette. Before that, how she showed up at his door. Before that, the beef with Eddie. He thought he remembered the phone ringing about the time Suzette took him into the bedroom. Had it also been ringing while they were in there doing it? He thought so but wasn't sure. Eddie, for certain, calling to say he was sorry. Or …

Shit. Darlene said she'd call on Thanksgiving. Eddie would have just walked over and knocked on the door. So it had been her. Had to be. And if it was also Darlene calling later on, while he and Suzette were doing it, then what was he going to tell Darlene when she got back and asked where he was and why didn't he answer his phone?

Plunk was not a fan of complications. He wanted life simple. But now he needed a plausible story to tell Darlene when she got back Sunday. Maybe he could say Pleasant Valley called to say his mother wasn't feeling well, so he went over to check even though it was late. No. That wouldn't work. Now Darlene expected to go with him to see Mom and she might mention it and somebody on the staff would say what, never happened. Okay. He'd tell her he and Eddie decided to go out to a movie, they got sick of football after watching it all afternoon. That might work. Except Eddie was mad at him. Well, he'd go see Eddie today, joke around some, smooth it all over. Eddie'd lie for a buddy. Guys stuck together in things like this.

The pain behind Plunk's eyes intensified as he remembered what he and Eddie had gotten into it over. If Eddie was telling the truth, Darlene was just looking for any guy who'd take her, as far as she was concerned the only thing special about Plunk was that he was willing.

He sat on the toilet and fumed thinking how she probably told a hundred guys she worked in the library and could copy them stories about whatever she thought they were interested in. When she got back Sunday he'd tell her to go make copies of stories for some other sucker.

Though the more Plunk thought about it, he realized it was really Darlene's fault he'd had all that Thanksgiving night sex with Suzette. If Darlene had come through after dinner Tuesday night, which is what any normal woman would have done, Plunk would have told Suzette no, thanks for offering but he had a girlfriend to be faithful to. He knew he would have said that because he was an honorable guy.

Plunk started to raise up off the toilet, feeling self-righteous and just a smidge less hung over, when he had the sudden mental image of what would happen when he told Darlene to go blow. She'd storm off acting like he'd done something wrong instead of her, women were so like that, and then probably throw away the list of all the Tail Man parties he was supposed to do just to screw him up. He sat back on the toilet, puzzling over this new scenario. If he didn't know where he was supposed to go as Tail Man and when, people would stop asking him, and he had to be Tail Man now, he loved it so much being the most famous man in Crowley. Maybe he wouldn't tell off Darlene.

And then Plunk started thinking about how Darlene had been the one to talk Hillary's mother into paying him to be Tail Man at her daughter's party, and how Darlene had come up with pin-the-tail-on-the-leopard-gecko and making gecko tails out of garbage sacks as party games for the kids. He remembered how she bought him the yellow work gloves and decorated them herself with black magic marker spots, and how she handed out the Tail Man business cards at the golf event.

He recalled the silly off-to-the-side topknot she had her hair in on Tuesday night, and the nervous hopeful way she said she was glad about them being together. Maybe Darlene had come on to lots of other guys before Plunk, but after she ended up with him she'd been loyal and helpful and sweet. She did act like a know-it-all but that's just the way she was, nobody's perfect.

Plunk got off the toilet. He'd get Suzette out of there in as kindly a way as he could, and then unlike Red he'd never, ever go back to the burger place where she worked again, even if they did have his Tail Man pictures pinned up. Then he'd go find Eddie, get things straight with him. He'd tell Eddie about Suzette, all the sexy details which Eddie would just love, and then they'd cook up a story for Darlene that Plunk would tell her when she got back Sunday. Life would go on just like before, except Plunk would now have some secret wildass X-rated memories to warm himself with on many a North Texas winter night. Everybody would be happy except maybe Suzette, but she'd soon find somebody else who'd had his picture in the paper to do her crazy sex stuff with.

This was the most thinking something through that Plunk had ever done in his life, and he hoped he'd never have to again. He came out of the bathroom, pulled on his clothes, and picked up the tail to move it to the living room. Suzette mumbled something. She was still wrapped in the covers. Plunk guessed he should offer her breakfast. With luck she'd eat fast and go. He needed to find Eddie, get things right between them and also get his alibi in place. Darlene might try calling from Florida again anytime, and he wanted to be ready.

Plunk clattered the coffee pot, and, like he'd hoped, the noise woke Suzette up.

"You here?" she called in a voice still thick with sleep.

"In the kitchen," he hollered. "Want coffee?"

"Yeah," Suzette said. The bedroom was separated at an angle from the kitchen by the short cramped hallway, but Plunk could see some flesh-colored movement and wondered briefly if they might do something one last time before she left. Better not.

The bathroom door slammed shut. Plunk got out cups and put them on the card table, first removing the bread, open jar of mustard, and brownish, curling ham slices that had been left out the night before. He stuck pop-tarts in the toaster and took the tail back into the bedroom so Suzette would have room to sit on the couch while she ate her hopefully hasty breakfast.

The toilet flushed and she came out of the bedroom wearing her sweatshirt pulled down over her ass but no jeans and probably not anything else, long bare legs reminding Plunk in a vivid way of how they'd wrapped around him not that long ago. Suzette wasn't in a hurry. She got her coffee, waved off the pop-tarts and slouched on the couch. Then she started talking, about her job as a waitress and how her feet hurt from being on them all day. Plunk was impatient but tried to act sympathetic. He felt like he owed it to her.

She was only waitressing to get enough money put aside for beauty college, Suzette said. Hairdressing was a great job, everybody was friendly and the pay was better. Waitressing sucked, the tips were lousy, guys kept grabbing at you, and at the end of the day your hair smelled like hamburger grease.

Then Suzette moved on to a more dangerous subject.

"So when are we seeing each other again?" she asked. "The girlfriend's gone 'til Sunday, right?"

"I guess," Plunk said. "Thing is, she's my girlfriend and also my business partner with Tail Man. I don't want her upset."

"She can't get upset about what she doesn't know," Suzette said. "Besides, the way you were last night I was thinking you might want a new girlfriend. Whatever way she helps you with the Tail Man thing, I bet I could do."

Suzette leaned back on the couch. The sweatshirt slid up and sure enough, nothing underneath. Plunk stood up, probably intending to lift her to her feet and tell her to get dressed rather than jump on top of her, and there was another knock at the door. Well, Eddie's gonna get an eyeful, Plunk thought, and he took off the chain and pulled the door open and there smiling at him was Darlene.

"You didn't answer your phone last night," she said. "I caught an early flight back from Florida because I just couldn't stand it. Did you miss me like I missed you?"

36.

Darlene stepped forward and Plunk slid in front of her, succeeding in blocking her from coming in but he couldn't block what was clearly visible behind him, Suzette sprawled on the couch with her sweatshirt riding up and her long bare legs showing. Not that Suzette looked upset or tried to cover up. She just stayed where she was, and Darlene looked past Plunk at her.

"Darlene," Plunk said.

She just kept looking, at the coffee cups and the plate of pop-tarts on the rickety card table and most of all at Suzette's pale naked legs scissored along the length of the couch. Darlene might not be the genius she usually tried acting like, but she was smart enough to realize what was going on right in front of her.

"Darlene," Plunk said again.

He could have stood it better if she'd gotten mad, if she'd screamed or slapped him or even tried to get past him at Suzette. But she didn't. Instead Darlene's face sort of crumpled in on itself, mouth opening to emit a low little moan, tears from the corners of her eyes, the expression of someone who's always known anything good in her life would somehow be ruined, and here was the latest proof. Her hands came up to her mouth and she moaned again, then turned and shuffled clumsily off across the parking lot. Plunk called her name for the third time and one of her hands waved briefly, meaning maybe leave me alone or go to hell, probably both, and then she went through the door into her apartment, gone just like that with not one word of accusation even though she was so obviously destroyed by what Plunk had done to her. Which made Plunk feel like the worst human being in the whole world.

He stood there staring across the parking lot at her door, a few people out in the parking lot looking at him curiously or with smirky smiles, a little free soap opera-style entertainment for them on the morning after Thanksgiving.

Plunk only turned around when Suzette called, "Hey, wanna shut the door? Getting drafty."

He closed the door and muttered, "Jesus."

"Don't take it so hard," Suzette said. She sat up on the couch and drank some coffee. "Now you don't have to worry she's gonna find out."

"She was really upset," Plunk said.

"Can't do anything about it now," said Suzette. She put down the coffee cup and came over to rub the back of Plunk's neck. "She'll live. They always do. How about lunch at my place? I'll cook you something."

Plunk moved her hand off him.

"Don't think so," he said. "I got to talk to Darlene."

Suzette shook her head.

"There's nothing you can say," she said. "Things happen, you move on. Maybe she's a nice person, but from what I saw you didn't lose all that much. Don't you think I'm cuter?"

She obviously was, but to Plunk now it didn't seem to matter.

"I guess you better go," he said to Suzette, and then her face got a look, too, not all crushed like Darlene's but still pained, even disappointed.

"Are we going out again?" she asked in a flat voice like she already knew the answer. "If I give you my number, you going to call?"

Plunk was too upset to lie.

"Probably not," he said. "I got to fix it with Darlene."

"Good luck with that," Suzette said, sounding sarcastic. She walked into the bedroom, and Plunk could hear rustling as she put on the rest of her clothes. Pretty soon she came back out, and went right by him to the door.

"The tail's not that great," she said. "Don't kid yourself." She went out into the parking lot, slamming the door behind her. Plunk heard tires squeal as she drove away fast.

He put the tail on right away, of course, but the familiar comforting feeling was missing. Plunk went into the living room, adjusted the belts so he could spread the tail out to the side, picked up his coffee cup and tried hard to think. His head still throbbed with a hangover but it seemed like his heart was hurting worse. He was scared of losing Darlene, and Eddie, and the Tail Man thing because Darlene was never going to forgive him and she probably wasn't the type who could separate personal from business. Before her, he was a guy who wore a fake gecko tail on Halloween. No parties, nothing on TV. No extra income to pay Mom's new bills. All these complications. Plunk hated complicated things.

So he sat there for what seemed like and maybe were hours. He had no experience with this kind of stuff, where you had to think of what to do. When Annie left that had been her decision, her doing. Sad but straightforward. This was different. Plunk didn't know what you said to your girlfriend after she caught you cheating. He had no idea how you patched things up with a friend who said your girlfriend came on to him, maybe she hadn't been Plunk's girlfriend yet but so what. He had no previous experience with his Mom losing her mind and not having anybody but him to pay for her getting help for that. The only thing he was absolutely sure of was he wanted to keep being Tail Man. It was suddenly just about the only part of his life without a shitty downside, and it was in jeopardy too.

Finally Plunk mumbled, "One thing at a time," and came up with a vague kind of plan. Darlene was the most complicated problem. Mom was his biggest responsibility. He'd start with Eddie. That was the simplest. He put on his Cowboys jacket and went over to knock on Eddie's door.

Eddie peered out. His eyes were bloodshot and his breath smelled like stale beer, which figured.

"What," he said when he saw Plunk there.

"Guess it got a little drunk out yesterday," Plunk said, sounding as upbeat as his hangover and heartache allowed. "I come in?"

"If you want," Eddie said. His apartment was dark. He had all the curtains pulled shut and only the light in the kitchen was on. There was some more light from the flickering screen of his TV set, an old model not nearly as nice as Plunk's. "I ordered pizza," he said, motioning toward a box on the counter.

Plunk's stomach was queasy but he took a slice to be polite. It was lukewarm and the cheese was gummy.

"The thing yesterday," Plunk said, figuring they might as well get right to it. "Pretty stupid."

"Shit," Eddie said. "*Lots* of beer, we had."

And from there it was pretty easy, especially since they never specifically discussed what Eddie had said about Darlene, and Plunk's reaction to it. This was, Plunk thought, why guys were so great. No hashing and rehashing like women would have done, just him and Eddie understanding they were both sorry it happened and so why go over the details? They joked about the amount of beer they'd had and how the Lions always stunk, and maybe in two or three minutes it was like nothing ever happened. Friends again.

"You can't see anything on that," Plunk said, gesturing at Eddie's TV. "Let's put the game on at my place." Georgia was playing Mississippi State; because of the holiday, it was being broadcast on Friday afternoon.

"I only got three beers to bring," Eddie warned.

"After yesterday, that's more than we need," Plunk said. "You have two, I'll have one."

As they went back to his place, Plunk looked over at Darlene's apartment across the parking lot. The door was still closed. Her car was parked in front. He wondered if she might be peeking out the window, seeing him and Eddie together out there, and if that might somehow make her feel worse. He wanted to walk over and try to explain, but he remembered her face being so sad and not angry and it was just something he didn't feel brave enough yet to do.

Even with the football game and beer and Eddie back as his pal, though, Plunk couldn't get the Darlene thing out of his mind. His preoccupation was obvious, because even dumbass Eddie picked up on it. When he asked what was the problem now, Plunk told him all of it, about Plunk thinking the knock on his door Thanksgiving night was Eddie but it was Suzette, and what he and Suzette did, and then how that morning there'd been the other knock and he thought it was Eddie again but no, it was Darlene, and how Darlene ran off crying and what Suzette said after Darlene was gone. It poured out. Plunk had never before in his life told so much personal stuff to anyone, because guys didn't do that. But it was like he couldn't help himself. He had to tell somebody. He hoped Eddie would say something comforting, maybe offer some useful advice.

When Plunk was done, Eddie whistled and said, "No shit, she really asked you to put on the tail?"

37.

On Friday night after Eddie left, Plunk tried to decide whether to call Darlene. That seemed safer than going over to see her in person. Plunk always wanted people to look at him but he didn't want anyone in the parking lot watching if Darlene slammed her door shut in his face. He put on the tail while he thought about what to do. It was probably his imagination, but it seemed to smell of Suzette and sex. He wet a paper towel and wiped the whole tail, remembering as he did with mingled pleasure and guilt what he and it had been doing with Suzette just the night before. No matter what, that was quite a memory.

Being so inexperienced at trying to figure out relationship issues, Plunk came to no conclusions. He still didn't feel well after all the Thanksgiving beer, so around ten he went to bed, first peering through his curtains at Darlene's apartment across the way. There was a light on behind her curtains. She was home. But he didn't want to face her until he'd decided what to say, and he hadn't yet. So he went to bed and of course thought the sheets smelled like Suzette too, he'd have to take them to the laundry. Maybe he didn't want to forget everything they did but he also didn't want physical evidence, just the X-rated memories to rerun in his mind whenever.

Plunk got up Saturday morning still unsure of what to do about Darlene, only that he had to do something. Her car was still in front of her place. He could walk right over, tell her he was sorry, see what she said. A couple times he started to do it but chickened out.

The weekend stretched in front of him in a desolate sort of way. There was college football on TV, then tomorrow being Sunday he'd visit Mom and afterward Eddie and Larry B. and Red would probably be over to watch whoever was playing, it wouldn't be the Cowboys because they'd played on Thanksgiving. He wondered what Red would do if he found out about Plunk and Suzette. Not much, probably. Red had lots of girlfriends, so it wouldn't be like it temporarily got between Eddie and Plunk. And then next Saturday Tail Man was supposed to be at Stretch's Chevrolet place in Fort Worth. Plunk and Eddie could go without Darlene, of course. But that would suck.

Plunk's reverie was interrupted by the phone ringing. His heart jumped because it might be Darlene, but it was Mr. Davenport from Quality Costumes in Crowley.

"I'd very much like to visit with you, Mr. Landy," he said. "You've become quite a sensation with our tail."

Plunk didn't like the way the guy said "our" about the tail. It was his and only his, he'd paid a lot of money for it, six hundred dollars or something.

"I guess so," Plunk said. "What do you want to talk about?"

"A business opportunity," Mr. Davenport said. "Something beneficial for us both. Are you maybe free later on today, could you come by?"

"I'm tied up," Plunk lied. Actually, he was so shook about Darlene that he didn't feel like talking any business with somebody, especially since it was Darlene who understood that so much better. Which gave him an idea. He told Mr. Davenport he'd probably be able to see him after work Monday, he'd call sometime Monday to make it definite. And the minute the guy was off the phone Plunk called Darlene.

She answered on the third or fourth ring. Her "hello" sounded wobbly.

"It's me," Plunk said. "Can I come talk to you?"

"Why?" said Darlene, sounding even wobblier. "There's nothing to talk about."

"There is, but that part can wait 'til you feel like it," Plunk said. "This is Tail Man business."

"Business," Darlene said, sniffling a little.

"Yeah, the guy from the costume place where I got the tail," Plunk said. He explained how Mr. Davenport said he had a business proposition. "I need your help because you're the smart one about this stuff."

Darlene was hesitant, but Plunk convinced her to let him come over. She said she needed an hour to get her place straightened up.

When he got there she was in one of her shapeless sweater/slacks outfits again. Her eyes were swollen and Plunk knew she'd been crying a lot for a long time.

"Sit down," Darlene said. She waited until Plunk sat on the couch; then she sat on a chair by the table where they'd eaten the bland chicken. Now instead of plates on it there was an open copy of Dr. Jennifer Nice's book *Face the Facts: Make Life Fair Even When It Isn't.* "Did he say exactly what he wanted?"

"Just that it was an opportunity," Plunk said.

"Opportunity," said Darlene, rolling around the word like it was a bad one, Plunk had no idea why. "Like what?"

"I don't know," Plunk said. "I hoped you would. You're good at this stuff, knowing what people are thinking."

"Maybe not," Darlene said, and as lousy as Plunk was at understanding women he still got that message. "I'll bet it's a personal appearance deal like the one at the car dealer. That would be logical. It's where you got the tail to begin with."

"Should I do it?" Plunk said, then quickly added, "Should we call him back and say okay for meeting Monday after we're both off from work?"

Darlene blinked behind her glasses; the lenses were all smeary.

"Why not," she said. "Since Tail Man's so popular with everyone." Again, Plunk got what she was really saying. Women knew how to cut you up with that kind of stuff.

"You got that list of all the things Tail Man's supposed to do," Plunk said. "I mean, we're still going to do them, right?"

"I guess," said Darlene.

"Because I know you're the one who helped Tail Man get so big. It wouldn't work as well without you. I found the tail, but you're smart."

Darlene nodded. They sat a while.

"I ought to say this," Plunk told her. "About the other thing."

"She's a thing?" Darlene asked.

"It was stupid. A mistake."

He thought Darlene might finally get mad, but she just started crying again, tears spilling down her cheeks from under her glasses.

"I came home early because I thought you'd miss me," she said, voice trembling in a way that bothered Plunk a whole lot more than the sarcastic stuff. "Thanksgiving night I called and called."

"Yeah," Plunk said.

Darlene wiped away some tears with the sleeve of her sweater.

"But you were with her."

It seemed wrong to lie.

"Yeah, I was."

Darlene took a deep breath.

"Who is she?"

"Just somebody. From this place I get hamburgers. Used to get them, not anymore. It's over, it doesn't matter."

"It does to me," Darlene said. "So tell the truth."

"I am. She doesn't matter. She's gone."

"Why? She looked really cute."

Damn women, Plunk thought. Suzette and Darlene had sized each other up pretty good in just a few seconds. He shrugged.

"I thought we were special," Darlene said.

"We were. Are."

"There are some women who can't resist celebrities," said Darlene. "They hang all over them. Getting famous like you are, they're going to be around."

"I shouldn't have," Plunk said, wishing to hell she'd go ahead and forgive him if she was going to. He was running out of apologetic things to say.

Darlene looked thoughtful. A corner of her mouth lumped up.

"Well, that's what men are like," she said as much to herself as to Plunk. He didn't reply because he figured he'd just proved she was right, men were like that. "It's what they have to have." She stood up. "Like Dr. Nice says, accept the facts. Find a solution. Resentment's not productive."

She'd confused Plunk completely. He stood up too.

"The way men are," Darlene muttered again. She reached out and took Plunk by the arm.

Her bedspread was light-colored and worn in places. She carefully moved shabby old stuffed animals off it before they lay down.

38.

By the time they walked to Quality Costumes on Monday evening for the meeting with Mr. Davenport, Plunk and Darlene were back together in a brittle kind of way. He understood he was on probation, sort of like when he worked at the grocery store. Following the Saturday afternoon sex she hadn't gotten all clingy like he'd thought she might. It was more like she'd decided that was something she had to do, so she did it. After they were done, and it was all right, though it hadn't been anything like with Suzette, Darlene was more old-fashioned that way like Annie had been, Darlene got dressed and started talking about what time Sunday they'd go to Pleasant Valley to see Mom. They moved back to the living room and Darlene got out the legal pad with all the Tail Man deals listed on it. There were nine Tail Man commitments in December starting with next Saturday from ten to two at Stretch's car lot. After a while Darlene said she had to work on her novel, Plunk should come by for her maybe at quarter past ten tomorrow for their visit to Mom at Pleasant Valley.

She gave him a quick kiss on the cheek as he left, just a peck.

So they did the Mom visit on Sunday, and Darlene was very understanding afterward about him needing to watch football with Eddie and Red and Larry B. She didn't even say Eddie's name like it made her want to spit. She said she'd use the time to work on her book some more.

Monday at six-thirty he got her and they walked to the costume place. Darlene didn't bump her shoulder into him but she did walk closer than she had on the way to Pleasant Valley the day before. There weren't any customers when they got there, costumes not being a priority for people during the start of Christmas shopping season. But Mr. Davenport still made a point of telling the clerk he was going into a very important meeting, don't interrupt under any circumstances short of store evacuation because of fire. Plunk was sorry the clerk wasn't the same girl who'd sold him the gecko tail just before Halloween. He would have enjoyed reminding her she hadn't thought the tail was something he could wear all on its own.

Mr. Davenport's office was small and messy. There were teetering piles of paper on his desk.

"We're getting ready for the seasonal run on Santa Claus outfits," he explained. "People rent them, you know, for Christmas parties. And parents get them for Christmas Eve. We need dozens and they're constantly going out and coming back in, sometimes in deplorable condition. How the spirit of Christmas gets honored by spilling whiskey on Santa's red coat is just beyond me. And sometimes there are stains from even worse things." He rolled his eyes, encouraging them to imagine what those worse things were.

Plunk wouldn't have minded jawing some more about Santa outfits. Costumes of all kinds interested him. But Darlene was all business.

"Mr. Davenport," she said. "You wanted us to come talk to you."

"Of course," he said. "I've been thinking about the tail Mr. Landy got from us. He's certainly made it very popular. In fact, since that piece on *Daybreak Metroplex* and of course the stories in the area newspapers we've had some people coming in looking for lizard tails of their own."

"Leopard gecko, not lizard," Darlene corrected.

"Yes, of course," Mr. Davenport said. He turned in his chair to face Plunk more directly. "Thing is, Mr. Landy, that kind of interest could offer some opportunity. I understand that Tail Man is going to keep making appearances, kids' birthday parties and such. You'll become even better-known."

"Well, I'm trying," Plunk said.

"My thought is a special line of Tail Man Junior tails for the children," said Mr. Davenport. "Sold exclusively at Quality Costumes with your personal endorsement. In return you would receive a small royalty, plus we would perform upkeep on your tail free of charge. Fix tears in the vinyl and so on."

"No shit," Plunk said, sounding inelegant but unable to choose his words better because he was so thrilled. "Tail Man Junior. For kids."

"What sort of tails?" Darlene said, leaning forward to get Mr. Davenport's attention back. "What kind of royalty rate? How much will you sell them for?"

"That will have to be determined," Mr. Davenport said. "There are so many factors. We'd want to manufacture them locally rather than all the way over in Hong Kong, which is where the original tail was special made. Of course, we wouldn't make all that many to start until we got a better idea of demand. You save considerably when you order materials in bulk, but since we won't do that initially we couldn't pay any substantial royalty at that point."

Made sense to Plunk, but not to Darlene.

"Tail Man is the key to your marketing," she said. "He's more important than the things you make the tails out of."

Mr. Davenport smiled in a chilly kind of way.

"Of course, we could offer the tails without involving Mr. Landy at all," he said. He looked right at Darlene instead of Plunk. "I doubt you have any copyright on the Tail Man name."

"We don't need one because everybody knows who Tail Man is," Darlene said. "Before we came over I looked it up. There are seventeen costume places in Fort Worth and around here. We could do a Tail Man deal with any of them, talk about it in the newspaper stories and when he's on TV. Your tails wouldn't be the official ones. If that's the way you want it."

This was a completely different side of Darlene. Plunk was floored. She'd looked up how many costume stores there were, just in case she needed to know?

Mr. Davenport backed right down. He said of course Mr. Landy was Tail Man, the only authentic Tail Man, and the agreement had to be satisfactory to all parties involved. At which point Darlene hit him with all right, how much will you charge for the tails, and though he'd said earlier he wasn't sure it turned out Mr. Davenport actually had a pretty good idea. He thought eighty-five was a good price, parents would back off getting their kids something that cost a hundred, what Mr. Davenport called "three figures." Of the eighty-five, perhaps Mr. Landy could receive 10 percent in return for regular store appearances promoting the Tail Man Junior product.

All Plunk could do was shake his head in wonder as Darlene told Mr. Davenport that was lowballing. Parents were happy to pay three hundred for Tail Man to come to birthday parties, she said. They'd spend half that, easy, to get tails for their kids. Charge one fifty, make sure you use good materials so the tails lasted and parents told other parents how good they were. And Tail Man himself would take let's say one-third for his official endorsement.

Plunk thought a third was outrageous, but Mr. Davenport said, "A third of net, of course. And net, assuming a sales price of one fifty after using reasonably-priced materials and labor would be what, sixty or sixty-five?"

"We'd have to see your worksheets," Darlene said. "Just to confirm." And Mr. Davenport agreed.

They decided—Mr. Davenport and Darlene decided, Plunk was

just sitting there—that Quality Costumes would make up some prototypes at the store's expense. Plunk would test them for quality and comfort of wearing, of course they'd be shorter and much lighter than his real one, these being for children.

"Perhaps we could also establish a line of adult tails exactly like Tail Man's," Mr. Davenport suggested. "For grown-ups who want nothing less than the real thing."

Plunk didn't wait for Darlene's response, whatever it would have been.

"No, absolutely no way," he said. "My tail's special. Nobody else gets one."

"Just the children's tails then," said Mr. Davenport. "If we hurry we can have prototypes sometime early in the New Year, maybe get them on sale by spring." He stood up. "Well. It will be interesting doing business with you, Tail Man, and also of course you." He shook Darlene's hand and nodded in the respectful way Plunk often saw heavyweight boxers use to acknowledge a tough opponent after a hard fight.

"One last thing," Darlene said. "Something Tail Man would like you to do for him. Real quick he needs a Santa hat, only in leopard gecko colors, yellow with black spots. Plus the usual white trim."

This was news to Plunk, but Mr. Davenport picked up on it right away. He said they couldn't do the hat in vinyl, they didn't have that on hand in appropriate colors, but there was a very nice bolt of leopard pattern rayon with a fluffy finish. It should work.

"We need it by Saturday morning," Darlene said. "For Tail Man's appearance at a big car lot."

"We can do that," Mr. Davenport promised, looking and sounding pleased. "Let me measure Tail Man's head so it will fit just right. Friday evening pickup, is that all right?"

"The hat's free of charge," Darlene said. "As part of our agreement. You said it would include upkeep of the tail. But we want the hat, too."

"Of course," Mr. Davenport said, less pleased but still cordial.

As they walked back to The Jacksonian, Plunk asked Darlene how she'd known to find out ahead of time how many local costume stores there were.

"I didn't," she said. "I just made it up."

Plunk had never felt more impressed. He impulsively reached down and held Darlene's hand all the rest of the way home.

39.

Starting with Stretch's Chevrolet dealership on Saturday, the next few weeks were maybe the greatest in Plunk's life. He'd always wanted to be somebody important, but he'd never imagined it could feel this good.

He and Darlene picked up the leopard gecko Santa hat Friday night. Mr. Davenport had it ready like he promised. Plunk looked in the mirror at the costume shop when he tried it on. The effect with the tail was just killer.

"We've got to keep freshening up the whole Tail Man concept," Darlene explained to him. "If something popular gets stale, people get tired of it and move on to something else." The Santa hat wasn't the only way she wanted Tail Man spiffed up for the holidays. Plunk would have settled happily for the hat, but Darlene, who never stopped thinking, was interested in smaller touches too. She bought a couple plastic sprigs of holly at a discount store and painstakingly painted the green stems black and the red berries gold to match leopard gecko colors. Then she tucked the sprigs into the wire at the tip of the tail where he attached the retractable leash. Bingo — leopard gecko Christmas holly that was brandished every time Plunk pulled the tail up. He asked her how she thought of this stuff and she said it just came to her.

The hat and holly made the appearance at Stretch's into a Christmassy occasion. Maybe a dozen kids and their parents were already waiting when Plunk, Darlene, and Eddie arrived. Stretch had put up posters advertising when Tail Man would be there. Plunk posed for pictures while Darlene set up pin-the-tail-on-the-gecko. By the end of the four hours there were so many holes in the thing that she had to laminate a whole new one at work the next week. Stretch being a smart guy had good prizes, Cowboys and Mavericks and Rangers sweatshirts and some passes to the movies. Kids kept showing up, so Eddie had his hands full keeping the lines orderly. There were too many kids to do the tail-making game, Darlene said she wouldn't have known how many garbage sacks and magic markers to bring anyway. Her question-and-answer session didn't go so well, the kids just wanted to touch the tail and get their pictures taken with Tail Man. While Plunk never allowed anybody else to put on his tail, he didn't mind letting one kid after another try on the Santa Gecko hat. Stretch hired a photographer to take all the pictures with Tail Man. If a kid's parents bought or leased or even test-drove a car that day, they got a complimentary 16x20 print attractively framed.

At 2 p.m. Stretch asked if they could stay another hour because it was going so well. Darlene pulled him aside and a minute later told Plunk okay, they would. Stretch was kicking in an extra two hundred, that made seven twenty-five for the day. It was so much money Darlene didn't even blink when Plunk said he wanted to give Eddie fifty right off the top.

Before they left Stretch booked another Tail Man appearance for the first Saturday in February, when he said people would be over the shock of Christmas bills and ready to think about new cars again. Darlene told him it would be six hundred for four hours, not five twenty-five, which had been an introductory rate, and Stretch said fine.

"You're really getting the business part down," Eddie said to Darlene on the drive back to Crowley.

"You kept the kids in line pretty well," Darlene responded. It sounded like a grudging compliment to Plunk, but at least she was making the effort.

"I gave out almost the last of the business cards," she added. "I think I've got enough for the birthday party tomorrow afternoon in Westlake, but we'll need more for the one Wednesday night in Waxahachie."

"I could get 'em for you after work on Monday," Eddie offered. "There's this quick print shop right across from the plant."

Tail Man appeared at eight different kids' parties over the next three weeks before Christmas. They all went pretty well, Plunk thought. The tail of course was a hit, the hat got lots of comments, and at each one there were parents wanting cards so they could book Tail Man for their kids too. Darlene once or twice said she was worried because she was seeing some of the same kids at several of the parties. She didn't want them to get bored with Tail Man like they had with Too-Fun Tex and his balloon animals.

"We'll think of some new gecko games for after the holidays," she said. "Maybe we could even buy a couple real leopard geckos, find a way to make them race each other or something."

Plunk let Darlene worry about that stuff. He just wanted to enjoy all the Tail Man attention, not to mention the money. Plunk never had any money before beyond what he scraped together for rent and food, gas and beer, and TV streaming bills. The six hundred extra for Mom's care every month had scared him, it seemed like so much. But after the first couple Tail Man appearances at December parties he was able to give Mrs. Jance at Pleasant Valley payment in advance for January and February, he'd paid for December already. When he did a couple more parties by the middle of the month, those plus his share of the seven twenty-five from Stretch totaled another thousand bucks. He got the bank to give it to him in hundred dollar bills, and sometimes he'd fan them out looking at all the Ben Franklin faces. Who'd ever have guessed? Keep this up, and sometime pretty soon, summer at the latest, Plunk thought he'd actually be able to afford something he'd wanted for so long but never thought he'd get—not a shiny new Ford 150, that was still too expensive, but surely a gun, and not just any ordinary handgun. Plunk had in mind nothing less than an AK-47 or AR-15, the ones that libs were trying to make illegal and that every real man in Texas wanted to own. Even though he sucked at using computers, Plunk managed to look up how much used ones cost on his computer at work—he knew Darlene would try to talk him out of it, women were like that. It seemed like ten thousand dollars would get him a fine weapon, and even though just a few months ago ten thousand might as well be a million, now Plunk just might be able to pull it off if the Tail Man business kept booming like it was. Plunk had no real idea what he'd do with the gun after acquiring it. For now, he just loved the idea of having it.

Meanwhile, he still had his day job. Austin always closed down Campbell Bolt & Screw for the last two weeks of the year because all the construction companies shut off operations for the holidays. If nobody was building or remodeling, there wasn't anybody to sell to. Of course, Austin didn't pay salaries during the shutdown, which meant except for himself and Kevin and Broc, everybody else—meaning Jessika, Red, Larry B., and Plunk—had to end their years short of dough. Plunk was pleased he wouldn't be starting the New Year broke thanks to Tail Man, but he still thought Austin could be a little more considerate of the low-end employees. He also still wasn't sure what Austin wanted to talk to him about after the holidays.

Austin always put on a company Christmas party at noon on the day they closed down for the year. He'd have Jessika get in a lunch of barbecue or pizza. It was the only time of the year he'd allow people to have wine or beer on the premises. Jessika would put up a little Christmas tree, and while everyone was eating Austin'd call them into his office one at a time. First he'd say something about thanks for all the hard work. Then some years he'd hand out envelopes with small checks inside, a hundred bucks or something like that, but more often baskets of cheese and sausage that everybody knew he got at a big discount from a company his sister managed. Everybody but Kevin and Broc would chip in to buy Austin something, a sweater or new golf shoes. The other two, being the boss's asshole buddies, got big Christmas bonuses and bought him their own expensive gifts in return.

So at this year's party Austin served barbecue, pretty nice brisket but dry tasteless ribs, and after a while he went into his office and called Red to come in. They all watched to see what Red would come out carrying, an envelope, which was what they hoped for, or a food basket, which they expected. Maybe two minutes later—Austin never took very long with this thank-you stuff—Red came back out and sure enough he had the basket.

Then Larry B. got called in, and the rest of them munched barbecue kind of grimly, because it was a gift basket year and nobody got to go home until everyone had their session with Austin. After Larry B., Plunk figured he'd get called but Austin wanted Jessika instead.

His turn now, Plunk thought, but Austin called Kevin and then Broc. Kevin came out with an envelope but Broc had the food basket. He looked really pissed.

"You, Plunk," Austin said. He went in and instead of handing him a basket Austin said to sit down.

"Going to make a change next year," Austin said, and Plunk's stomach lurched, he couldn't help it. Even though Austin had hinted at some kind of promotion when they spoke right after the golf tournament, he was always changing his mind about things. Plunk could imagine what was coming next. Business was bad, somebody had to be let go, sorry.

But Austin had in mind something different. Sometime right after the New Year Broc was going to seek new opportunities, he explained. That was because Broc really didn't see Campbell Bolt & Screw as a collective effort, everybody doing everything they could to benefit the whole team.

"I want you to consider taking over Broc's accounts after he leaves in a month or whatever," Austin said. "Makes a lot of sense. You call on the people who make large orders, and word'll get around with the big boy customers that Tail Man is part of our company. Maybe you can put on the tail, go to their company parties if they ask, or do stuff for their kids on their birthdays. They buy from Campbell Bolt & Screw, they get preferred access to Tail Man."

Plunk wondered what Darlene would think.

"Better money guaranteed, Plunk," Austin continued. "Broc gets eight-fifty a week draw plus 5 percent, and of course that's 5 percent of a lot bigger orders than you get from your little guy customers. You'll think about it these next two weeks, right?"

Mind whirling, Plunk said he would.

"Great," Austin said. "Meanwhile, Merry Christmas." He handed Plunk an envelope. Plunk waited to open it until the party was over and he was in his car. The check inside was for two thousand dollars.

40.

On Christmas Eve Plunk was Tail Man for the residents at Pleasant Valley. Mrs. Jance asked if he would. She reminded him they always had their big holiday gathering the night of the twenty-fourth because it was hard for people to come visit on Christmas morning, church and so forth. And of course most of the staff wanted to spend Christmas with their families.

It was storming like a mother, so Plunk, Darlene, and Eddie drove to Pleasant Valley instead of walking. Plunk didn't want rain getting on his tail. When they got there they found all the old folks and their visitors herded into the dining room again. There wasn't a turkey dinner on the tables like at Thanksgiving, just plates of store-bought holiday cookies, along with big bowls of orange-colored punch that nobody was drinking. The Christmas tree in the corner was big and glistened with all kinds of lights. Plunk spotted Mom sitting off to the side with other people from the constant care ward. Darlene whispered to him not to worry, she'd go sit with her, just put on the costume.

Plunk went into a room to change. He put on the leopard-spotted Santa Gecko hat at a jaunty angle and cinched the tail on tight. He knew from visiting Mom there on past Christmas Eves that each resident got some little gift from the staff. Mrs. Jance wanted Tail Man to hand them out this year.

So he did, and it was fun. Eddie got most of the old folks lined up and they came one by one to where Plunk stood by the tree. There was a big gift bag there and Plunk would reach down into it for the presents. All of them were the same, this year everybody was getting mittens, a silly gift in Plunk's opinion because how many of these people ever went outside in the cold anymore? But they seemed to like the idea of getting any present at all. Plunk really got into it until the last residents were brought over for their turns. They were the ones from constant care. Their expressions were dull and though they reached mechanically to take their gifts they just sort of held them afterward until staffers took off the wrapping paper for them.

Mom went last of all. When Plunk was growing up she'd been one of those nuts about Christmas, wanting to decorate the house as soon as Thanksgiving was over. She'd put out a plastic manger scene and tack up stockings, these really red socks she'd bought at the Dollar Store, and wrap the three-foot artificial tree with construction paper chains Plunk made in elementary school.

But now she just stood there in front of him, eyes as blank as all the other constant care zombies. Darlene, who'd guided her over to Plunk, said, "Your son has a present for you, Mrs. Landy." Mom didn't react until Plunk held out the package. She took it and then just stood there like she was waiting for somebody to tell her what to do next.

Plunk couldn't help it. He started to cry. Not woman sobbing, but tears anyway while his throat ached and seemed to close up completely. Darlene was nice enough to act like she didn't notice. She gently took the package from Mom, opened it and showed her the mittens. Then she took Mom back to her room.

After he changed back to his regular clothes Plunk went to wish Mom a Merry Christmas. He was ashamed of crying and wished he could have kept the tail on longer for comfort's sake. He was carrying it under one arm but it wasn't the same. When he got to the room he saw that Darlene already had Mom in bed, the covers pulled up to her chin.

"She's tired," Darlene whispered. "That's why she was kind of slow out there. Look, she's already asleep. When she wakes up tomorrow she'll be fine."

Plunk knew that wasn't really true, Mom was never going to be fine again. She was never going to understand that her son had become the most famous man in Crowley. She would have been so proud.

"Merry Christmas, Mom," Plunk said. He leaned over to kiss her cheek. Her breath smelled like medicine. Darlene went over and kissed Mom too, a nice gesture Plunk really appreciated.

They were delayed in leaving because they couldn't find Eddie. Plunk realized he hadn't seen the butthead since he'd gotten the residents in line to get their gifts. He asked Darlene if she thought Eddie might have gotten bored and headed home, and Darlene said who knew but the two of them should just go on anyway.

"It's time for our Christmas," she said. "If he gets left behind he can find his own way."

But Plunk insisted that they look around for Eddie, and they finally found him in the staff's break room cuddling on a couch with a woman Plunk recognized as the one who handed residents their pills at mealtimes. Eddie introduced her as Kendra.

"I got to go with them, but I'm gonna call you tomorrow, wish you Merry Christmas," he promised her. For some reason Kendra seemed pleased to hear it.

"She wants Tail Man to do her daughter's birthday party, but I don't think she can afford three hundred," Eddie said as they drove away. "That's how we got to talking, she asked what we charged. You think I can maybe tell her it would be for less or even free?"

"No freebies," Darlene said sharply.

"The one tonight was," Eddie said.

"It was for Plunk's mother. You're not his mother."

"We'll talk about it later," Plunk said. "Christmas Eve. Let's everybody act like it's joy to the world."

Back at the apartments Darlene told Plunk to give her a minute and then come over. He went back to his own apartment and got paper towels to dry off the tail, drops of rain water probably wouldn't hurt vinyl but there was no sense taking chances. There weren't any decorations up in his place. Darlene's apartment was decorated enough for both of them. Part of Plunk wished he could just strap the tail back on, get a beer and watch ESPN. There was a Mavericks basketball game on. But he had obligations to Darlene, she wanted him to come over. So he dried off the tail, then reached under the bed to get Darlene's present. He'd done his best to wrap it up fancy but he'd never been any good at that, so the brightly colored paper was wrinkled in places and Scotch tape stuck the torn parts together.

Darlene's apartment was a freakin' Christmas wonderland, big tree decorated with the kind of delicate fragile-looking ornaments lots of women liked, Santa figurines on every flat surface, holiday music playing in the background.

"I've got eggnog," she said, and served Plunk a cup of syrupy crud. She started telling him the history of eggnog, Darlene had this endless supply of information about things no regular person would care about. But he acted interested. They were a couple after all, though they were still working out some of the details. Since all the stuff at Thanksgiving they'd had sex maybe five or six more times—okay, two. Otherwise they kissed a lot but stopped whenever she said, which was most of the time. Plunk felt like this was his punishment for Suzette. His mistake with her gave Darlene extra girlfriend power where sex was concerned. Plunk had no idea how long that was supposed to last. He wasn't going to ask, though—the last thing he wanted was to talk about Suzette again.

Darlene rattled on some more about eggnog, which she said once upon a time used to have meat juice in it. Plunk took a couple polite sips of his and then put the cup down on the coffee table by the computer. When Darlene paused for breath he said, "Not working on the book tonight?" in hopes it would get her off the eggnog subject.

"Not tonight or tomorrow either," Darlene said. "It's our first

Christmas together."

"I still feel bad you aren't with your parents," Plunk said. "Your sister went back down there."

"No more holidays apart," Darlene said firmly, and Plunk of course knew why.

After a while Darlene pretended she'd just noticed the badly wrapped package Plunk brought along.

"Is that for me?" she asked. When he nodded she said she had something for him, too. She went into her bedroom and came out with two things, a wrapped package and an envelope.

"We always used to open presents on Christmas morning," she told Plunk. "Daddy was strict about it."

"We can wait," Plunk said. "Doesn't make any difference. If you like doing it Christmas morning, okay."

"I want us to make our own traditions," Darlene said. "Presents on Christmas Eve is fine if that's the way we want to do it."

She handed Plunk the package and envelope, but he grabbed her present and said, "You first." Darlene took it, exclaiming over the size and weight of the rectangular gift.

"Sorry about the wrapping," Plunk said.

Darlene ripped the paper off, then said in a stunned voice, "You bought me a new laptop?"

"Girl at Best Buy said Dells were good," Plunk said. "This one's supposed to be extra fast or something. I thought you could use it to work on your book even if you were visiting your folks."

"It must have cost so much," said Darlene.

"Well, that's thanks to Tail Man," Plunk said. Actually he'd used Austin's big Christmas bonus, which he hadn't told Darlene about yet. That, and the pending promotion. He still wasn't sure how she'd feel about Tail Man doing stuff as part of his job at Campbell Bolt & Screw.

"You're awesome," Darlene said. She leaned over and kissed him. Then she pulled back, clapped her hands like a little kid and said, "Your turn. Open yours."

The package turned out to be a framed copy of the Tail Man golf picture in the Dallas paper.

"I called them and bought it from their photo department," Darlene said.

"I like it a lot," Plunk said, and he did.

"But your main present's in the envelope," said Darlene.

Plunk opened it, thinking it sure was a Christmas for envelope-getting. But there wasn't a check in this one. Instead, Darlene got Plunk a hundred dollar gift certificate at a bookstore.

"I thought you could use part of it for Dr. Nice's new book about goals," she said. "You're just out of the habit of reading. If you start doing it again you'll love it."

"Huh," was all Plunk could manage.

Darlene talked about how publishers often waited to put out self-help books like Dr. Nice's until after New Year's because that was when people took stock of their lives and decided to live differently. During Christmas they were too caught up in holiday celebrating. Plunk pretended to listen. When Darlene showed no signs of stopping he said, "Okay, that's great." He kissed her, she kissed him back, and she took him into her bedroom.

"You got me a laptop," Darlene mused as they lay there afterward. "I can't believe it."

"And you got me books," Plunk said. "I can't believe it either."

They wished each other Merry Christmas and for the first time Plunk spent the whole night at her place.

41.

Eddie and Kendra turned into a couple. Not a week into the New Year Eddie asked if he could start bringing her along on Tail Man appearances. Plunk didn't see why not but Darlene said he had to tell Eddie no, there wouldn't be anything for Kendra to do except get in the way. Plunk didn't tell him that last part. He said there wasn't room in the Ranger, what with them and Darlene and the tail.

So sometimes Eddie started not coming, because most Tail Man jobs were on weekends and that was when Kendra was off work and had time to do things with him and her seven-year-old daughter. He sort of apologized to Plunk for not being available as much, and Plunk told him not to sweat it. Hell, Plunk himself was scheduled out the ass, usually some Tail Man thing every Saturday and Sunday afternoon, he wasn't catching any of the NFL playoff games. You always had to give up something to get something better, Plunk figured, and maybe not much beat pro football on TV but wearing the tail and getting paid for it did.

If he didn't see Eddie as much, suddenly he didn't see Red and Larry B. hardly at all except at work. It had always been Plunk left behind when other guys got girlfriends or busy with something and couldn't come over anymore to watch sports on TV. Now he was the busy one with Darlene and Tail Man stuff. Red and Larry B. understood. They bought a widescreen TV and started watching games at their own apartment. They invited Eddie to come over but he was usually tied up with Kendra and her daughter.

The couple times Plunk was able to have him over for TV games and beer, Eddie ignored the football to go on and on about Kendra, he thought he might marry her. He was worried about her kid, he hadn't been a father before, but maybe he could do it.

"The other two I married didn't have kids," he said.

Plunk about spit out his mouthful of beer.

"You been married twice?" he said. "I didn't know that."

"You never asked," Eddie replied.

Plunk asked Eddie as a special favor not to mention marriage anywhere near Darlene. He was starting to worry she had it in mind.

Though she hadn't come right out and said so, Darlene was starting to use the words "we" and "us" much more than necessary. It made Plunk uncomfortable. He'd been married once and it hadn't worked out. Maybe it had been fifteen years ago but he wasn't sure he was ready to try it again. Not that he didn't like Darlene a lot. Maybe he loved her. He didn't want to analyze how he felt, he just wanted to enjoy feeling it without any extra pressure.

Darlene also began talking about them getting a bigger place together. She still lived in her one-bedroom and he lived in his across the parking lot. He liked the arrangement because when he was alone in his place he wore the tail when he wanted, which was most of the time. He didn't tell Darlene that. He told her the separate apartments were good so she could have a quiet place to work on her book.

Darlene tried twice to bring her new laptop over and write at Plunk's. But when Plunk watched ballgames or Fox on TV he tended to yell at the screen a lot, and this distracted Darlene. After the second time, she said if they had a bigger apartment Plunk could watch football in the living room and she would write in the spare bedroom.

For now they were too busy with Tail Man stuff to even think of apartment-hunting. Most weekends for the rest of January and February were booked solid with kids' birthday parties. Sometimes they had one on a week night. Darlene thought if the February appearance at Stretch's car lot went well she could start drumming up more of what she called "big ticket" jobs, six hundred for three or four hours instead of the three hundred for two hours that they charged for the kids' parties. And she thought if demand kept up like it was they'd bump the party price to three fifty or even four hundred, where else would those parents find entertainment as good as Tail Man?

By the middle of January word got around Campbell Bolt & Screw that Broc was leaving. Jessika, Red, and Larry B. speculated how Austin might replace him. Jessika said that Austin's wife had a brother who was looking for work. When she told Red and Larry B. this, she winked at Plunk behind their backs because she knew exactly what was going to happen. Red and Larry B. said Austin should promote from within but wouldn't.

Plunk didn't say anything, but he could have told the two of them a lot. Austin had pulled him aside to say Broc was looking for a sales job in Dallas or San Antonio but it was tough going. So Austin told Broc that he had a job through February and maybe March if necessary but no longer than that.

"Even though he wasn't loyal to me I'm going to be loyal to him," Austin said. "Soon as he's gone, you're in, okay?"

It was fine with Plunk. The extra income from being Tail Man already had him feeling rich. He was able to pay Mom's constant care bills even without his promotion at work. He could wait until March, no problem.

Plunk turned forty-three on January ninth, and since he hadn't used his book store gift certificate yet, Darlene dragged him down there and insisted he use part of it to buy *Set Them, Get Them: Why Goals Are Better Than Dreams, and How To Achieve Them*, the new book by Dr. Jennifer Nice that had just come out. She told him reading it would probably change his life, and he told her he didn't want anything in his life changed, it was already just the way he wanted. Darlene somehow took that as a compliment and gave him a huge hug. Then she insisted on going to the Chinese place for his birthday dinner. At least they had sex when they got home, so Plunk did get something he wanted for his birthday.

A couple days later an assistant in Congressman Rod Argent's office called Darlene to ask if Tail Man would participate in something. Tail Man was just amazingly popular with area children, the assistant said. The congressman wanted publicity for a new bill he was proposing to fund more playgrounds for kids. On the afternoon of the nineteenth he'd invited the media to a playground in Fort Worth that represented the kind he wanted more of. It had a basketball court and swings and climbing bars and places for mothers to sit while they watched over their kids. He'd like Tail Man to come along. The congressman and Tail Man would pose together for pictures, and maybe Tail Man could say something about the importance of safe places for kids to get good healthy exercise. Could Tail Man be there? Darlene said yes.

"It's great free publicity," she told Plunk. He wondered how it could be free when it would actually cost them money—the nineteenth was a Saturday and Darlene would have to cancel a Tail Man party appearance so they could do the thing with the congressman. But he went along because where business was concerned she'd convinced him she knew what she was doing.

It snowed on the nineteenth, which was odd for North Texas but not altogether unknown. They had to clear the stuff off the basketball court so Plunk and Congressman Argent could play on it while the photographers took pictures. The congressman had a pretty nice jump shot, but he also had an advantage because it was tough for Plunk to guard him while wearing the tail. Then the congressman talked into the microphones for a long time. When it was Plunk's turn he kept it short and sweet, just like he and Darlene had rehearsed. She'd explained to him about sound bites.

"We need to bust our tails to get more playgrounds for our kids," was all he said, and the people standing around watching clapped louder for him than they had for the Congressman. That night it was on all the TV news shows, and there was a photo and story in the next morning's Fort Worth paper. Darlene was right, you couldn't buy that kind of publicity.

42.

Monday night Darlene's cell phone buzzed while Plunk was over at her place. They'd just had dinner that included more strange salad. Darlene didn't think there were enough vegetables in his diet.

Now he ate dinner at Darlene's on Monday and Wednesday nights. Tuesdays and Thursdays she had her writing class at the junior college. Friday nights he took her out to eat if they didn't have a Tail Man job. Weekends were Tail Man plus the Sunday Mom visit and maybe if he was lucky Plunk got to watch one football game with Eddie. All this combined into a new routine for him to get used to, but he liked routine.

Part of the Monday and Wednesday deal was that after dinner they'd sit a little while, then Plunk would say Darlene needed to work on her book. She'd agree, and after a kiss or two he'd go back to his place, strap on the tail, and watch ESPN. Tuesdays and Thursdays since she was in class he microwaved his own meal and watched TV with the tail on. He didn't see her when she got home from class because she still had to write her two pages on the book, obeying Dr. Nice's rules about achieving goals. Friday nights he didn't get to wear the tail because that was when Darlene let him stay over. He made up for it by getting to wear it a lot on the weekends at the Tail Man parties and appearances. If somebody asked him to choose between Darlene and the tail he wouldn't have known what to do, but nobody was asking so he had the best of both.

On Monday night he was deciding it was about time to say okay, you need to get back to your book, when Darlene's cell phone rang. She picked it up and Plunk listened to her half of the conversation.

"Oh? What can we do for you?"

"Really? On Friday? Of course."

"He can talk about that."

"Who else is on? Oh, I see. Sure."

"Right, five-thirty. No, it's not too early."

"I know about your new format. I watch every morning. I like it a lot."

"I understand, five minutes. The first person gets longer. No, that's okay. That's fine. We're happy just to be invited."

"Will you give the guard my name, too? I always come with him."

"Thank you so much for calling. This is very exciting. We'll be there."

Darlene closed the cell phone and said, "That was the assistant producer from *Daybreak Metroplex*. They want you on this Friday."

"More of that film stuff they shot with me and the congressman on the basketball court?" Plunk asked sourly. "'Cause I know I'm not great but I can play better than that. The tail slowed me down."

"No," said Darlene. "This time they want you in their studio in Dallas as a real guest, not just a tape of something. You sit in a chair and they interview you."

"What about?"

"The guy, his name is Tony, the assistant producer, said they liked what you said about busting tails for kids. They just want to talk to you about being Tail Man, how you started doing that, and also what he said was your commitment to youth."

"I guess," Plunk said. "If that's what you call it."

"Of course you're committed to youth," Darlene said. "From the beginning, even before Tail Man. All the times you dressed up and went out on Thanksgiving. You can tell about that."

"I could talk about Warrior Mascot," Plunk said. "I still can't believe those buttheads changed it to Tornadoes."

"That might be too long ago," Darlene cautioned. "Better just stick to Tail Man and maybe a little before."

She put off working on her book for another hour to tell Plunk more about the great opportunity this was going to be. *Daybreak Metroplex* was the most-watched morning show on local TV, she reminded him, and cohost Bonnie Woody had been voted most popular TV personality two years in a row in the Dallas paper's reader poll. A few weeks ago they'd changed the way they did the show, it was different since Plunk watched it that one time after the golf event. Now they still had traffic and weather reports, but the last half hour Bonnie and cohost Tim Carter sat with a couple studio guests to chat like they did on the big network morning shows and also on the nighttime shows with big name stars as guests.

"Who else is gonna be there besides me?" Plunk asked.

"Tony said they were still lining up guests," Darlene said. "Usually a day or two before they know exactly and start mentioning who's going to be on. We'll watch every morning this week so you can see how it works, and probably by Wednesday they'll be saying who's on Friday besides you. This is amazing. Everybody sees the show. You need to mention how to get in touch with us for appearances. I bet we get a hundred Tail Man calls afterward. It's a big, big step."

Darlene came to Plunk's just before six the next morning so they could watch on his widescreen. The first ninety minutes of *Daybreak*

Metroplex was exactly like it had been, Bonnie and the Tim guy joking back and forth plus lots of breaks for traffic and weather reports. There were quickie interviews with unimportant people, somebody from Meals on Wheels looking for volunteer drivers and somebody else from the highway department telling the audience how to drive safely on icy roads.

But just after 7:30 the show switched to Bonnie and Tim sitting on easy chairs with a couch between them. Tim said they were so lucky, a talented actress who'd first become famous on *NCIS* was in Fort Worth to play Liza Doolittle in *My Fair Lady* at Bass Hall. Bonnie said she'd loved her on that series and let's welcome her. The actress sort of swept out and as soon as she sat down said it was so exciting to be in Texas, where she'd wanted to perform for so long.

"This is always where they have the most important guest," Darlene explained. "They'll talk to him or her for the whole segment, I think it's like eight or ten minutes. Then after commercials they bring on another one who gets a five minute interview. That's going to be you on Friday. Then there's a final five minutes or so when both main guests are talking with the hosts."

"I'm not the most important one?" Plunk asked, sort of kidding.

"It's still great publicity," Darlene said. "You're going to overshadow whoever the first guest is anyway. Tail Man is very charismatic."

The actress told Bonnie and Tim about the many movie opportunities she turned down to come to Bass Hall and do *My Fair Lady*. Bonnie asked her for some makeup tips. Tim said he'd had her poster on his bedroom wall all through college.

"This is boring," Plunk said. Darlene shushed him.

The less important second guest was a nutritionist who'd written a book about losing weight while eating all the chocolate you wanted.

"Everybody says sugar is bad, but you need some every day for energy," he explained. "You have enough energy, you stay on your feet doing things, and that gets the weight off."

Bonnie asked why the sugar had to come from chocolate, why not get your energy from natural sugars like in fruit? The guy told her that not everybody liked fruit, but he'd never met anyone who didn't like chocolate. Diets only worked long-term when people could still eat things they loved.

During the final five minutes the actress and nutritionist talked about how much chocolate she should eat just before going on stage, and Bonnie jumped in once to say she wished somebody would invent a diet that let you eat all the Toll House cookies you wanted, that was her favorite food.

When the show was over Darlene asked Plunk what he thought.

"I think I want a chocolate bar," he said.

43.

When Plunk finally got to work Tuesday morning, he explained to Jessika why he was late. She thought it was exciting and started telling everybody else.

"We'll all have to get in late on Friday, 'cause we'll be watching you on the show," Jessika said. "That Tim guy on it is just so cute."

"Don't you think he kind of looks like me?" Red asked her.

"Not even a little," Jessika said. "Your nose is too big."

That got them fun-arguing over the size of Red's nose, which Plunk thought was getting off the more important topic of him being on *Daybreak Metroplex*.

"Guy told Darlene they want me to talk about my commitment to kids," Plunk said. "I guess I'll tell them about the birthday parties and everything."

Austin came out of his office just then with a list of customers he told Jessika to call. They were behind making their order payments and he wanted them reminded.

"Who wants you to talk about what?" he asked Plunk. Before Plunk could answer Jessika did it for him, telling Austin about *Daybreak Metroplex* on Friday and how everybody would have to come in late because of course they all had to watch Plunk on it. Austin frowned and told Plunk to come into his office for a minute.

"I know I'll probably miss a little work time Friday," Plunk said. "If you want to dock me for it."

"Not at all," said Austin. He went into a cupboard and got out his putter and the metal glass and some golf balls, plus another putter. Plunk never realized he had two in there. Austin set the glass on the floor across the room and started putting balls toward it. He motioned for Plunk to do the same.

"I like to do this while I think," he said. "Relaxes me for some reason." Plunk understood because he felt the same way about wearing the tail. He putted a few balls toward the glass himself, but they didn't come very close.

"This TV thing Friday," Austin said. "I don't watch the show myself but Leanne does. The second half. She puts it on while she fixes breakfast, gets Timmy ready for school."

"Sure," said Plunk, wondering where this was going.

"Popular show," Austin said. "You go on it, lots of people will see you. An opportunity."

"Darlene thinks we'll get a hundred Tail Man calls," Plunk said.

"Right. But I was thinking about another kind of opportunity."

Austin leaned his putter against a cabinet and sat down behind his desk. Plunk put aside his putter and sat down too.

"Free advertising's a great thing," Austin said. "Not many chances like this. I was thinking about your Tail Man outfit. We put 'Campbell Bolt & Screw' on it where it's easy to see, also our phone number. You go on that show, camera's on you, and there's our company name and contact information. Better than any billboard."

"I don't know," Plunk said. "I mean, where on me would it be? And the TV people might not let me."

"Not their choice," Austin said. "People do it all the time. You watch golf on TV, every one of them including Tiger Woods has logos and company names on his hats and shirts and golf bags. That's what they call precedent. We'll just do it, you show up, they're not going to tell you to take the costume off and go home."

"But where would the name and everything go?" Plunk asked. He knew Darlene wouldn't like this. He wished she were there to talk to Austin about it instead of it having to be him.

"The tail would be best," Austin suggested, and Plunk couldn't help himself, boss or not. He shook his head violently from side to side. Austin got it.

"Okay, then," he said. "What about a new sweatshirt. One you wore to Timmy's party looked like shit anyway, all faded. We get you a new one, top of the line from Target or wherever. Have the name and number put on it, you wear it on the show. Simple."

"I'm on the show Friday," Plunk said. "Can they make one that quick?"

"Jessika'll find a place," Austin said. "I'll get her on it right away." He leaned back in his chair. "See, this is what I mean by everybody helping the team. I got plans for this place. No reason with the right breaks we can't be one of the big guys, too. You as Tail Man in on all of it. You know I'll take care of you, aren't I proving it?"

"You are," Plunk said. "Promoting me and all."

"No later than March, I promise," Austin said. "I'll even call some people in San Antonio myself, tell them how Broc's so great. We might get you a desk in here with me, be a little quieter for you."

"I'm okay out with the other guys," Plunk said. "In fact I need to get out there now, see who I should call on today. But tomorrow and Thursday I might be a little late again, Darlene wants us to watch the show so we can decide what I should say. And Friday I'm on it, so late again."

"Not a problem," Austin assured him. "Send in Jessika, will you? We got to get her on the sweatshirt thing."

Wednesday morning Plunk and Darlene watched *Daybreak Metroplex* again. She had a pad and pen and took notes during the last part when Bonnie and Tim interviewed the head Dallas Mavericks cheerleader in the star segment and the director of the Mid-Cities YWCA in the secondary five-minute slot.

"Why doesn't the star go last?" Plunk asked.

"I think it's because the longer the star is on, the longer people stay around to watch the whole show," Darlene said. "And if you put the biggest name on last, some people might feel like they can't wait that long before they leave for work."

The final part had the cheerleader and YWCA director agreeing how self-image was critical to young women. The cheerleader suggested cheerleading and the YWCA director thought community volunteerism was good.

"They want the two guests to interact at the end," Darlene said. "We need to remember that on Friday, think of what you should say to whoever the other person is. They're announcing tomorrow's guests now and maybe Friday's too."

The camera pulled tight on Bonnie as she said, "Tomorrow on *Daybreak Metroplex* we'll visit with the Dallas mayor himself, the honorable Hector Melara. He's just grown a great beard and I think he looks so handsome. Mayor Melara's going to tell us about an exciting new city program to increase use of libraries."

"And we'll also meet Curly Bourgeois, the Texas Rangers' new conditioning coach," Tim said as the camera switched to him. "He's going to show us some simple exercises that will increase joint flexibility, and maybe explain why the Rangers didn't have sufficiently flexible joints to make the playoffs last season."

"Don't you dare ask him that!" Bonnie said, giggling. "Then on Friday we're going to have maybe our biggest show so far this year. You certainly won't want to miss the *tail end* of the program."

"I bet I know who you mean, Bonnie. And it's going to be?"

"The one and only Tail Man himself, my old golfing buddy. He'll talk to us about the importance of children getting lots of exercise, and maybe about how he got that tail in the first place."

"Be sure to mention the Tail Man Juniors coming to Quality Costumes," Darlene instructed. "Get them that publicity."

Plunk thought this might be the time to tell Darlene about the sweatshirt and Campbell Bolt & Screw getting some publicity too, but as he started to speak Darlene held up her hand to shush him.

"Here's the name of the other guest," she said.

Bonnie clapped her hands and said, "We're so thrilled that besides Tail Man on Friday, we'll be joined by perhaps America's most popular author of books that explain how to change your life for the better."

"She's sold about a bazillion copies of all of them," Tim added.

"Right," Bonnie said. "Friday on *Daybreak Metroplex*, here to tell us all about her latest number one bestseller will be the famous author of *Set Them, Get Them: Why Goals Are Better Than Dreams and How to Achieve Them*, none other than the most popular life advice-giver ever, Dr. Jennifer Nice."

Darlene put down the pad and pen.

"Oh, my god," she said. "Oh, my god."

44.

If Plunk thought Darlene talked a lot before, she probably came close to a world record Friday morning on the way to the *Daybreak Metroplex* studio. It was in downtown Dallas, where Plunk didn't go a lot. It was hard to see the street signs because it was not much after five and still pitch dark. Plunk wanted Darlene to read the signs for him, they were supposed to turn into the studio parking lot off Ross Avenue, but she was yapping nonstop about Dr. Nice and what she would say when she met her.

"I mean, so many people must tell her how she's changed their lives. I want to say something original," Darlene said.

"'Nice to meet you' would work pretty swell," Plunk said. "What was that street we just passed?"

"I didn't look. But it's got to be around here somewhere. I should tell her about my book, don't you think? Maybe she'll ask to read it."

"Maybe," Plunk said. "Look, you might not get to talk to her at all. I don't want you to get disappointed."

"I *will* meet Dr. Nice," said Darlene. "Don't you worry about that."

Plunk was going to say that he wasn't worrying about it, she was, but then kind of by accident he saw a sign for Ross and made the turn. Up ahead he saw a chain link fence with an open gate, and a big building behind it. Plunk drove through the gate. There was a little guardhouse where he had to stop. The guy in it was shivering.

Plunk rolled down his window and said, "Cold this morning."

Darlene leaned across him and told the guard, "This is Tail Man, a guest on *Daybreak Metroplex*."

"Yeah," said the guard. "Park there by the door with the light over it."

"Has Dr. Jennifer Nice gotten here yet?" Darlene asked.

"Don't know her, but if she's a guest too she hasn't come through," the guy said. He pulled back into his little guardhouse and slammed the door shut.

"Tony the assistant producer said just to come in and tell the person at the desk we're here for the show," Darlene said as Plunk parked. "You have to go to makeup and then we're in the Green Room."

"If I'm only on the last part, why do I have to be here so early?" Plunk asked.

"It's the way they do it. Just cooperate. You remember what you're supposed to say?"

"Yeah."

Darlene had rehearsed him all last night. He'd say something about kids and playgrounds, but then it was important to sell Tail Man. That was the word she used, "sell." Tell about getting the tail, the excitement at parties and business appearances. Mention the Tail Man Juniors coming to Quality Costumes. Repeat the Tail Man contact number at least twice, more if possible.

They went inside. After the drive through the dark, the bright lights made Plunk blink. The woman at the desk looked pretty wide awake for five-thirty in the morning. She didn't stare when she saw Plunk was carrying the tail, wrapped up in several towels to protect it from the sleet. He figured she'd probably seen a lot of things if she'd been working there for long.

The woman called Tony, who came to get them. He was young, Plunk figured late twenties, long hair and an earring. Plunk could never understand why a guy would wear an earring. Tony shook hands with Darlene and then with Plunk, whom he called "Mr. Tail Man." Plunk kind of liked it. Tony said they could wait in the Green Room for just a few minutes while the makeup people got set up, and then he'd come take Mr. Tail Man to them. They got to the Green Room by walking past the *Daybreak Metroplex* set or rather two sets, one with a couple desks for Bonnie and Tim and the other with the two easy chairs and couch for the later interview segments. Bonnie and Tim were already at the desks studying notes or something. To be friendly, Plunk yelled, "Hey, Bonnie," and wished he could also wave. He couldn't because he was lugging the tail. Bonnie looked up briefly but didn't say hi back.

"They're going on the air soon, so they have to concentrate," Tony said. "You understand."

Plunk and Darlene sat in the Green Room. There was a coffee maker and some mugs with *Daybreak Metroplex* on the side. Plunk wondered if he could maybe grab one for Jessika at work but decided not to risk it. He got himself coffee and offered to pour some for Darlene, but she said no.

"What if she asks if I brought what I've written so far and I have to say I didn't bring it?" Darlene said. "I guess I could get her address and send it to her."

Plunk thought maybe Darlene should stop worrying so much about Dr. Nice and start making sure he was all right. He was about to go on TV and should be feeling nervous to the point of barfing, though in fact he wasn't nervous at all. It was like this was what he was supposed to be doing, being interviewed on a big important show and everybody in and around Dallas-Fort Worth watching. But it would have been nice for Darlene to worry about him anyway.

Plunk drank his coffee and unwrapped the towels from around the tail. He was wearing the black jeans and tennies. The sweatshirt

Jessika had made up for him was in a paper bag; it had *Campbell Bolt & Screw* on the front and back as well as the office phone number. Darlene still hadn't seen it. He wanted to put on the tail right there in the Green Room, not to calm his nerves because he wasn't nervous but just to have it on, get the good feeling from it. But like grabbing a coffee cup with the *Daybreak Metroplex* logo for Jessika, he thought he better not. For a big TV show, this Green Room wasn't all that big, just some chairs that were worn on the armrests and a TV in the corner, turned on but the screen blue and blank. Kind of disappointing. But the coffee was pretty good.

Tony stuck his head in the door and said, "Makeup in maybe ten minutes. Got a guy talking about a homeless shelter in Fort Worth and some kid who won a singing contest to do ahead of you. The short little vignette segments during the first part of the show. We don't even bring them into the Green Room, they're on and off so fast, not like the major guests."

Plunk liked the sound of "major guest."

"Is Dr. Nice here yet?" Darlene asked.

"Actually, she's not arriving 'til just a little before she goes on," Tony said. "Her publicist called, said they got in late last night from Philadelphia, so they'll show up here around seven, seven-fifteen. We get that sometimes from big name authors on book tour. They've got posses almost, publicist and driver and sometimes even their own makeup person like they're movie stars or something. Go figure."

Just then the picture and sound came on the TV. *Daybreak Metroplex* was on the air. Bonnie and Tim, looking a lot more bright-eyed than they had when Plunk saw them on the set a little earlier, told their audience hi. Bonnie said they were going to have a great show, bestselling self-help author Dr. Jennifer Nice was on and also the very popular Tail Man.

"Now, there's a combination," Tim said. "I wonder if Dr. Nice ever met a man with a tail before."

They bantered a little bit more and switched to the first traffic report, which advised everybody coming into Dallas from the north and east to allow extra time getting to work because there had been a few accidents, nothing major but there were some traffic backups.

Plunk glanced over at Darlene and saw she looked very pale. She wasn't quite hyperventilating but she was breathing hard.

"You okay?" he asked.

Darlene managed a sickly smile.

"It's just so much," she said. "Everything that's happened in a few months. I can't help wondering what's coming next."

"I think it's me on TV and you maybe meeting your hero," Plunk said. "Enjoy it."

"I'm trying," Darlene said. She reached over and held his hand. Her hand was clammy, but Plunk's was warm and dry. He felt great.

They sat there in the Green Room holding hands. Tony came in a couple minutes later and told Plunk they were ready for him in makeup.

"Just got a call from Dr. Nice's publicist," he said. "They're on their way. Should be here any minute."

"Watch the tail for me," Plunk said to Darlene. She didn't even look at him. Instead she pulled a brush out of her purse and began yanking it frantically through her ponytail.

45.

Makeup wasn't too bad. Plunk joshed some with the woman who patted powder on his face.

"The lights burn down on you pretty good out there," she said. "Why they have you on, anyway?"

Plunk told her about Tail Man, and she asked another woman in the room if maybe they should check the tail because this guy here says it's vinyl.

"Just on the outside," Plunk said.

"Vinyl's shiny," she said. "We ought to give it a light dust or something, cut down the glare."

"No makeup on the tail," Plunk said firmly.

He looked at his watch when they told him he was done. Seven fifteen. He hoped Darlene hadn't wet her pants if Dr. Nice showed up while he was gone from the Green Room.

But when Tony took him back Dr. Nice still hadn't arrived, even though she was supposed to be on in about twenty minutes and her publicist had called Tony on his cell twice more to say they were nearly there.

"What if she doesn't get here in time?" Darlene asked Tony.

"They always do," he said. "They just like to cut it to the last possible minute."

Right then a woman came into the Green Room. She told Tony she was Maddy McMillion, Dr. Nice's publicist, and the woman at the desk had said to take Dr. Nice straight into makeup.

"So she's on her way there," Maddy said. "She's supposed to go on in what, ten minutes?"

"About," Tony said.

"All right," said Maddy. "Remember we've been promised two close-ups of the book jacket. And she has to be out of here no later than ten past eight. We've got a flight to LA, she's on Jimmy Fallon tonight. Which we hope the hosts of your show will mention."

"We'll try, but it's another network," Tony said. "They got rules about that."

"This is Dr. Jennifer Nice," Maddy said. "I would think that makes a difference." She turned and walked off in the direction of makeup.

"You see the kind of attitude we get," Tony said to Plunk and Darlene. "I better go to makeup, see if her highness wants anything."

Plunk thought Darlene looked stunned, but it turned out she was impressed.

"To have a publicist like that," she said. "Making everything right for you. When my book comes out I'm going to have one too. I'm sure that the publishing company supplies them, the author doesn't havc to pay."

"Real good," Plunk said. "I guess I better get dressed."

He put on the tail before the sweatshirt, which he finally took out of the paper bag. Distracted as she was by being so near her idol, Darlene still noticed.

"What's that on your shirt?" she demanded.

Plunk looked innocently down.

"Oh, just something Austin wanted," he said. "Hardly anybody's gonna notice."

"You can't wear that," Darlene said. "It distracts from Tail Man. It's disgusting advertising."

"You want me to mention our contact number, and also about the Tail Man Junior thing," Plunk said. "Don't you call that advertising?"

Darlene got a look and Plunk thought she was going to order him not to wear the sweatshirt and wondered what would he do then? Because Darlene was his manager but Austin was his boss. But Darlene never did say whatever she was going to because Dr. Jennifer Nice was led into the Green Room by Tony and her publicist Maddy.

Plunk's first impression was, this is what a star is like, all calm and confident like being on *Daybreak Metroplex* was okay but nothing special.

"Is there coffee, Maddy?" Dr. Nice asked, although there obviously was, the coffeemaker was right there on the table in front of her. Maddy got the coffee and Dr. Nice looked at Plunk and Darlene.

"Well," she said to Plunk. "That's quite a tail you've got there. I can't wait to hear you talk about it on the program." She sipped from the cup Maddy handed her and gave it back. "I think I'd like just a little more creamer in this." Then she turned to Darlene. "Now, tell me who you are."

Plunk had to give it to Darlene, even at this moment the girl was incapable of being struck speechless.

"I'm Darlene Quaverley, Dr. Nice," she said, her voice shaky at first but then picking up steam with every word. "I'm Tail Man's manager, and I know you hear it all the time but I've got to tell you that you've changed my life. All your books, I've learned so much from them."

"How lovely of you to say so," Dr. Nice said. "I could never get tired of hearing something like that." Maddy handed her the coffee cup back, and this time after taking a sip Dr. Nice nodded at her.

"You've inspired me with my novel," Darlene continued even though Plunk could tell Dr. Nice thought her conversation with Darlene was over. "Before I read *Set Them, Get Them* a few months ago, don't worry, I work in a library and we got an advance reader's copy, I didn't steal one from your publisher. I was trying to write a novel and not getting anywhere, doing the same two chapters over and over again. Just dreaming of writing a bestseller."

"Really," said Dr. Nice.

"But like you said in *Set Them, Get Them* I turned it into a step toward a goal instead, writing two pages every night," Darlene said. "Now I'm almost done and I've got the next steps to the goal worked out, getting an agent and getting the book published. Kind of like you do."

"Of course," Dr. Nice said. "Maddy, are we about to go on? Because I need the ladies' room."

"I'm sure there's time," Maddy said.

"We need to get her microphone on," Tony said.

"In just a minute," Maddy told him. "Jen, I looked and the powder room is right there down the hall."

"Well, then," said Dr. Nice. "I'll see you out there," she said to Plunk, and to Darlene, "I'm sure your book will be wonderful. I can't wait to read it."

"I could send you a copy of what I've got now," Darlene said.

"Certainly," Dr. Nice said. "You'll have to do that."

She went down the hall to the bathroom.

"I'll be waiting by the side of the set," Tony said. "To get her mike on."

"She'll be right there," said Maddy.

"You can stay here and watch her on that TV," Tony suggested, but Maddy said she would stand right off-camera in case Jen needed anything.

"Can I stand there too?" Darlene asked Tony.

"Why not?" he said. "Join the parade. Mr. Tail Man, you want to come along? I'll get you all miked and you'll be ready when it's your turn."

"What the heck," Plunk said, and went with them. The tail sloofed behind him on the carpet.

46.

Bonnie smiled widely and said, "What a thrill it is for Tim and me to introduce one of the most famous authors in America. She's taught us how to find true love, how to nurture relationships, and how to do just fine even during those inevitable times when life isn't fair. Now she's got a new book, *Set Them, Get Them: Why Goals Are Better Than Dreams, and How to Achieve Them*. We welcome Dr. Jennifer Nice."

Dr. Nice sat comfortably on the side of the couch nearest Bonnie's chair.

"Thank you, Bonnie," she said. "I'm honored to be a guest on your wonderful show."

"Number one rated morning program in Dallas-Fort Worth in the latest public poll," Tim said. His chair was by the empty end of the couch, where Plunk assumed he'd be sitting. "And Bonnie's been voted the Metroplex's most popular morning TV personality two years in a row."

"Congratulations," said Dr. Nice. "That's quite an achievement. Not just this year, but last year, too."

"You use the word achievement," Bonnie said. "That's a big part of your new book, isn't it?"

"That's called a segue," Darlene whispered to Plunk.

Dr. Nice said that was absolutely true. She'd thought for a long time that most people didn't realize dreams were actually self-destructive, as opposed to goals, which were productive. When people said they had dreams, they meant they had something they yearned to do or be but no idea how to actually make it happen.

"Like a little boy saying he wants to grow up to be a cowboy," Dr. Nice said. "It sounds exciting but he has no idea of how to make it really happen."

Ambition can only be satisfied by setting goals and taking the specific steps required to achieve those goals, she continued. You figured out what you wanted to do, and then you used common sense to determine what steps were necessary. Her own life and career were cases in point. She spent about ten years as a very successful therapist in Scarsdale, New York, helping people with problems. But that didn't satisfy her. She wanted to help many more people than she ever could in private practice.

"But to accomplish that goal, as opposed to dreaming about it, I had to sit down and determine what steps were necessary, and in what order," Dr. Nice said.

"Using common sense," Tim suggested.

"Exactly."

Dr. Nice said she saw how self-help books were very popular, but most of them lectured instead of discussed, never putting things in plain terms every reader could understand. So she went back to school at night to take writing courses, because you can't write books if you haven't trained yourself to be good at expressing things in print.

"That's what I'm doing!" Darlene hissed in Plunk's ear. "This is so inspiring!"

Then Dr. Nice took her next steps. She began writing and submitting articles to magazines and newspapers, "but not those boring professional journals that want you to use big words no one but other therapists can understand. My first few got turned down, but then I had one accepted in *People* and also a guest editorial in the *Washington Post*. They got good responses, especially the editorial in the *Post*, and then I was a guest on *The View* and talked about finding true love as opposed to mythical Romeo and Juliet love. After that broadcast, a publishing company contacted me and asked if I would like to expand what I'd said on that program into a book."

"*Realistic Romance: Using Common Sense to Find Love That Lasts*," Bonnie said. "The rest, of course, is bestselling history."

Dr. Nice modestly admitted it was. She added that this new book was by far her most important yet. Everyone needed to know the crucial difference between dreams and goals.

"A dream is something you want to happen," Dr. Nice said. "A goal is something that you actually make happen by taking a series of steps, each of which brings you closer to achieving the goal. If you do this properly, there's nothing wrong with aiming high. Once you have a goal as opposed to a dream, then the only thing that absolutely guarantees you'll never achieve it is if you stop trying. Otherwise, the potential is always there."

"We can't all become bestselling authors," Bonnie said.

"No, but more of us could," Dr. Nice said. "I did, and here I am on *Daybreak Metroplex* and I go from here to Los Angeles to appear tonight with Jimmy Fallon. I especially recommend my book to those who have achieved limited success at something but still yearn to break into the really big time. You, for instance, Bonnie."

Bonnie looked confused.

"But I'm one of the ones who's achieved my goals," she said.

Dr. Nice shook her head.

"Bonnie, let me guess. When you were a girl you saw someone else on television and thought, 'That's what I want to do, that's who I want to be like.' Am I right?"

"Dana Bash," Bonnie said. "She's so wonderful."

"I'm sure lots of girls who saw her on television felt the same way. But unlike almost all the rest of them you, Bonnie, made it a goal instead of a dream, by starting with the step involving education."

"That's right," Bonnie said. "I majored in RTF at Arizona. I grew up in Scottsdale."

"And since you got out of school what, a dozen years ago, there have been several jobs on TV, I'm sure, each one a step up the ladder."

Bonnie nodded.

"Though my first job was as a weather girl on a small station in Pocatello. From there I got to do early news in Amarillo, then in Syracuse, then cohosting that station's morning show, and finally here on *Daybreak Metroplex*."

"So what step is next, Bonnie?" Dr. Nice asked. "To achieve your goal of becoming the next Dana Bash. Dana is a personal friend of mine. She didn't get featured on CNN by settling for being an intern at NBC, which is what she once was."

"I like my job here at *Daybreak Metroplex* very much," Bonnie said.

"Of course, and viewers must like you back, since you've been voted most popular local TV personality two years in a row."

"Got a couple hundred fewer votes than last year, though," Tim butted in. "I myself moved up from sixteenth to fifth."

Bonnie shot him a nasty look.

"Getting back to your book, Dr. Nice," she said.

"But we are. This is what my book is also about, encouraging the partial achievers not to settle. When people who settle grow old, they inevitably find themselves believing their lives have been wasted, because deep down they know they could have done more. But that takes effort, and also involves risk. They settle because they feel like they're comfortable, safe, where they are. Do you really want to settle, Bonnie? At night, don't you still fall asleep imagining you're a national star on CNN like my dear friend Dana? If emulating Dana is your goal, then the job you have now is just one more step. The month shouldn't go by that you don't send tapes to producers at CNN."

"I love being where I am," Bonnie said. "I don't think I'm settling."

"Then you really need to read my book," said Dr. Nice. "Dana says if she'd had my goals versus dreams advice, she'd have been a big TV star ten years sooner. Bottom line: Dreams aren't real. But goals are achievable, and the higher you set them, the better."

"Dr. Jennifer Nice, author of *Set Them, Get Them: Why Goals Are Better Than Dreams and How To Achieve Them*," Bonnie said, her smile quivering around the corners of her mouth. "And after this break for messages, we return with the tail end of our program."

"The popular Tail Man from Crowley," Tim said. "His real name is Plunk Landy, and he's going to talk about how important it is for kids to exercise, and maybe how he got a tail in the first place. We'll be right back."

The cameras on the set swung aside. Bonnie glared at Dr. Nice, who didn't seem to notice. Instead, she complimented Tim on his jacket.

"Light blue is a good color on you," she said.

"I want to end up on CNN myself," Tim said. "Like Wolf Blitzer. Or else on Fox, like Sean Hannity. The best news guys. I'm trying to move from morning talk to hard news, so I'm going to get your book."

"I know it will be helpful," said Dr. Nice.

Tony said to Plunk, "Time to get you in there." Plunk turned to tell Darlene she should wish him luck. She was staring raptly at Dr. Nice.

"Don't you think she was kind of mean to Bonnie?" Plunk asked.

"No, Dr. Nice is being helpful," said Darlene. "She's saying like she writes in her book that partially successful people often need to force themselves not to settle."

Plunk followed Tony onto the set and Dr. Nice shifted slightly on the couch to make a little more room. Plunk reached down and unbuckled the two thigh belts so he could pull the tail off to the side while keeping the main belt cinched around his waist. He rested the tail over the arm of the couch. The tip curled on the floor.

The cameras swung back, and somebody said, "In three, two, one."

47.

"We're back on a cold Friday morning," Tim said. "This is *Daybreak Metroplex* and it's 7:48. I'm Tim Carter with Bonnie Woody, and we've been having an amazing talk with Dr. Jennifer Nice, author of the bestselling *Set Them, Get Them*, all about how we need to set goals rather than waste time with dreams, and how we shouldn't settle for partial success. Important life-changing stuff. Everybody should read this book."

"But now we have another guest," Bonnie said, sounding just a bit sharpish. "From the Fort Worth suburb of Crowley, this is Plunk Landy, better known as Tail Man. Plunk, welcome to *Daybreak Metroplex*. Or should I call you Tail Man?"

"Either one's okay," Plunk said. He was trying not to squint because the makeup woman had been right, the lights were very hot and bright.

"This is your first in-person visit to our show, but we've seen you on tape twice in the last months. First at a charity golf event benefiting Cook Children's Medical Center in Fort Worth, and then with Congressman Rod Argent supporting a program to build more outdoor playgrounds for our area children. So I guess we can assume kids are the motivation behind your Tail Man character?"

Plunk handled it just like he and Darlene planned. He said Tail Man was all about kids, he was glad to make charity appearances for them, because nobody could argue kids' hospitals and clean safe playgrounds weren't very good things. And he also enjoyed appearing at kids' birthday parties and business events like when he'd be at Stretch's Southwest Chevrolet in Fort Worth a week from tomorrow.

"I just want to help people have fun," he said. "This world could use more fun, don't you think?"

Everyone nodded, even Dr. Nice.

"Tell us about the tail," Tim urged. "How you found it, what made you decide to wear it."

So Plunk told about Halloween and going out in homemade getups every year, then the griping about President Trump. How he went to Quality Costumes, fell in love with the tail and had to have it.

"Very expensive?" Tim asked.

"I can't remember exactly, I think just about a thousand or something," Plunk said. Afterward Darlene told him that was when he should have talked about the Tail Man Jr. tails, how they'd be available at Quality Costumes soon, but Plunk plain forgot. Instead he related how he had to figure out how to walk around with the tail on without scuffing it. He jumped up, buckled the thigh belts on, and demonstrated how he could raise or lower the tail with the retractable leash.

"So now your life is dedicated to Tail Man appearances, helping out with good causes for kids and also helping everyone around you have fun," Bonnie said. "Are you Tail Man 24/7?"

Plunk unbuckled the thigh belts again and twisted the tail to the side so he could sit down. He said no, he had a day job in sales with Campbell Bolt & Screw in Fort Worth.

"My boss asked me to put our number on my sweatshirt here," he said. *That* would please Austin, and hopefully not piss off Darlene too much.

"Do you eventually hope to be Tail Man full time?" Tim asked.

"Ah, I haven't thought about it," Plunk said. "Like I want for everybody else, right now I'm just having fun."

"Well, you're doing a wonderful job, and Tail Man is really becoming an integral part of the greater Fort Worth community," Bonnie said. "Maybe we can be partners at the next charity golf tournament, but you've got to promise not to hit me with the ball like you nearly did Congressman Argent. Let's see that tape again."

For the thirty seconds or so the tape played, Plunk became aware that Dr. Nice was studying him carefully. It reminded him of how he felt back in high school when one of the really strict teachers kept him after class to talk about something he'd done to make everybody laugh but interrupted the lesson. Dr. Nice had the same intense expression, like inside her head a calculator was whirring and clicking, reading his mind, figuring him out.

The way she was looking had him so distracted that he was caught off guard when the tape ended and Bonnie asked, "Was that the world's strangest hole in one ever?"

"Uh," said Plunk, then, "It wasn't really a hole in one. Stretch the Chevrolet guy pushed the ball in with his golf club. But it came close."

"So what's next for Tail Man?" Tim asked. "Will you be joining Congressman Argent for more appearances promoting new playgrounds?"

"I will if he asks," Plunk said. "But otherwise I'll keep doing what I'm doing. If somebody wants Tail Man at a birthday party or company thing, call my manager and I'll be there." Through the glare of the lights he glimpsed movement on the side of the set. Darlene was gesturing at him. It took a second, but he got it.

"Can I give her number?" he asked Bonnie.

"Why not?" she said, so Plunk did.

"And now we've got some *other* commercial messages," Bonnie said. "Please stay tuned, because we're going to be right back with Tail Man and also bestselling author Dr. Jennifer Nice. I'm sure they'll have more interesting things to talk about before we have to say goodbye and send you on your morning way."

The cameras swung aside again. Plunk immediately rubbed his eyes. The freakin' lights were just brutal.

"Aren't you interesting," said Dr. Nice. She wasn't looking damn near through him anymore. It was like Superman turned off the x-ray vision. "The whole thing with your tail."

"Thanks," Plunk said uncertainly. He wasn't sure if she was complimenting him or not.

"Just perfect," Dr. Nice said. "I couldn't have invented anybody better."

"Beg your pardon?" Plunk said. But Dr. Nice just sort of nodded to herself. Maddy the publicist came over and asked Dr. Nice if she needed a tissue or anything.

"Oh, I'm just fine," she said. "But is the car going to be waiting right when we're done here? Because I know we have to get to the airport."

"He'll have the motor running," Maddy promised.

Darlene came up.

"Say the phone number again if you can," she told Plunk.

Darlene looked past Plunk at Dr. Nice like she hoped Dr. Nice might say something to her, but she didn't. There was a shout of "on in ten." Maddy and Darlene turned to go back to the side of the set.

"I need to get Dr. Nice's address to send her my manuscript," Darlene said.

"I'll give you my card when we're done here," Maddy said. "You can send it to me. I'll see she gets it, I handle all her reader mail."

"Here we go," Dr. Nice said to Plunk. He wasn't sure, the lights were still bothering his eyes, but he thought she might have winked.

48.

"I can't remember a *Daybreak Metroplex* when we've had two such intriguing but very different guests," Bonnie said. "We've got Tail Man, who just wants to help people have fun, and bestselling author Dr. Jennifer Nice, who just wants to tell people what to do."

"Not tell, Bonnie," Dr. Nice said. "It's more along the lines of offering common sense guidance. I'm sure you realize that often the best advice may initially seem a little stern, may even temporarily hurt someone's feelings. The term 'tough love' isn't contradictory."

"I know I've learned a lot this morning," Tim said. "Don't mind me saying everybody should read your new book."

"Of course I don't mind," said Dr. Nice. "*Set Them, Get Them* is the bestselling book in the country thanks to people like you, Tim, who are determined to achieve their ultimate goals, rather than waste time on dreams or settle for getting partway there. And I'd like to demonstrate with Tail Man, if he doesn't object."

"I guess not," Plunk said.

"It's so clear you're enjoying your newfound notoriety," Dr. Nice said. "Helping people have fun is an admirable goal. But of course that's a goal directed toward others. I wonder what are Tail Man's personal goals."

"Like I said, help other people have fun and also have fun myself," said Plunk.

"As Tail Man in and around Fort Worth," Dr. Nice said. "Mostly on weekends, correct? You have your day job. We can read all about it on your sweatshirt."

"Yeah, sales rep at Campbell Bolt & Screw," Plunk said. He had no idea what she was getting at.

"Then let's compare, Mr. Landy. Do you enjoy selling things as much as you do being Tail Man? Do you look forward to your workday at Campbell Bolt & Screw as much as you do playing in area celebrity golf tournaments with popular local personalities like Bonnie, here?"

"I guess not," said Plunk. "But you gotta work for a living, you know. That's why they call them *jobs*."

"I take it you charge for most Tail Man appearances," Dr. Nice said. "Birthday parties, programs at car lots, and so on. Are you making enough from them to perhaps give up your day job?"

"Not really," Plunk said. "I got some extra expenses now. My mom's not well."

Dr. Nice tilted her head slightly, eyebrows rising with refined professional curiosity.

"Why not schedule more Tail Man appearances so you in fact earn whatever income you need, and then you can make your entire living doing what you love most instead of being stuck at a day job you like much less? Is it your goal to remain a full-time salesman and part-time Tail Man, or would you rather be Tail Man without the necessity or rather the distraction of being a salesman at all?"

"Careful," Plunk said. "You could get me fired." Dr. Nice kept looking at him. "Well, sure. I guess I'd like to be Tail Man all the time."

"Then why aren't you setting goals to make that happen, Mr. Landy?" Dr. Nice asked. "We all heard you say how you dress up every year for Halloween. You thrive on attention from others. It's fine to say you portray Tail Man on behalf of children, but the truth is you're also doing it for yourself. It's when you're happiest."

"I like kids," Plunk said plaintively.

"I'm not suggesting you don't. But since you've become Tail Man, people pay more attention to you. It's the most gratifying, exciting time in your life."

"Yeah, I guess so."

"So why haven't you thought about how to make it your whole life instead of just the best but limited part? Why aren't you quitting your job, committing yourself to aggressive Tail Man marketing and making your full-time living doing what you're happiest doing?"

"I dunno," Plunk mumbled, completely forgetting he was on TV with people watching.

"Well," said Dr. Nice, "I do know. You've gotten a taste of doing what you love, and of course you like it very much. But you're settling. You're a partial achiever who's settling. Perhaps deep down you're afraid to set your goals higher, afraid if you do you might lose what you've already got. But if people stop striving, stop trying to achieve more, then most of the time they end up losing the limited success they've previously gained. You either move forward toward your ultimate goals or you fall back away from them. Tim, didn't you say in that viewer popularity contest Bonnie got fewer votes this year than last?"

"I still outpolled the runner-up almost two to one," Bonnie said before Tim could reply.

"What about next year, Bonnie?" asked Dr. Nice. "How many

more votes will you lose then? But right now we're talking about Tail Man. Mr. Landy, how many birthday parties in the Fort Worth area can you be hired for before most of the kids who want to see you and your tail already have? What will you do when those calls stop coming? After what you've had in the past few months, the ongoing thrill of being a celebrity, could you ever be happy going back to dressing up as Tail Man only once a year on Halloween? Because if you don't push yourself, set higher goals than remaining a part-time local Tail Man, then that's what I predict will happen."

"It might not," Plunk said. Sweat sluiced down from his armpits to his sides.

"But it probably will. I'm not trying to be cruel, Mr. Landy. I think your Tail Man persona is wonderful. That's why you ought to be thinking about quitting your sales job, committing yourself wholeheartedly to the goal you deep down really want, which is being Tail Man full-time and famous on a bigger scale, even on a national basis."

"I don't think about stuff like that," Plunk protested.

"Then start thinking about it, Mr. Landy," said Dr. Nice. "Over the next days and weeks, ask yourself if being part-time Tail Man is what you really want to settle for. Be honest with yourself. Why be a temporary local celebrity rather than a long term national star? As I prove in my new book *Set Them, Get Them: Why Goals Are Better Than Dreams, and How To Achieve Them*, often the worst thing that can happen to us is almost getting what we want. Get everything you want, Mr. Landy, be an achiever and not a dreamer. Just like anyone who reads my book can be."

"And we're out of time," Tim said. "What a show this morning, Bonnie. We want to thank Tail Man and Dr. Jennifer Nice, whose new book about goals being better than dreams is taking the whole country by storm. You two can come back on our program anytime."

"It's been a pleasure, Tim," said Dr. Nice. "I look forward to being interviewed by you on Fox News or CNN someday soon. And Bonnie, best of luck with maintaining your career on this station."

Plunk didn't say anything. He just nodded.

"Monday on *Daybreak Metroplex*, meet rising rap star Shaniqua and Ed Charles, the director of Arlington parks services," Bonnie said. She looked and sounded really pissed. "Have a great Friday, and a wonderful weekend." As soon as the cameras swung away she stalked off.

Dr. Nice extended her hand to Plunk.

"I can't thank you enough," she said. "I'm sure that we sold some books this morning."

Dr. Nice had her microphone unhooked and was walking away with Maddy before Plunk even realized she'd gotten up off the couch. They disappeared down the hall.

Darlene came over.

"Maddy forgot to give me her card," she said.

49.

Just like that, Plunk wasn't happy anymore. From the moment he left the *Daybreak Metroplex* set, everything in his recent life that thrilled him suddenly seemed limited and depressing. He'd spent his life deliberately not thinking about goals. As soon as he started doing it, he came to a discouraging conclusion:

Dr. Nice was right. He was falling short of what he really wanted. Even if he hadn't realized it before, it turned out he did want certain things.

Some were pretty basic, like something better than a shitty one-bedroom apartment. When he was home now he looked around with growing disgust. He was Tail Man, the most famous man in Crowley. Why should he have to sit on a saggy couch or a cheap chair that had a spring digging into his back? Why did he have to eat off a rickety card table that damn near fell over every time he dug his fork into a microwave dinner? Why, for Christ's sake, did he have to live in such limited space that he and his tail had to share a bedroom? Why not a bigger place so the tail could have a room of its own?

And his Ranger. What it must look like for people to see Tail Man driving around in a crummy pickup with duct tape covering a hole in the windshield. A sleek Ford F-150, or even better an imposing Hummer, those were the kinds of cars important people like pro football stars drove. A ride that made a statement—hey, look at me, I'm big time. Which, without better goals, was something Plunk Landy wouldn't ever be.

Even Plunk, who in taking stock of his life for the first time was thinking more dutifully than creatively, knew the cure for the car-apartment ills. Money. He had more than he'd ever had before, but he needed much more than that, and he wasn't going to be able to earn it under the present circumstances.

Broc got a job in San Marcos a couple weeks after Plunk appeared with Dr. Nice on *Daybreak Metroplex*. Austin wasn't real happy about the way the show had gone, but he promoted Plunk anyway. And like Austin promised, he made more, maybe twice as much, with a lot less effort. Where before he had to spend his workdays driving around frantically on small-dollar sales calls, now he maybe talked to a half-dozen customers a day, often just over the phone, and they usually made whopping orders. So on the work front Plunk was doing a hell of a lot better, now no worrying about paying Mom's monthly bills for extra care. That was good, but it didn't fix the bigger problem. Even if he made enough money at Campbell Bolt & Screw for a new car and bigger apartment, Plunk wanted to afford these things from what he earned as full-time Tail Man because that was his real goal. Dr. Nice taught him that.

Which forced him to focus on something else. The way he was being Tail Man wasn't right, either. Because it wasn't going to make him permanently famous, the goal he wanted most to achieve.

He still loved putting on the black jeans, the black tennies, and the new yellow sweatshirt Darlene bought him that had no reference to Campbell Bolt & Screw on it. The magic of wearing the tail remained. It felt special, it made him special. Just not special enough, and he couldn't blame the tail for that. The tail was holding up its end. Plunk was the one letting the side down. He wasn't letting the tail reach its full potential.

Appearing at birthday parties held no further pleasure. Dr. Nice nailed it when she said how many parties could there be around goddamn Fort Worth before the kids got bored with it? Too-Fun Tex was right—a local party guy couldn't go on forever. Because there were only so many times Plunk and area kids could pose for pictures and play pin-the-tail-on-the-gecko and have lizard races with tails made out of plastic garbage bags. Darlene promised to come up with some new gecko party games, but she hadn't—she was frantically trying to finish her book so she could get to the next steps of her goal to become a famous writer. So Plunk began finding fault in what had so recently seemed like the most incredible break of his life. Three hundred extra bucks once or maybe twice a week for appearing at a birthday party? Small time. No longer acceptable to Tail Man. He yearned for bigger and better.

Same thing with his appearances for businesses. Tail Man's second visit to Stretch's Southwest Chevrolet fell flat, at least for Plunk. Families came, Plunk and Darlene did the pictures and games thing, Stretch paid them in full, six hundred bucks, but he didn't mention booking them again and Plunk could tell he was thinking maybe two Tail Man appearances were enough. There was only so much Tail Man business in and around Fort Worth and its nearby communities. Like Dr. Nice said, settling was dangerous. Darlene, when she wasn't thinking or yapping about her still unfinished book, started talking about something she called "the law of diminishing returns." Plunk assumed she was saying if he stayed only local the Tail Man calls were eventually going to stop coming. Which, with Dr. Nice's help, he'd already figured out.

Even a summons by Mr. Davenport to check out the first Tail Man Jr. prototypes at Quality Costumes in Crowley did little to lighten Plunk's funk. He thought that the half dozen mini-tails were crappy, cheap plastic and Styrofoam stuffing except for the one that was just plastic—you blew it up like a long skinny balloon. He went through the motions of trying them on before telling Mr. Davenport to decide which ones to use. Later he drove to Fort Worth and went into one of the big chain stores. Plunk looked at all the superhero toys on its shelves, Avengers and Harry Potter and *Star Wars*. If something didn't change, the only place the Tail Man Jr. shit would ever be displayed would be at Quality Costumes in goddamn Crowley. They'd sell maybe a hundred, not gazillions like with a national deal. Plunk wanted his signature products in classy stores like Target and Wal-Mart. Better quality Tail Man Jr. tails and also action figures and bubblegum cards. Why shouldn't he have all that?

Plunk's winter of discontent intensified when Eddie moved out of The Jacksonian and in with Kendra and her daughter. One morning he was just gone. He broke his lease, crammed his stuff into his car, and headed off. Sometimes Plunk still had a Saturday or Sunday free to watch TV sports, but now Eddie pretty much never did. On weekends Kendra liked doing family things and that meant Eddie couldn't come over to watch the games, basketball now since football season was over and baseball hadn't started yet. Plunk was surprised to find he missed the butthead. Red and Larry B. stopped coming, too. They were pissed because Plunk got the promotion at work. They acted so shitty to him now, like inviting Jessika to go to lunch but not him, that Plunk accepted Austin's offer to share his office. Sometimes they putted together. Plunk still couldn't get his ball in the glass. Austin talked about planning some Tail Man appearances for customers and their kids, but it still being winter with pissy weather they'd wait for spring to do that. Also Plunk wouldn't get paid extra for doing these—his new work salary included Campbell Bolt & Screw customer events.

The upshot was that for the moment when Plunk wasn't at work or being Tail Man at birthday parties or spending time with Darlene he was all on his own, and now he was plagued by thoughts about goals, about how to break out of *this*, the life that seemed just fine until Dr. Nice on *Daybreak Metroplex* taught him better. Once you started thinking about things, Plunk discovered, it was practically impossible to stop.

So he was actually relieved, around the end of February, when Darlene said they needed to talk.

"Not about us exactly, but about goals," she said. "It's time to really set them, get them, like Dr. Nice says. Have you finished reading her book yet?"

"No, but I don't need to," Plunk said, who hadn't even started reading it. "I already know what's in it. I understand what she's saying."

"I still wish you'd read the whole book," Darlene said. "There's a lot of nuance. I've reread it four times at least and every time I get more out of it."

Plunk didn't know what "nuance" meant. But he did know Darlene was right about it being time for goal-setting. She said come over for dinner the next night, they'd eat and talk until they figured everything out. Plunk agreed, then went back to the apartment he now hated to watch sports on his widescreen TV, which he still loved. The only good thing on was pro wrestling. He and the tail watched for a while before turning in.

50.

"It's Tuesday night, how come you're not at your writing class?" Plunk asked Darlene. They'd just finished another of her tasteless meals, baked chicken and limp-leafed spinach salad. Darlene always fixed chicken because she knew he liked it. Which he did, but something that didn't cluck would have been a welcome change.

"I'm not going to go anymore," said Darlene. She carried their plates out to the kitchen. "I feel like I've learned everything the professor has to teach me."

"But you said he was hot stuff," Plunk said, sitting on the couch. "He had a book published in New York."

"I know, but I've been trying to apply Dr. Nice's ideas about goals," Darlene said. "I don't want to be a student anymore. I want to be a real published author. The time I spent in class took away from work on my novel. The step of taking the class is over. The step right now is finishing the book. I'm moving on so I don't fall back."

"But maybe the guy was just about to teach you something that would help you write better," Plunk said.

"No," said Darlene. "Being completely honest with myself like Dr. Nice recommends, I realize that I'm already a very talented writer, I think probably more talented than the professor is. I've learned what he had to offer. Staying in his class when there's nothing more to get out of it is settling, and I'm through settling."

She picked up a pen and legal pad, and came over to sit beside Plunk. She moved the spiffy laptop he'd given her for Christmas out of the way on the coffee table and set the pad down so she could write on it.

"In her book Dr. Nice says to start serious goal-setting by first deciding what your ultimate goals are," Darlene said. "After that you work out the necessary steps to achieve them. Which is what we're going to do now. Get it down to the most basic things. What do you really, really want? Will you tell me?"

"Sure," Plunk said, "but don't make fun of me."

"I won't if you don't do it to me."

Plunk took a deep breath.

"Okay. I want to be famous. Really famous, not just somebody around here."

"Famous as Tail Man?"

"Of course, Tail Man."

"Fine," said Darlene. "And I want to be such a successful author that when the girls who were mean to me in high school google me they'll get jealous." Plunk knew that Darlene herself did a lot of googling about girls she knew back in high school, finding out what they did for a living, who or if they married, even seeing pictures of them sometimes.

"Why do you care what happened to them?" Plunk asked.

"It's just natural," Darlene said. "Because you want to know, especially about the girls you didn't like, the ones who were stuck up and hateful. I want them to see me on TV and my book on Amazon and just tear their hair out because I'm so successful."

In capital letters she wrote FAMOUS TAIL MAN/BESTSELLING AUTHOR at the top of the page. She asked Plunk if that seemed right and he said it did.

"Okay, then what's the first obvious step?" Darlene asked. "To make these goals happen."

"I know that one," Plunk said. "At least for me. I got to start doing Tail Man someplace else, someplace bigger. And as soon as I can, something better than birthday parties and car lots."

"It's kind of the same for me," Darlene said. "You can't become really famous unless you're in a big city, what they call a media hub, New York or Los Angeles mainly. Because that's where you're on shows and go to important parties and they keep showing you on TV. So I think those two places are our options."

Plunk was stunned. "New York? LA? No way. Those places are weird."

"Of course, New York and LA if you want to be famous," Darlene said. "Where else did you think?"

"Well, Dallas, for starters. We mostly do our stuff around Fort Worth, but Dallas is a lot bigger. We got a leg up in Dallas because I've already been in their paper and on their TV. Then maybe San Antonio. Houston's almost as crazy as New York or LA, but it's at least still in Texas. Get Tail Man going in those places, newspapers and TV. After that, West Texas, I guess. El Paso for sure."

Darlene scrunched up her face. "I thought you wanted to be famous."

"That's what I've been saying."

"Well, if you just keep being Tail Man in Texas, you're never going to be really famous, someone everybody everywhere knows about."

Plunk had an answer for that. "The Dallas Cowboys did it in Texas. So has Willie Nelson."

Darlene shot back, "They come from Texas, but they play all over the country."

Which was why Plunk tried never to argue with Darlene. She always came up with unnecessary facts.

"The best example for you is Kelly Clarkson," Darlene said. "She was just this girl from Burleson, I think she worked in some restaurant there. Then she went to LA and got on *American Idol* and got to be maybe one of the most famous singers in the country. She even got her own talk show."

"I heard the name, but I guess I don't know much about her."

Darlene took the deep breath she always took when she was about to start one of her long-winded explanations.

"Then you need to learn everything about Kelly," she said. "That girl ought to be your role model. She knew that to reach her goal, which I read in *People* magazine was to be famous and have people always looking at her—sound familiar?—she needed a big break and of course that was getting on *American Idol* and everybody in the country watched her and that's how she achieved her goal. A good step toward your goal would be to get on a show like that, a reality show on national TV. There are like hundreds of them. People go on and do all kinds of things. I mean, you must have watched some."

"I guess not," Plunk said. "You know sports and Fox are mostly what I watch."

"Which is why your perspective is so limited. But that's all right, because you have me and I know all about them. I watch them not for entertainment but because as a writer I need to know where the culture is, what people respond to, and that's why I know Tail Man is such a natural for a reality show. The people running them would be crazy not to put you on. Everyone watching will love you, and then you'll be like Kelly, famous all over the place. So you need to go where those shows are. Los Angeles and I guess probably New York, between them they have everything."

"Look," Plunk said. "I just like living in Texas. I understand it here. I don't understand anything about LA or New York."

"You could if you really tried," Darlene said. "Tail Man's got to be more than just Texas. You need to understand that. I'll put it on the list." She wrote "PLUNK LEARN ABOUT KELLY, NEW YORK AND LA" on the legal pad in big capital letters. "There. That's settled."

"I don't think so," Plunk mumbled, but Darlene said firmly, "It's on the list. We need to keep going." She added "MOVE TO NEW YORK, LA???" on the legal pad.

"We're moving together, of course," she added, saying it fast like maybe if Plunk didn't agree he wouldn't have time to say so. But he nodded.

"Together," he said, knowing it was a commitment to something more down the road. Why not? Darlene had made the first Tail Man jobs happen. She was the one who'd known about Dr. Nice. He wasn't sure he exactly loved her, but he knew he needed her.

"So move to which place?" Darlene asked. "East Coast or West Coast?"

"You'd know better than me," Plunk said. He was still trying to deal with the idea of leaving Texas.

Each city had its advantages, Darlene said. For Tail Man to get famous he needed media exposure, and for him TV was better than print because the whole tail thing came off better when people could see it waving in all its glory rather than printed words describing it with maybe a picture alongside. So LA was probably better for Plunk's goal. After becoming a reality TV star he would be on TV talk and entertainment news shows that were national like Jimmy Kimmel and *E!* instead of regional like *Daybreak Metroplex*, and also have a chance to maybe get his own TV series, a sitcom or even star in a reality show where a camera followed him around all day recording everything he said and did. "It worked for the Kardashians," Darlene said. "And they didn't even have tails." And then there was Hollywood and the movies. Right after winning *American Idol*, Kelly Clarkson starred in a movie about herself. Darlene remembered going to see that movie when she was just a little girl. A Tail Man film, she thought, might be a big hit like the Muppets or something.

"Tail Man's very loveable," Darlene assured him.

"What about you, writing?" Plunk asked.

Darlene thought New York would be better for an author. All the major publishers were there and also the big-time literary agents who could get her lots of money for her novel. She could be part of the New York author social set.

"I bet Colleen Hoover lives there," she said. "She's originally from Texas like us, but I'm sure she lives in New York now. We move there, she and I could be friends."

Problem was, Darlene said, that Tail Man's chances for fame weren't quite as good in New York. There were the national morning TV talk shows broadcasting live from Rockefeller Center, but not as much opportunity to get a TV series since it seemed like most of those were based in LA. Though what they had in New York were Broadway musicals.

"Do you think you could sing and dance with the tail on?" she asked.

"Well, I couldn't play good basketball with it," Plunk replied. "But we can go to New York if it's better for you."

"No, I think LA," Darlene said. "My novel will be made into a movie anyway, so being there would give me a head start that way. I would be right there for meetings with Spielberg or whoever, and they'd pay me lots to write the movie version of the book. I could just commute to New York when I had to. You need to be in LA."

She crossed through NEW YORK on the pad and underlined LA. Then she scratched out the question marks.

"Okay, we've got the big things," Darlene said. "LA it is. You're going to be famous as Tail Man. I'm going to be a bestselling author. Actual goals like Dr. Nice says, with ambitious but sensible steps to achieve them."

"LA," Plunk mumbled. He wondered if he could be okay away from Texas. He'd have the tail with him. Darlene too, of course. And as a famous guy, also undoubtedly rich, he could come back to visit Texas whenever he wanted to. Maybe even see a Cowboys game in person.

"But I still gotta act like me, not like some liberal California asshole," Plunk said. "I'm Texan through and through, never changing that. Don't try to make me."

"I never would," said Darlene. "It's just smart to be in LA, that's where goals get achieved. I mean, even for Dr. Nice, who for all her writing success continues having goals. It says on her website that she's moving from New York to LA. She's getting her own cable TV talk show there. I bet we can be guests on it, you as Tail Man and me when my novel is published. But Kelly Clarkson will be helpful, too. She's such a friendly girl. We'll get her phone number and ask her which reality show producers we should meet with."

"And we can trust her cause she's from Texas," Plunk said. "You think of everything." He leaned over and kissed her.

"I try," Darlene said, and kissed him back.

51.

They didn't leave until the end of March. They had eleven Tail Man birthday party appearances lined up before that for Plunk to do, plus one time when he played golf with a Campbell Bolt & Screw customer. But they didn't make any Tail Man commitments for April or beyond because they knew they'd be in California then.

Darlene used the month between deciding to go and leaving to finish her novel. It was almost two hundred pages long. She said Plunk could read it if he wanted. He said he probably should wait until they were in Los Angeles, thinking maybe she'd forget she asked him by then. He really did hate to read.

"First thing when we're settled, I'll find out if there any literary agents in Los Angeles," she said. "I think probably most of the good ones are in New York, but we'll see."

The money from the Tail Man appearances in March gave them a nest egg of just over four thousand, plus Darlene had a savings account with almost three thousand more. Plunk would have had a couple thousand from the Tail Man jobs in January and February, but he used that money to get Mom's extra care paid up four more months in advance. Leaving her behind was tough.

"As soon as we get our place and everything we can send for her," Darlene promised. "We'll find her something nicer than Pleasant Valley in Los Angeles. And if it takes you a little longer than we expect to get on TV and make some money, we can use mine from selling my book."

"You gonna sell it that quick?" Plunk asked.

"It's a very good novel," said Darlene. "Every publisher in New York will want it. I expect a bidding war."

They decided to go ahead and sell Darlene's car. It was much smaller than Plunk's Ranger and they needed room for suitcases and the tail. When they took Darlene's car to Stretch he offered seven hundred. Darlene was insulted, but the next two dealers only offered six hundred and six twenty-five. Darlene took the six twenty-five because she didn't want to go back to Stretch and admit his offer was the best. After she sold her book, she said, she'd buy herself a new car, maybe one of those hybrids.

Darlene also yakked about them needing a Tail Man website as soon as they were settled in LA. She'd be too busy with her book to go around handing out Tail Man business cards, she said, but Plunk shouldn't worry. A really great website with candid photos and also videos of him in Tail Man getup would bring in thousands of appearance requests.

"We'll need to find somebody with real technical skills to build the website," Darlene said, lecturing Plunk as usual. "And after it's up, we'll probably need to hire someone to run it. Unless you want to."

"Not me," Plunk said. "Got to be somebody else." He immediately thought about Jessika. She handled the Campbell Bolt & Screw website, and it would sure be nice to have another Texan around in weird-ass LA besides Darlene and Kelly Clarkson after they made friends with her. But he didn't mention Jessika to Darlene just yet, because what Plunk was really hoping was that with everything involved in moving and getting her book sold, she might not get around to the website. The Internet, to Plunk, was menacing. You never really knew what might happen if you hit a wrong key or something.

52.

Two weeks before they left, they gave notice at their jobs. Darlene said the head librarian told her she'd been the best library assistant they ever had, and if things didn't work out in California she could always come back. Austin didn't say something similar to Plunk. He told him he was being an idiot, he'd get eaten alive out there.

"People in California hate Texans," Austin said. "No matter what you say or do, they'll say it's stupid and prejudiced and wrong. You'll see. And after that, don't come crawling back. Campbell Bolt & Screw's going to be fine without you. You're not a team player."

But Plunk still got a going-away party. Jessika ordered a cake shaped like a tail. Red and Larry B. acted like they'd never been mad at him. Probably they both hoped to get promoted in his place. Austin ate two slices of cake but only gave Plunk a half-hearted goodbye handshake, not a parting bonus. Plunk hadn't expected one but he'd still sort of hoped. From everything Darlene could pick up on the internet, Los Angeles was more expensive than Crowley, and especially Venice Beach, which she'd seen on some TV shows and where she thought they might like to live. Darlene kept saying all the beachfront rental houses there couldn't be as much as the real estate websites said, they'd get a motel room and shop around until they found a bargain.

"Just because we've got seven thousand dollars or whatever doesn't mean we have to spend it all," she reminded Plunk. They might have had about nine hundred more but when they told the manager of The Jacksonian they were breaking their leases he insisted on keeping their deposits.

They told Mr. Davenport at Quality Costumes that the Tail Man Jr. deal was off. He didn't seem sorry.

"If you're moving away everybody'll forget about Tail Man anyway," Mr. Davenport said.

"Don't count on it," said Plunk.

"And we never did sign anything with him," Darlene told Plunk afterward. "So when Tail Man gets famous out in LA we can do any kind of endorsement deals we want."

53.

About this time Plunk thought of something that bothered him to the point it became hard to think about anything else. He already knew that California had lots of liberal crazies. Some of them were bound to hate his tail just because they hated anything that regular people liked. What if they started screaming that the tail was wrong, that it was unfair to lizards or something? They loved doing shit like that. Maybe they'd try to make the tail illegal, they might actually try to take his tail away. What would he do then? So Plunk decided that anyone trying to take his tail had better watch out. He was planning to buy a gun anyway, which of course he hadn't mentioned to Darlene because she was one of those women who wouldn't understand the need to own a gun no matter how patiently you explained it to her. And not that Plunk would ever actually shoot somebody. What he imagined was a mob of libs coming after the tail, and him firing a few shots in the air and them peeing their pants and running away. People-loving, fun-making Plunk Landy had never thought about such things before, but hey, he finally had something special and he was damned if any buttheads were going to take it away from him just because he was in California and they wanted to. Things like that happened even in Texas, look at Two-Gun Tex and his squirt guns, but if the people on Fox were right libs did it all the time in California. A guy with a tail had to be ready. Plunk didn't share this with Darlene. She was so excited about moving to LA. He was a man and it was his responsibility to protect what he loved when they got there.

54.

The week before they left, Eddie and Kendra took them out to dinner. Darlene wanted to go to the Chinese place one last time. She still didn't like Eddie much but she got along with Kendra all right. Kendra loved reading Colleen Hoover books too.

Talk turned to Plunk's worries about leaving Mom. She was paid up at Pleasant Valley through the end of the summer, Plunk wasn't really worried about that part. But he thought she'd be lonely without Sunday visits even though she'd pretty much stopped knowing who he was.

"I don't like her sitting there with nobody coming to see her," Plunk said.

"Not a problem, buddy," said Eddie. "Sometimes I got to go over there and pick up Kendra after work anyway. I'll make sure I drop in on your mom. If I think there's something you need to know, I'll give you a call."

Plunk was very grateful.

"Tell you what, when the school year's over you and Kendra and the kid ought to come visit us in LA," he said. "Swim in the ocean, that stuff. Disneyland. We're gonna have a big place, plenty of room for you to stay as long as you want."

"Yes," said Darlene, not enthusiastic but trying.

That Saturday night Plunk and Darlene got a Rand-McNally road map and planned their route from Crowley to Los Angeles. Best they could figure, they would head west to El Paso and then follow Interstate 10, a little under two thousand miles. Darlene said if they split the driving and didn't stop too much they could do it in three days, but Plunk had seen Darlene drive just like a grandma and knew it would take another day at least.

55.

Sunday morning they loaded Plunk's Ranger. They didn't have all that much to bring, mostly clothes. Darlene had put her books and furniture in storage until they had their place in LA. She brought her laptop, though, and two flash drives of her novel, plus all four books she had by Dr. Nice. She told Plunk the books were for inspiration.

Plunk was only bringing his clothes. None of his furniture was worth paying to move all that way, so he left it in the apartment. Whoever moved in next could keep it or throw it away. His only beloved possession, even more so than the TV, which Eddie was keeping for now until Plunk sent for it, was the tail, and of course the tail was coming with him. He and the tail were inseparable.

They crammed everything in the pickup truck bed and covered it with a plastic tarp from Home Depot. Darlene shoved a couple grocery store sacks with sandwiches and fruit in the narrow back area of the Ranger's cab, next to where Plunk had carefully placed the tail across the fold-down seats. She said there was no sense stopping at fast food places on the road because all that food was overpriced, but Plunk hoped they would anyway. Darlene had traveled some, but this was his first great road adventure. He'd heard of places like Carl's Jr. and wanted to try them out if they passed one.

When the pickup was all loaded, they drove to Pleasant Valley so Plunk could tell Mom goodbye. Even though it was a warmish spring day, Plunk still wore his Dallas Cowboys jacket. He intended to wear it during the whole trip, and maybe most days when they got to LA. It would set him apart from California weirdos wearing T-shirts made from trees.

Ida sat in the chair in her room and patted her bun while Plunk explained that he and Darlene were moving to LA, but not to worry because they'd be sending for her soon.

"We'll get you a place there where you can see the ocean, Mom," he promised. "And your own TV so when Tail Man's on shows, you can watch."

Darlene whispered some things in Ida's ear, and then the aide came to take Mom to lunch so it was time for them to go. Plunk leaned in for one more hug and whispered, "I love you, Mom."

"You know, I do like Annie," Ida said, suddenly smiling in Darlene's direction. It was the first thing she'd said to Plunk in weeks.

"I'm glad," Plunk said. "I like her, too."

Darlene was buckling her seatbelt when Plunk noticed in his rear-view mirror that the tail was getting all squished up in the back with the overflowing grocery sacks of food. He got out, opened the side door and tried to rearrange things so the tail had more room, but it was hopeless.

"It needs to be out kinda straight," he complained to Darlene. "If I let it stay bent like that the pointy end might get permanently twisted." He kept moving things around but it didn't help.

Finally Darlene said, "Do you want me to sit in the back so you can give the tail more room in the front?"

"Would that be okay?" Plunk asked. "Because you don't have to."

"It's fine," said Darlene. "I know you like to take care of your tail."

"Well, it's gonna be my meal ticket in California," Plunk said. "So I guess if you don't mind."

Darlene got in the back and shoved the food sacks as much to the side as she could, then squished herself into a fold-down seat. She had her copy of *Set Them, Get Them* to read. Plunk buckled the tail into the front seat belt, with the thick end on the floor and the tip at eye level.

"Here we go," he said, and eased the pickup out of the parking lot. As they drove toward Crowley's city limits, he kind of choked up. Plunk was thinking about how strange it would feel to drive over the Texas state line for the first time.

Darlene was already engrossed in *Set Them, Get Them*. But she picked up on the nervous note in Plunk's voice and reached over to pat his shoulder.

"Be happy," she said. "I think this is going to be very exciting."

Plunk stretched out his right hand and rested his fingers on the tail.

"Let's find out," he said.

About the Author

Jeff Guinn is a former award-winning journalist and bestselling author of both fiction and nonfiction. He lives in Fort Worth.

www.ingramcontent.com/pod-product-compliance
Lightning Source LLC
Chambersburg PA
CBHW060805310726
48980CB00002B/240
* 9 7 8 0 8 7 5 6 5 9 3 5 0 *